GIRLS
of SUMMER

Book five of
Girls of Summer

by Kate Christie

SECOND GROWTH

Copyright © 2019 by Kate Christie

Second Growth Books
Seattle, WA

All rights reserved. No part of this book may be reproduced or transmitted in any form or by any means, electronic or mechanical, including photocopying, without permission in writing from the author.

This is a work of fiction. Names, characters, organizations, events, and incidents are either the products of the author's imagination or used in a fictitious manner. Any resemblance to actual organizations, persons (living or dead), events, or incidents is purely coincidental.

Printed in the United States of America on acid-free paper
First published 2019

Cover Design: Kate Christie

ISBN-13: 978-1-0810394-5-5

DEDICATION

To the petitioners in *Obergefell v. Hodges*: April DeBoer and Jayne Rowse; Jim Obergefell and John Arthur; David Michener and William Ives; Georgia and Pamela Yorksmith; Kelly Noe and Kelly McCraken; Joseph Vitale and Robert Talmas; Brittani Henry and Brittni Rogers; Gregory Bourke and Michael DeLeon; Randell Johnson and Paul Campion; Jimmy Meade and Luther Barlowe; Kimberly Franklin and Tamera Boyd; Maurice Blanchard and Dominique James; Timothy Love and Lawrence Ysunza; Johno Espejo and Matthew Mansell; Kellie Miller and Vanessa DeVillez; Ijpe DeKoe and Thomas Kostura; Valeria Tanco and Sophia Jesty.

Thank you.

ACKNOWLEDGMENTS

As always, I offer my sincere gratitude to my two trusty early readers/editors, Kris and Margaret. The Girls of Summer series wouldn't be the same without you.

CHAPTER ONE

"What do you think?" Jamie asked, tapping her phone case nervously with her thumb as Ellie gazed around the one-bedroom apartment.

It wasn't quite the exposed brick walls and high ceilings Jamie had been looking for, but after a solid week of apartment hunting, her list of desired qualities had shifted. Noise, car pollution, and the scent of cigarettes and other smoking products was not a good combination, she'd discovered while looking in the hipster neighborhood she'd thought she wanted to live in. Burnside, home to the apartment they were currently viewing, was quieter and more residential, and offered easy access to Washington Park and its wooded trails, decorative gardens, and the city's resident zoo.

The building was historic, nearly a century old but carefully maintained and recently updated, according to the property manager. The wood floors were in good shape, the kitchen counters and appliances had been recently replaced, and the windows looked clean and functional. Windows which, incidentally, looked out over Providence Park only a block and a half away. That meant she would be within walking distance of Thorns (and Timbers) home games, only two and a half miles from Ellie's house, and twenty minutes from the team's training facilities in Beaverton. Not only that, but—and this had made the decision for her, really—there was a Fred Meyer *and* a Chipotle across the street from the stadium. Jamie could walk to most of the necessities in life, an advantage that trumped wall surfaces and ceiling heights any day.

"I like it," Ellie announced, gazing around at the gleaming wood floors and the three wide windows in the living room.

"It isn't too white?" Jamie asked. The walls and most of the wood trim had recently been painted a nearly blinding white.

"Well, this is Portland we're talking about," Ellie joked.

"Ha ha. I meant the interior."

"No, really, I think the white makes it seem bright in here."

That had been Jamie's impression, too.

"Burnside isn't cheap, though," Ellie added, lapsing into what Jamie thought of as mom mode. "Is the rent doable?"

She shrugged. "It wouldn't have been before. But now… Besides, I could cover the lease with my savings if I had to."

She was hoping—planning—that she wouldn't have to do that. She had yet to receive her first permanent roster paycheck from US Soccer, and the Nike deal wouldn't offer a payout for a little while yet, but she'd been earning more than league minimum while living rent-free at Ellie's, not to mention her Champions League bonus for making it to the semis. Even without additional compensation, she could afford the deposit and a few months of rent without taking too much of a hit.

"All right, then," Ellie said, grinning at her from across the empty apartment. "I think you should go for it."

"Good," Jamie said, her return smile a bit crooked. "Because I signed the lease an hour ago."

"Are you kidding? It's yours?"

"At least for the next year," Jamie confirmed.

During the open house that morning, there had been multiple applications submitted on the apartment. Fortunately, the property manager was some form of queer, Jamie was pretty sure, as well as a self-avowed fan of the Thorns and Timbers. The place was Jamie's if she wanted it, the manager had told her when she dropped off a completed application, giving her a smile that let Jamie know she was getting the preferential queer treatment that every once in a while made life as a non-binary lesbian easier to deal with. Or maybe the manager just liked the idea of having a soccer player in the building. Either way, Jamie had taken the apartment on the spot, only a little nervous as she signed the lease and handed over the deposit and first month's rent. Signing the checks had made it real in a way that even filling out the lease hadn't done.

Now she took a deep breath as she gazed around her first solo apartment. She was definitely going to need to find some furniture. But that was what Craigslist was for, wasn't it?

"Aw! My kid is growing up!" Ellie said, her arms opening wide as she approached Jamie.

"For fuck's sake," Jamie said, steeling herself for one of her soon-to-be former roommate's signature bear hugs. But she was smiling, too.

"Have you told Emma yet?" Ellie asked as she released her.

"I had her on FaceTime during the open house."

"Nice. So when do you move in?"

"This weekend." As Ellie gave her a surprised look, she shrugged. "I know, I'll barely be here for the next couple of months, but I wanted to have a place to come home to after Canada. You know?"

Ellie nodded and threw her arm around Jamie's shoulders. "I know exactly. Now show me the rest of it. This place is definitely bigger than my basement."

"You mean your daylight basement, right?" Jamie said as she led her toward the kitchen and dining room.

"Sure, buddy. Whatever you say."

The tour didn't take long, because while the apartment was decently sized for a unit of its kind (Jamie felt like an expert on Portland residential properties after the past week), it was still only three large rooms plus a walk-in closet.

"Holy shit," Ellie said, turning a circle inside the closet. "This is huge."

"I know," Jamie said, grinning as she surveyed the space. She could practically fit her car in here, which wasn't saying much given it was one of the smaller automobiles on the road, but still.

"Well done," Ellie said, holding up her hand.

Jamie slapped it hard, laughing at Ellie's wince as the sound echoed through the empty apartment. This was her new place. Her place. *Hers*.

A few hours later, though, as she lay in the guest bedroom in Ellie's basement going through her nightly meditation routine, she found herself distracted. Upstairs she could hear the occasional rumble of a voice, punctuated by the creak of a floorboard and the whoosh of water surging through pipes. Usually, these sounds were white noise, but tonight they engendered an almost panicked nostalgia. In a matter of days, she would be sleeping alone in her new building several miles away, surrounded by strangers in separate, locked apartments.

But maybe she didn't actually have to move just yet. Ellie wouldn't mind if she figured things out after the season ended, would she? The property manager might let her rescind her application. It wasn't like they wouldn't be able to fill the space.

As anxiety swirled through her, Jamie closed her eyes. *Thinking*, she told herself, trying to pick up the threads of her lost mantra. She refocused and made it through the exercise twice more before the wave of nausea subsided, leaving her tired and slightly empty. She went through her mantra a few more times, continuing until, finally, she could feel the peace of meditation in every part of her body and mind. *May all beings everywhere be happy and free. Including me.*

But she wasn't free, and it was possible she never would be.

In the middle of the night, she awoke from a dream so real that it took a full thirty seconds for her to realize that it was only a nightmare. Even after her eyes grew accustomed to the dark and she understood that she was in a house in Portland and not in the back room of a bar in France, the dream that was in fact a memory lingered, its inky fingers probing her mind. She huddled under her comforter, sweat making the short hair at the back of her neck itch. She was too hot, but she couldn't stand the thought of baring her skin to the cool air. So she lay where she was, shaken and shaking, and tried to trick her mind into thinking different thoughts.

At first she conjured an image of Emma the last time she'd visited Portland, but that wasn't quite right. She tried another memory, one from their recent trip to Lyon—but no, that was wrong, too. The idea was to escape the nightmare, not revisit it. Finally, she remembered their last camp in Carson. On movie night, Emma had sat beside Jamie on one of the beds, their hands clasped loosely, friends and teammates all around. Jamie had felt completely at ease even though she was still technically on the bubble. It had helped that Jessica North had been cut before New Zealand.

At the thought of Jessica North, a tiny spark of outrage flared in her brain. Quickly, Jamie seized on it, fanning it carefully until it became an actual ember that burned away the remaining dark tendrils of the dream. Jessica North didn't deserve to represent the stars and stripes. Ultimately, it didn't matter if you were the most skilled player on the soccer field; you had to be a good teammate, too. Jamie had seen it in the men's game in London again and again: a team made up of superstars who couldn't seem to find a way to work together on the pitch. That was why seemingly inferior teams were often more successful—their players struggled less with subjugating their egos to the team.

The flame of righteous indignation did its job, and soon the sweat was cooling on her skin and she was burrowing into her comforter for warmth rather than safety. Ellie's basement really was cold, even now that spring had sprung in Portland. In a matter of days, Jamie would be sleeping far above the earth on the third floor of—

She cut off the thought and pictured instead Emma in her condo at the top of Seattle's iconic Queen Anne Hill. Buyer's remorse once again threatened to settle in, but she pushed it away. She needed to think of good things, like the smell of fresh mown grass, the morning dew sparkling on a sunlit soccer field, the softness of her cleats after she rubbed shoe polish into the leather. These memories were easy to summon. Soccer had been the one almost daily constant in her life since she could remember. Even if she wasn't in season, she was always training for the next pre-season, the next opening match, the next championship run.

When her soccer career was over, how would she mark the passage of time? Maybe she would coach, maybe not. Either way, there would be kids to teach the ways of the beautiful game. She and Emma were both clear on that. Which meant kiddie practices and Saturday mornings at the local soccer complex, wherever that might be. Would their daughters (sons?) someday play at Emma's high school, following in their mom's—and Michelle Akers's—footsteps?

The thought made her smile, and the gesture pushed out the remaining darkness gripping her mind. She breathed deeply and concentrated on the images that always calmed her. Soon, before she even knew it was happening, she drifted into sleep where she remained until the world beyond her daylight basement was suffused again with light.

#

Her nightmare the following night was more of a morning-mare. She awoke at five a.m. sweating and gasping, certain once again that the dream was real. But it wasn't, of course. She was in Ellie's basement, not her new apartment, and—THANK GOD—there wasn't actually a faceless man standing beside her bed, silent and ominous.

Jamie held her chest where she could feel her heart pounding. Blood rushed in her ears, muffling the silence of her bedroom and making her feel oddly disconnected from reality. What had she been thinking? She clearly wasn't ready to sleep by herself in her new apartment. She'd romanticized the idea of living alone without taking into account what it would actually feel like, and now the reality was creeping in.

The sky was already growing light outside. What she really wanted was a long, hot shower, but the noise would wake Ellie and Jodie. Instead, she slipped out of bed, pulled on warm socks and sweats, and went through the exercises and stretches she always did before starting a tai chi session. With her crazy travel schedule, it had been difficult the past few months to keep up her routine. Why was it that even when you knew something was good for you, you couldn't always make yourself do it?

As she began her tai chi moves, she remembered an article Lacey, the national team's fitness coach and chief of torture, had shared a couple of months earlier. The trick to making a habit stick, the author had written, was to start small; schedule the new practice after an existing step in your daily routine, like brushing your teeth; and associate the action with a pleasurable reward. A square or two of dark chocolate wouldn't be a violation of the team diet, Lacey had stressed unsubtly, especially as studies showed that dark chocolate was good for the human brain.

Maybe Jamie should pick some up. According to Ellie, Trader Joe's chocolate selection was the best, and Portland had at least three TJs in the city limits, one of which was only a few blocks from her new apartment. It might help her work her mental health regimen back into her daily routine, something she obviously needed. The incident with Jenny's stalker and the trip to Lyon were hitting her at last, judging from her dreams.

Freaking PTSD. Every time she thought she'd gotten past Lyon, it came back to bite her in the ass. Or, to be more precise, in the brain. During her recent trip to France, Jamie had been surprised how little angst she'd felt strolling the narrow avenues of the city where she'd been assaulted. She would have thought she'd be looking for the guy everywhere, and she did occasionally think of him and what had happened. But even if she had crossed paths with him, she doubted either of them would have been the wiser. A decade was a legitimately long time, and she was such a different person now. Being in Lyon didn't have the power to hurt her like she'd thought it would, maybe because Emma had been there, too.

At the second leg of Champions League semis, Emma hadn't hidden in the stands in a baseball cap and sunglasses, but rather insisted on sitting directly behind the visitor's bench at the Parc Olympique Lyonnais stadium, her blonde ponytail defiantly uncovered. When Jamie had asked worriedly if she was sure she wanted to be so public, Emma had touched her shoulder and said, voice calm and confident, "Yes. Don't worry, okay?"

And then she had taken off her sweatshirt and turned away, and Jamie had realized she was wearing an Arsenal jersey. Jamie's Arsenal jersey, to be exact. For a United fan, this was nearly akin to proposing marriage. Britt must have had similar thoughts because she'd slapped Jamie in the arm during warm-ups and waved toward the seats where Emma was posing for a fan photo with her back to the camera, smiling over her shoulder with "Maxwell" and Jamie's number clearly visible.

"Do you think she'll take your name when you get married?" Britt had asked. "Or wait, I know—you could both change your name to Blakewell!"

"Shut it," Jamie had said, but she couldn't help smiling. Emma was definitely working hard to make up the whole lying to her thing. To be honest, it was working.

Emma's presence had been the best thing about the match against Lyon. That, and scoring first only five minutes in. But Arsenal had ended up losing 2-1, and even though beating Lyon at home had been a long shot, the loss had still stung. Flying home in first class with Emma had been an excellent distraction, though, Jamie had to admit.

First class travel, an apartment of her own, and enough money in the bank to pay off her car, if she wanted. Or even to buy a different model. If the Nike contract turned out to be as lucrative as Amanda, her new agent at Sparks Sports Management, had suggested—especially if the US won the World Cup—then maybe Jamie would trade in her tiny Kia for a car more befitting a world champion. Like a Beamer, or maybe a Mercedes… She stopped herself. No need to get all status-conscious. She lived in the Pacific Northwest, so a Subaru would be the best bet. Then she and Emma would have matching cars.

And yeah, no. That would be a little too saccharine even for her taste.

She used to fantasize about what she would do with money. She'd lived month to month for so long, never certain where her future income would come from. Her first professional job with FC Gold Pride in the WPS had come to a sudden, disastrous end, leaving her with the sense that no job in women's sports was ever guaranteed. Even now she knew plenty of NWSL players who lived with host families. If Ellie hadn't offered up her basement, Jamie might well have pursued a host situation herself. But with a US Soccer contract and a growing list of sponsorship opportunities, everything had changed—except who she was. All she really needed was a quiet place to sleep, a gym membership, cooking supplies, and comfortable furniture. Well, and maybe some updated electronics. Her laptop was ancient, and she'd never actually bought a television. But she didn't really need much more to be happy. As long as her car could get her to Seattle and back, she was good.

She breathed in through her nose and out through her mouth as she moved through the familiar tai chi patterns, allowing the breath to expand her abdomen before tightening her muscles again on release. Energy buzzed in her fingertips each time she extended her hands away from her chest. That was how she knew she was doing the movements correctly. As relaxation flowed through her, she wondered if she even needed to trick her brain with chocolate to make tai chi part of her daily routine.

Wait—why would she pass up the opportunity to eat sweets that had been pre-approved by the USWNT fitness coach? Looked like a visit to Trader Joe's really should be in her near future. Ellie would be happy to come along, and maybe she would even let Jamie treat her to a stack of chocolate bars. It was the least Jamie could do, given Ellie's help over the past year and a half.

Almost as if Jamie had conjured them, steps sounded overhead. Probably Jodie getting ready for a pre-work run. As Jamie headed for the shower, she reflected that she owed her soon-to-be former roommates so much more than a stack of chocolate bars. Whether or not they would ever let her repay their kindness, however, remained to be seen.

CHAPTER TWO

"Wow," Emma said, staring up at the cream stucco edifice. The natural wood door was so polished it shone, while the concrete foundation and stone and wooden accents had been painted a deep, rich brown. The overall effect was of an older, very well-tended building.

"I know, right?" Jamie said from beside her, cheeks pink and eyes bright as she lifted a box marked "misc." out of her car. She was practically preening—or at least as close to preening as Emma usually saw her. On the soccer field she always had a bit of a swagger, but in real life, she was typically less assuming. "Could you get the door, though?"

"Oh. Of course."

Emma unlocked the glass-plated front door with the keys Jamie handed her. Then she grabbed an unmarked box from the double-parked hatchback and joined Jamie inside her new building.

"Sorry, there's no elevator," Jamie said as she led the way to the stairwell.

"That's it, I'm out," Emma joked as she followed Jamie up the narrow stairway.

"Are you, though?" Jamie asked, smirking at her.

"After Champions League, I'd say there's a pretty good chance."

Emma still occasionally woke up in the middle of the night kicking herself for wearing a replica jersey with Jamie's name on it to Arsenal's last game. She was a United fan; how could she not regret the momentary lapse in judgment? But so far, her plan to stay off most social media platforms (as the national team's PR manager had advised) seemed to be working. There may have been a meltdown of epic proportions on Tumblr or Twitter after Arsenal's match in Lyon. If so, Emma was none the wiser. Her stress and anxiety levels dropped a little bit more every week she stayed offline. Good timing, too, given the upheaval the World Cup was guaranteed to bring.

Jamie's apartment was even nicer than the building's exterior. A large corner unit on the third floor with a view of the Thorns stadium and downtown, the space possessed the sort of vintage charm Emma suddenly realized her own recently constructed condo lacked. The wood floors looked like actual hardwood instead of the ever-present laminate, the ceilings were high with intricate crown molding and classic light fixtures, the kitchen cabinets were white and classic in design, and the large windows in the living room and bedroom let in plenty of light. The bathroom tub was deep, the tiling and sink newer but vintage in style just like the kitchen. Emma's favorite feature, though, was the huge walk-in closet with built-in drawers and shelves.

"There's also a hall closet," Jamie told her. "And a corner closet, too. Oh, and the manager said there's a wine nook in the kitchen."

"I'm impressed," Emma admitted, gazing around. "And maybe even a little jealous."

"Don't sound so surprised."

"No, I'm serious. First apartments in big cities are

rarely this nice."

"It isn't exactly my first apartment, Emma, and London is bigger than Portland, you know."

Emma lifted a brow and stared at Jamie, wondering why she was being defensive. Then she remembered that Jamie had been sleeping in their mutual friend's guest room for the past year while Emma owned a condo in one of Seattle's most expensive neighborhoods. The defensiveness actually made perfect sense.

"Anyway," Jamie added, turning away to stand at the windows that overlooked the soccer stadium, "it's pretty nice, isn't it?"

"It's beautiful," Emma said, and crossed the room, her trainers noiseless against the wood floor. "And so are you." She slid her arms around Jamie's waist from behind, pulled her closer, and leaned up to kiss her cheek. "Thanks for inviting me for your first night here."

Jamie's arms folded over hers, holding her securely in place as she leaned back into Emma. "Thanks for being here."

They stood quietly like that for a few minutes, listening to the sounds from West Burnside a couple of blocks away, and Emma was quietly, peacefully happy.

"Just one thing," she said. "Where exactly are we going to sleep?"

"Oh, we're not sleeping here tonight," Jamie said, laughing.

"Thank god. I'm pretty sure my old lady back couldn't take camping out on the floor."

She had driven down to Portland immediately after her game that afternoon—her last Reign game before World Cup residency camp. On Monday, she and Jamie would leave for Carson via Berkeley, where they would spend a night with Jamie's parents on their way down the coast to Southern California. After a short training camp in

Carson, the team would head north to San Jose for a game against Ireland in the first of three World Cup send-off matches. Jamie was thrilled that she would get to play in front of her family and friends, especially now that she was officially a member of the national team, and Emma was thrilled for her. She only hoped the Irish bitc—*player* who had broken Jamie's ankle two and a half years earlier wouldn't get any ideas.

Though if Emma did somehow end up with a red card, at least she would return from suspension in time for the final send-off match in New York. Priorities, obviously.

"I thought we could go furniture shopping tomorrow," Jamie told her, moving a few steps away to lean against the kitchen counter and type something into her phone. "It looks like there's a bunch of places within walking distance. Although, I guess if we're going to buy a bed, we should probably borrow VB's truck. I'll text her. I think she said she isn't flying out until Tuesday."

"So, *we're* buying a bed, are we?" Emma asked, closing the distance again.

Jamie glanced up from her phone, eyes widening as she took in Emma's half-lidded stare. "Um, yeah?"

"Good." Emma grasped Jamie's belt buckle firmly. "Because I, for one, would like to break in your new apartment properly." She leaned in slowly, enjoying the audible gulp she drew from her girlfriend, and placed a kiss on the soft skin behind her ear. "I mean, assuming you don't mind."

"I wouldn't say I *mind*, exactly," Jamie said, and pulled Emma closer the better to kiss her.

Hmm, Emma thought as Jamie's hand slipped inside her T-shirt. Maybe they didn't need that bed, after all.

#

"What about this one?" Ellie asked, flopping onto a queen-sized mattress with a frame that looked like it might collapse under her weight.

Emma saw Jamie wince and turn away. With a slight glare at Ellie, Emma followed suit. She reached for Jamie's hand and tugged her closer. "You okay?" she asked, her voice quiet so that their fellow shoppers wouldn't hear.

Jamie glanced back at the bed where Jodie was now lying with her head on Ellie's shoulder while Jordan VanBrueggen and Ainsley Meyer, another Thorns player who had hovered just at the edge of the national pool for years, were testing a rustic four-poster frame that probably cost more than Jamie's car had.

"This place isn't really what I had in mind." Jamie waved at the cavernous warehouse that had been converted into a high-end furniture gallery featuring organic mattresses and live-edge furniture. "Isn't there a United Furniture Warehouse or something around here?"

Jamie said the store name in a sing-song tone that Emma recognized as part of the chain's jingle, and she couldn't help laughing. But Jamie didn't join in. "Oh, you're serious."

"Super observant of you," Jamie said, and stalked away.

"What's her deal?" Jordan asked, appearing at Emma's elbow.

"She's got sticker shock, doesn't she?" Ainsley put in. "This stuff is crazy expensive."

"No, there's just a lot to do before we leave," Emma said, and followed Jamie to the living room section of the gallery.

Jamie was standing beside an elegant desk, running her hand over the wood surface that, according to a sign, had been fashioned from a city tree that had come down during a wind storm. She looked up as Emma neared. "Sorry."

"For what?"

"For being an ass."

"You kind of were, weren't you," Emma agreed.

"Hey!"

"What? You said you wanted honesty from here on out, so…"

"I can't believe you would bring that up right now." But she was half-smiling as she said it.

Emma drifted closer and set her hand on top of Jamie's. "Do you want me to buy this desk for you? It could be an apartment-warming gift."

"Jesus, Emma." Jamie had started to soften, but now she straightened again and pulled her hand away. "You know what? I'll be outside."

Again, Emma watched her walk away, but this time she didn't follow. Instead, she headed back to where their friends were still jumping on beds like the overgrown children they were.

One look from Emma and Ellie extricated herself. "What's wrong? Where's Jamie?"

"Outside. I think she wants to try a different store."

"Really? I totally thought this stuff would be up her alley."

"I don't think the furniture is the issue." Emma hesitated. Jamie wouldn't mind her telling Ellie, would she? "The prices, on the other hand…"

Ellie literally slapped her forehead. "Crap! I'm such an idiot."

"No, I know. Me, too."

Ellie ushered the others together, and soon they were headed across town again, Jamie leading the way this time to a mattress shop whose name contained the word "Superstore." Jamie seemed more at ease as she browsed the impressively large selection. By lunchtime, she'd ordered a mattress and mission-style frame that was simple but tasteful, and she'd even found matching nightstands in her price range. Jodie and Ellie were storing a couch she'd bought from one of their neighbors, along with a dresser, two bookshelves, and a kitchen table she'd found on Craigslist. For now, she announced, she should be set. The final decorative touches could wait until they were back from Canada.

After lunch at Ainsley's favorite vegetarian restaurant, they backtracked to Ellie and Jodie's house to load VB's extended cab pickup, a hand-me-down from her parents. It didn't take long to maneuver Jamie's furniture and boxes of books and papers outside onto the sidewalk in front of Ellie's house. Her athletic bags, backpacks, and luggage were already in her car, accompanied by a couple of trash bags of shoes and jackets. She wore them all, she insisted when her Thorns teammates teased her about the overflowing garbage bags.

The main moving challenge was getting the multiple team captains in the group to agree how to fit the accumulated furniture into the back of the truck. Finally, VB announced that since it was her truck, she would make the final decision. This resonated with everyone else, although it didn't prevent snarky comments and less-than-subtle smirks when VB's packing sense revealed its imperfections. But they finally managed to fit the last of the dining chairs into the truck bed, and the caravan of friends and movers was off.

Unfortunately, finding street parking in Jamie's new neighborhood was no easy feat. Emma had volunteered to drive Jamie's car, and as she circled the block for the fifteenth time (okay, maybe it was only the third), she vowed to look up parking space rental rates in the area. Jamie may not want to spend her newly acquired income on such a luxury, but Emma had no such qualms. 2015 was a major tournament year, so they would be together more often than not. Same with 2016 and the Summer Olympics. But if they were still playing on separate NWSL teams in 2017, Emma wasn't about to waste time looking for parking when it was her turn to make the road trip.

To be honest, Emma had fantasized more than a few times about trying to convince the league to trade Jamie to Seattle, even though she wasn't sure how Jamie would feel about such a trade. Emma would have considered moving to Portland, but the STP rivalry is REAL, y'all, and she was a native Seattleite, so that wasn't a realistic option. Then again, the Thorns played in a professional stadium where they led the league in attendance while the Reign averaged less than half Portland's attendance figures in a stadium that felt like a World War Two bunker. Actually, that was pretty accurate, Emma thought, given that Memorial Stadium had been built in 1948. They didn't have changing facilities or showers on site, and add in the fact that the playing surface didn't meet US Soccer's professional league standards…

Clearly, if Emma was smart, she'd try to get traded to Portland—assuming Jamie even wanted her to. But that was a conversation that could wait until after the World Cup. Even, possibly, after the Olympics.

By the time she found a spot two blocks away and hoofed it back to Jamie's building, she'd missed much of the unloading process. Jamie and VB were in the truck bed as she approached, each at one corner of the queen mattress, while Ellie and Ainsley were standing at the rear of the double-parked truck, arms outstretched, ready.

"Hey," Jodie said, nodding at Emma from the curb where she stood, phone in hand.

Ellie's fiancée was seldom without her phone. Emma was tempted to share the power of unplugging with Jodie—*you feel so free, and mentally healthy, and less stressed!*—but at the last moment recognized the proselytizing urge for what it was.

"Hey," she said instead, drifting to a stop beside Jodie. "Street parking sucks."

"It really does. I somehow forgot about all the countless hours I wasted circling the block before I moved in with Ellie."

"Selective memory, which most definitely does not suck."

Jodie flashed her a sideways smile and went back to her phone.

"A little help here?" Jamie asked, eyebrows rising as she glanced at Emma.

Her tone was more than a little hassled, and Emma momentarily considered turning around and walking away. Fred Meyer on Burnside would be deliciously cool inside, and she could use a smoothie right about now. But she only sighed long-sufferingly, straightened up, and muttered just loud enough for Jodie to hear, "I'm not the one without a designated parking space." Lifting her voice, she added, "Whatever might I do to assist thee, Lord Maxwell?"

"Ha ha." Jamie nodded at the dining room chairs sitting on the sidewalk. "Those aren't going to move themselves."

Emma wasn't entirely sure she was going to move them, either. But then she took another look at Jodie, who was on her phone pointedly ignoring the exchange. Better to deal with cranky Jamie than be lumped into the useless girlfriend category. Without another word, she picked up all four chairs and headed inside Jamie's building through the propped-open front door.

"Careful!" she heard Jamie call, her voice alarmed.

Whatever. Emma could bench press Jamie. Or, high school Jamie, anyway.

On the second floor landing, Emma's bravado abruptly deserted her as she faced another set of stairs with the awkwardly arrayed chairs. They weren't heavy, and two would have been a cinch. But four in Portland's early summer heat? Ah, silly pride. Definitely coming back to bite her in the—

"Whoa," a laughing voice said from behind as she tried to rearrange the chairs and nearly fell over. "Need some help there?"

She blew her hair away from her forehead and glanced over her shoulder to see a guy and girl about her age emerging from the second floor hallway. "Actually, yeah. Thanks."

The pair moved a few steps toward her, hands outstretched. Emma sensed the moment the guy recognized her—it wasn't difficult, since he froze, hands still half-extended toward the chairs that were probably leaving permanent dents in her hands by now.

"Babe, what…?" The woman trailed off, her eyes going wide as she followed his gaze, locked onto Emma's face. "Holy shit. You're Emma Blakeley!"

Emma reached deep and mustered a semi-professional smile, quelling the panicky knee-jerk reaction at being spotted in Jamie's new building. She was unplugged, remember? *Free, mentally healthy, less stressed.* And about to drop Jamie's chairs on their apparent fans. Actually, Jamie's fans. They were in Portland, after all.

"Does that mean you're not going to help?" Emma asked. "I promise, I'm friends with the Thorns players off the field…"

Both of her would-be rescuers leapt forward as if poked with a cattle prod, and Emma hid a smile as they relieved her of one chair each—predictably, the guy tried to take two, but Emma rebuffed him firmly—and accompanied her up the final flight to Jamie's apartment.

The front door was held open by the extended bolt, and Emma heard the couple murmuring to each other as they kicked their shoes off before following her into the dining area. There, they set the chairs down beside the two she'd carried, glances curious as they took in the half-empty apartment.

"Wow," the guy said. "I wondered if the corner units were as spacious as advertised. Check and check."

"Thanks for the help," Emma said, extending her hand. "I'm Emma, as you already deduced."

"Jackson," the guy said, shaking her hand gingerly.

"Hannah," the girl added, smiling as she took Emma's hand in turn. "It's so great to meet you. We're huge fans. Like, *huge*."

"Even if you play for the Reign," Jackson added.

"Speaking of, you're not moving into the building, are you?" Hannah asked, her head tilting.

They had recovered their equilibrium faster than Emma would have expected. Maybe seeing her sweaty and unmade up in shorts and a ratty "I heart NYC" T-shirt had set them at ease, or maybe it was the twenty-something Portlander quotient. Hipsters were not supposed to be intimated by mildly famous peers.

"No, I live in Seattle. This apartment is…" She trailed off as voices echoed down the hallway. In another moment, Jamie appeared in the doorway, swearing as she backed inside wrestling the mattress. "Hers."

Jamie glanced over her shoulder, eyebrows knit. Emma could tell she was about to snap again when her eyes fell on the couple who were now gazing avidly between them. *Doh*.

Whoever was in the hallway failed to notice Jamie's pause, probably because the mattress took up most of the doorway. Jamie yelped as it bonked into her and nearly knocked her over. "Hold up," she called, rearranging her grip. Then she continued into the apartment, shooting Emma and their impromptu visitors a harried smile before guiding the mattress into the bedroom on the opposite side of the apartment. VB, who was at the other end of the bed, nodded at them briefly.

"Jamie Maxwell," Hannah said, and it was clear she wasn't asking. "Jamie Maxwell is moving into our building, and you and Jordan VanBrueggen are helping her."

At that moment, Ellie and Jodie ducked into the apartment with pieces of the bed frame, followed by Ainsley with more wood sections, and Emma had to hide another smile as Hannah reflexively clutched her boyfriend's arm.

"You okay there?" Emma asked as the guy visibly paled.

"No, yeah, I mean, um," he mumbled, eyes still glued to the national team's current captain and leading scorer and, in Emma's opinion, shoo-in for the hall of fame.

The players emerged from the bedroom a moment later, and there were introductions all around. Then VB mentioned that the truck was double-parked, so they should probably get back to it… Jackson and Hannah said they understood, and chatted amiably with Jamie about the building's quirks and the management company's responsiveness as the group returned to the ground floor.

"You're going to love living here," Hannah assured Jamie. "The tenants are mostly young professionals who are really active. Oh! And there are lots of cute dogs here, too."

Jamie gave Emma a meaningful look, and she knew instantly they would be having the "why we can't get a puppy in a World Cup year" conversation again that night.

Jamie's new neighbors helped them move the rest of her belongings in, and then, back on the street again, asked if they could take a selfie with the group. Naturally, the players complied. Jodie even offered to take a picture of the pair with the Thorns players arrayed around them—and Emma too, of course.

"It's so great meeting you," Hannah enthused after the photo had been taken, looking for a moment like she might try to hug Jamie.

Emma inserted herself into the space between them and extended her hand again. "You, too."

As Jamie shook hands with their moving help, she asked, "Actually, could you maybe keep that photo private? I'd rather not have the whole world know where to find me just yet."

"Oh, right, of course you don't," Hannah said, nodding quickly.

"Totally," Jackson echoed, similarly struck. "We won't post it on social media."

"Thanks, guys," Jamie said with an easy smile that Emma envied. Then again, Jamie liked people in general in a way that Emma could honestly say she didn't.

As they headed down the sidewalk toward Burnside, Emma heard Hannah whisper to Jackson, "I told you they were together!" His response, however, was lost to the long blast of a nearby car horn.

Emma exchanged a look with Jamie, who only shrugged and said, "I mean, she isn't wrong." Then she reached for Emma's hand and gave it a quick squeeze. "Sorry I was a dick before. It's just so effing hot."

"I know, right?" Emma agreed.

Seattle and the Bay Area definitely had better climates to offer than Portland. Maybe she would be able to convince Jamie to move north, after all. There was plenty of time to work on her.

CHAPTER THREE

"I love Chipotle!" Jamie said, sighing as she closed the lid on her now empty to-go dish.

"Well, yeah. Why wouldn't you?" Emma asked, pushing a last few grains of rice onto her spoon and trying not to pout over the fact that she had finished her burrito bowl. "Their food is the nectar of the gods."

They were alone in Jamie's living room, the evening sky darkening beyond the windows. Jamie had invited their moving help to dine with them at Chipotle, but everyone had claimed to have some place else to be. So Emma had treated their friends to takeout and she and Jamie had come back to the apartment to eat dinner on the coffee table Jamie had bought on Craigslist. The food had tasted just as good on the wood veneer surface as it would have on a live-edge table built from a reclaimed urban redwood. At least, Emma assumed so.

Jamie turned sideways on the couch and eyed her. "Nectar, seriously? You are such a dork. I can't even."

"*I can't even?*" Emma echoed. "What are you, a teenager?"

"Not last I checked." Jamie's blue eyes narrowed as

she set her Chipotle dish on the mission style coffee table and reached for Emma's. "Didn't you say something about breaking in my apartment properly?"

"I think we did that last night, didn't we?" Emma said, trying not to think about the couch's previous owners. Jamie had vacuumed and washed it with baby wipes—a cleaning hack she'd found online—before moving it in, but even so, the fact that the gently used furniture had lived in someone else's home for the past few years creeped Emma out. What if the previous owners had been meth users? Just because they lived across the street from Ellie and Jodie didn't mean they couldn't be addicts. Admittedly, it would be difficult to afford the mortgage in Ellie's neighborhood if they were, but still.

Jamie smiled. "I meant in the bedroom, Emma."

"Oh, thank god! In that case, yes. But how about a shower first?"

"You read my mind."

Ten minutes later they were standing close together in the clawfoot tub, water streaming from the gleaming chrome shower head. There was no shampoo, but Jamie had brought along her lavender soap from Ellie's, and soon they were soaping each other, movements languid as they washed the day's grime from one another's skin. The water pressure wasn't quite as strong as at Emma's place, but she didn't think either of them minded as they watched each other through the rising steam. This was her favorite Jamie, quiet and vulnerable and so strong, her hands gentle and her eyes warm with affection and something else Emma couldn't quite define but that she knew was probably reflected in her own face. It didn't matter that they'd sniped at each other half the day. Their relationship was strong enough to survive moving tensions exacerbated by Portland's cloying heat.

A belly full of Chipotle didn't hurt, either.

Clean again, they backtracked to the bedroom where Jamie made sure the blinds were closed. Then they climbed naked between the sheets on the brand new bed, giggling when the mission-style frame creaked slightly. Their friends had teased them earlier about breaking the place in, citing thin walls and the proximity of neighbors, and now Emma realized that they were completely right. The 1920s building was charming and attractively renovated, but the older construction offered significantly less insulation than she was used to.

"Music?" Jamie asked, grinning, her short hair tousled and damp.

"Why not?" Emma said, smiling back at her.

Which was how they made love for the second time in Jamie's new apartment in the bed they had bought together accompanied by Beyoncé on the Bluetooth speakers it took Jamie ten minutes to locate in the very last box she checked: kitchen supplies, naturally. Unlike the previous night, this time was slow and silly, with plentiful shushing and laughter, and it felt like college all over again but not in a bad way. Being with Jamie in Portland was still so different from being with her in Seattle, where Emma knew the city and had arranged her life rigidly so that her down time from soccer would be as comfortable and stress-free as possible. But that difference was more intriguing than anything—at least, now that the worst of the move was over and the overhead fan was cycling cooler evening air through the apartment.

Jamie's arms were loose about her as their breathing and heart rates slowed and settled, her lips warm against Emma's forehead as she stroked one hand lazily up and down her arm. Street noise drifted up through the open window, car engines and voices from neighboring blocks muffled by the distance. City lights filtered in through the gaps and around the edges of the blinds, white and yellow and, in one window, noticeably blue.

"Is that the Volvo sign?" Emma asked.

Jamie's bedroom faced a Volvo dealership with an old-fashioned neon sign that dwarfed the five-story building that housed it. Fortunately, the sign faced downtown, as did Jamie's apartment, so Emma found the blue light more romantic than obtrusive.

"Totally," Jamie said, her voice slightly gravelly after sex. "I told the team I could see it from my living room window, and they were all, 'That's so cool!'"

"It is cool," Emma agreed, turning her head slightly so that she could inhale the scent of soap and *Jamie* lingering at her girlfriend's collar bone.

"You know what's even better, though? There are three coffee shops between here and the stadium."

"Aw, did you have me in mind when you were apartment-shopping?"

"Of course." Jamie pressed another soft kiss to her forehead. "I always have you in mind."

Emma felt tears prick her eyes and blinked them back. Silly post-orgasmic hormones.

A few minutes later, Jamie pulled away and sat up, elbowing a pillow higher against the headboard. "Actually, can we talk about something?"

Emma swallowed down her fear of the phrase that had signaled an end to every relationship she'd ever been in: *Can we talk?* "Of course," she said, trying to channel magnanimity as she sat up beside Jamie. "What's up?"

Jamie looked down at the cream-colored sheets Ellie and Jodie had given her as a housewarming gift, brow knitting as she smoothed a wrinkle away. "I'm not really sure where to start with this."

Emma took a calming breath and channeled her mom's bedside manner. "Take your time. You can talk to me about anything, you know."

Jamie's tone was wry as she said, "I know—in theory. It's just harder to do in practice."

Emma was a little relieved to see that she wasn't the only one who struggled with talking about feelings. Predictably, though, Jamie didn't struggle for long. She took a deep breath, released it, and launched right in.

"Remember how I said being in Lyon was anticlimactic? Well, as it turns out, I might not have been entirely accurate about that."

Emma tried not to let her concern show as Jamie's words from all those weeks earlier on the moonlit Breton beach washed over her: *I wanted it all to go away. I felt like I couldn't stay in my skin.* "What do you mean?"

Jamie squinted at her, head tilting sideways. "Um, I might have invited you to spend my first night here with me not just because it's romantic but because, well, it's *possible* I was nervous about staying here by myself."

"That's understandable," Emma assured her. "I'm still nervous at my place sometimes, too. I think it's part of being raised female in this culture—knowing you might not be safe anywhere, not even in your own home. Actually, not just in this culture. In this world."

Half of Jamie's face was in shadows as she faced Emma, her features barely discernible in the filtered blue light from the Volvo sign. "It's not just that," she admitted. "I—well, I've been having nightmares since we got back from Lyon. And I've been struggling with some other signs of PTSD, too."

Emma's heart sank as Jamie checked off the list of symptoms she'd been dealing with since Lyon. Nightmares? Check. Obsessive showering? Check. Panic attacks? Check.

"I'm so sorry," Emma said, reaching for her hand and squeezing it tightly, wishing she could somehow inoculate

Jamie with her touch against the trauma that had never quite left her.

"It's not as bad as when I was younger," Jamie said, squeezing her hand back. "Probably because I recognize what's happening and I have ways to short-circuit some of it before it can really take over. But, well, I wanted you to know. In the spirit of being honest."

"I'm glad you're telling me," Emma said, running her thumb over the back of Jamie's hand in what she hoped was a soothing manner. "Was it the trip to Lyon that triggered everything, do you think?"

"Partly. But I think it was what happened with Jenny in St. Louis, too. I've been thinking about that, trying to imagine what Shoshanna would say about it, and I think she would have said that it was a test that showed how far I've come. I mean, I didn't just freeze up and tune out. I stepped up, you know? I *acted*. I didn't let him hurt any of us. I think Shoshanna would say that's a good thing."

Emma nodded slowly, digesting what Jamie was saying. She hadn't thought of what had happened in St. Louis in those terms. Mainly she had been furious with Jamie for risking herself against an uncertain threat. Now, though, she could see how empowering Jamie's actions might have felt. She wasn't the same girl who had lain unmoving while a drunken stranger assaulted her in the back of a French bar, nor the same girl who had fled the country the next day without telling anyone about the attack. She had grown into a strong woman who, when faced with a potentially similar situation, had taken quick, decisive action to protect herself and those she cared about.

Shoshanna, Emma suspected, would say that was a *great* thing. Except that there were nightmares, apparently, and obsessive behavior. And panic attacks.

"And yet…?" Emma asked.

"And yet, then we went to Lyon, and now I think my mind is trying to reconcile what happened in St. Louis with the experience of being back in the city where—well, you know."

Emma did know. Lyon was where Jamie had lost so much that she'd had to become an entirely different person. A stronger person in many ways, but different all the same.

"Would it help to talk about everything?" Emma asked, her hand still tight around Jamie's. "Or would it be too much?"

"I don't know," Jamie admitted.

Emma lay quietly, allowing Jamie the time and space to make up her mind about what she needed. After a minute or so, Jamie pinched the bridge of her nose and sighed, her hand tense in Emma's, her face shadowed by more than blue light from the blinds.

"It was my decision," she told Emma, "not to go after the guy. A US embassy rep in France reviewed the case, and given the lack of physical evidence… I think I told you before I took a shower after I got back to the hotel, and the rape kit my mother insisted we do at the hospital only had my DNA, so there wasn't really anything to go on. The embassy rep we met with in San Francisco said it would be an uphill battle to get anyone in France to take me seriously. I mean, I went to the bar willingly and my friends and I accepted drinks from the guy, so…"

Emma tried to smother the angry sound that rose in her throat. "Accepting a drink in no way implies consent for anything else. And besides, you were fifteen!"

"No, I know." Jamie smiled a little, picking at the sheet again. "You should have seen my mom. She was all, 'Are you trying to say the attack was my daughter's fault?' She gave him her glare, and he, like, quailed before it. Understandably."

Emma nodded. She'd never actually seen Jamie's mother's famous Death Glare, but the legend preceded the smallish woman.

"He was like, 'No, of course not, ma'am. I'm simply saying this would be a difficult case to win.' I don't think he was wrong, either. I totally botched the whole thing."

"Understandably," Emma said, echoing Jamie's own words. "You were just doing the best you could to get through it."

"I know. But it meant there wasn't any evidence. So after that meeting, I pretty much begged my parents to let the whole thing go, and they agreed even though they clearly didn't want to. It was my decision, and they said they supported my choice. At the time, I was just relieved the whole thing was 'over.' But now…"

She paused, her eyes closed briefly, and said, her voice low in the quiet bedroom, "Now I kind of wish we'd gone after the guy. If nothing else, it might have stopped him from trying the same thing with some other girl who didn't know how to fight back."

Emma winced, because she understood why Jamie might think that. If Emma were in her shoes, the "what ifs" would drive her slightly batty. Or maybe a whole lot batty.

"The people at the bar might have known him," Jamie added, turning her head to stare at nothing. "Maybe the police could have tracked him down even without DNA evidence."

"And then what?" Emma asked. "You were here, in a totally different country. Could you really have gotten him arrested?"

She shrugged. "Maybe not. At least I would have been able to say I tried."

And yeah, Emma got that. But what if Jamie had tried and failed? Emma remembered the post-France Jamie, the girl who flinched if you came too close, the girl whose smile didn't reach her eyes, the girl who played soccer like it was the last game she might ever get to play. "I think that who you are now could handle what an investigation and trial would take, but who you were then? I don't know. I think she made the right decision."

Jamie expelled a long breath and glanced over at Emma. "Yeah, you're probably right."

"Duh," Emma said, and poked her in the side.

Jamie caught her hand and held it. "You know what else gets me, though? How he knew just by looking at me that I wouldn't fight back."

Emma's heart broke a little. "Jamie…"

Her smile was lopsided. "One of my friends in college who knew about France asked me once if I thought the rape made me gay. She didn't realize I'd already come out."

"I don't think assault could change someone's sexuality," Emma said, frowning a little. "Do you?"

"No, not really. I told her I thought it happened *because* I was gay. You know, like he knew and that's why he picked me. Did you know that trans people and bisexual women experience the highest rates of sexual assault? It's like straight men need to punish us for daring to be who we are."

Fucking straight men, Emma thought. Who did they think they were? She remembered the rage that had overtaken her, hot and fast, after Jenny's stalker called Jamie a dyke. She remembered wondering in Lyon if any of the faces they passed belonged to the man who had hurt Jamie. She remembered wishing she could get that guy alone in a room just once. With her anger and Dani's kickboxing classes, she felt confident she could take the son-of-a-bitch.

Violence might not solve anything, but it would feel good. At least, in theory.

"I'm sorry, Jamie," she said, moving closer until they were sharing the same pillow. "I wish I could say something or do something to undo it all. I really do."

"I know. But it's made me who I am, so I'm not sure I would change it even if I could." Jamie paused, and then she shook her head. "Actually, that's not true. I would love to go back in time and lock myself in that hotel room. If only time travel were a thing."

Emma knew exactly what she meant. She hesitated, but—no more secret-keeping. She'd promised. "As long as we're talking about this, I think there's something I should tell you."

Jamie drew away slightly. "What is it?"

"Well, you know how your mom hasn't always been the best at keeping what happened in France to herself?"

Jamie scooted up the bed even further. "Who else did she tell now?"

So Emma told her, haltingly, about her mother confronting her club coach about what had happened the last night of the trip.

"What the fuck?" Jamie hopped out of bed and paced across the hardwood floor, her body naked, both hands on top of her head. "She fucking told Pete and didn't tell me? Not that that should be surprising." She stopped suddenly and faced Emma. "Wait. How do *you* know all of this?"

"Um, Jo told me? She and Pete apparently go way back. That's all I know."

Jamie's eyes narrowed. "When exactly did you and Jo talk about this?"

Emma bit her lip. "Brazil. The night we told the coaches about us, Jo called me up to her room to discuss the online situation, and, well, it came up."

"Jesus Christ, Emma!" Jamie reached for her T-shirt and shorts at the end of the bed and yanked them on. "I can't fucking believe you right now!" And with that she turned and stalked out of the bedroom.

Emma waited, ears straining for the sound of the apartment door slamming, but it didn't come. Instead, she heard Jamie rifling through boxes in the kitchen muttering to herself. Finally, there was the sound of water running and the gas flame on the stove being lit. Tea, Emma guessed. Jamie was making tea.

By the time she pulled on her own discarded clothes and made her way to the kitchen, the kettle was poised to whistle and Jamie had two mugs and an assortment of tea out on the counter. Emma honed in on the two mugs and started to breathe again. Jamie wasn't going to send her packing. At least, not without a farewell beverage.

"I'm sorry," Emma said, drifting to a stop a few feet away. "I know it probably doesn't make much of a difference, but I didn't tell you because I was trying—"

"—to protect me," Jamie finished for her. "Yeah, I know. Mint? Or lemon ginger?"

"Lemon ginger," Emma said, and watched as Jamie poured the hot water over the tea bags. "Jo didn't let on she knew because she said if you wanted her to know, you would tell her."

Unexpectedly, Jamie's gaze shifted as if she was focused on another place and time. "No free passes—right."

Emma wasn't sure what that meant, but she didn't feel like she could ask, either.

"Do you want honey?" Jamie asked.

"Yeah. Sure."

Emma watched Jamie open two different cupboards before she found the honey. Ainsley and VB had helpfully unloaded a few grocery bags, which had Jamie lamenting that she would never find her stuff. Good thing the kitchen wasn't that big to begin with.

"Come on," Jamie said a minute later, motioning her closer. "I know you don't like your tea as sweet as I do."

Emma stole a glance at Jamie as they traded the plastic bear-shaped container of honey back and forth. She didn't look quite as angry anymore, but she didn't look happy, either.

"I'm sorry," Emma said again, even though she was probably saying it too much.

Jamie side-eyed her. "I know."

She didn't say it was okay. She didn't say much at all as they took a seat on the couch and scrolled through their phones while they drank their mugs of tea. But she did let Emma curl up at her side without comment, and even once pressed the ghost of a kiss to the side of Emma's head. That was how Emma knew everything would be okay. Because even if she fucked up again and again—which, apparently, she was determined to do—and even if Jamie had PMS or PTSD or both and was legitimately bitchy for a solid week, neither of them was going anywhere. Jamie loved her, and she loved Jamie, and they would figure it all out somehow because that was what they had both decided to do.

The US really wouldn't lose the World Cup because of them, Emma realized once again as the lemon ginger tea started to settle the queasiness burbling in her belly.

Thank freaking goodness for that.

CHAPTER FOUR

Jamie buckled her seat belt and reached for the auxiliary audio cable Emma kept in her glovebox. Leaving at an ungodly hour meant they would miss Portland traffic *and* get to Berkeley in time for dinner, if all went well. Although after Emma's bombshell the previous night, Jamie wasn't entirely sure she wanted extra time with her parents right now.

"Hold up," Emma said, watching Jamie connect the cable to her phone. "What happened to my car, my music?"

Jamie smiled at her, taking in Emma's messy bun and the sunglasses that held back the usual wisps. "I made us a mix."

"You—oh." Emma's pre-coffee frown eased, and she even smiled back. Almost.

"I mean, it's our first real road trip," Jamie added.

"That's sweet," Emma decided, and turned the key in the ignition. As the opening bars of Rachel Platten's "Fight Song" filled the Subaru's interior, Emma's half-smile morphed into a snort. "I stand corrected."

"Come on, it's catchy!" Jamie said, laughing as Emma

guided the car toward Burnside. "Besides, it's totally appropriate, *Rocky*."

"Too soon, Jamie. Or maybe it's just too early. Why exactly did we decide to leave at the ass crack of dawn? And don't say *traffic* because I'm pretty sure we're doing the reverse commute."

"Oh, look," Jamie said, pretending to be surprised. "A drive-through coffee stand. Do you think we should stop on our way out of town?"

Emma was already turning into the half-circle drive. "Come to Mama," she said, eyes lighting up as she surveyed the menu.

Thank god for coffee. Maybe Jamie would have to get a magnet or some other trinket that said as much.

"The mix is actually pretty good," Emma admitted a little while later as they drove down I-5, her entire being sunnier thanks to the addition of caffeine. "Jenny might have some competition."

Jenny Latham held the unofficial title of team DJ, which came with the responsibility of mixing the official Game Day playlist and any and all travel mixes.

"Hello, she already does," Jamie said. "Lisa's boyfriend is literally a professional musician."

"*Lisa*? Are you kidding? She listens to the Eagles and, like, Fleetwood Mac. Can you imagine Maddie's reaction if Tom Petty came on in the locker room before a big game?"

Jamie shuddered. Tom Petty's voice creeped her out. No way she was the only one, either.

They talked music and concerts for the first leg of the journey, accompanied by Jamie's boppy travel mix, before moving on to books and movies. When Emma revealed that one of her favorite books was still *To Kill a Mockingbird*, Jamie commented, "It's a great book, obviously. But I don't know. I wish it wasn't about a woman who accuses an innocent man of rape. I mean, how often does that actually happen?"

"Okay, but there's a long history of African American men being wrongfully accused of sexual assault," Emma pointed out, "and then sent to prison or executed by white mobs in the name of 'justice.' Like the Scottsboro Boys, or even the Central Park Five."

"I get that. But if you look at it statistically, false accusations are super rare. Most rapes actually go unreported, and those that are? Something like *one percent* of accused rapists are convicted. African American men are totally more likely to be falsely convicted, and Harper Lee was calling attention to bullshit racist scapegoating. I just wish a book that is taught to teenagers wasn't centered around a girl who lies about being raped."

Emma was silent for a long moment, her eyes on the road ahead. "I never actually thought of that. But it makes sense that you would. Given your experience and all."

The phrase reminded Jamie of something. What was it? She couldn't quite remember.

"Okay," Emma added. "You've convinced me. *To Kill a Mockingbird* is no longer one of my favorite books."

Jamie expelled an irritated breath. "That wasn't my point. I'm not trying to tell you how to feel about it, Emma."

"I know," Emma said, and smiled sideways at her. "Don't worry. In case you haven't realized by now, I'm not easily swayed by the opinions of others."

Except that she was, Jamie thought, watching the Oregon countryside race past Emma's Subaru. Otherwise, she would have already come out publicly. "Whatever you say, Blake."

It wasn't until later in the day when Jamie was taking a turn at the wheel and Emma was dozing beside her that Jamie remembered why the phrase "given your experience" felt familiar. The first time they'd kissed in high school, Emma had freaked out afterward and gone radio silent. Finally, a few days later, she'd reached out to Jamie and apologized in a text. Her apology for not seeking Jamie's consent before kissing her had included the cringe-worthy phrase: *Given your experience.*

In all the time they'd been together, they'd never discussed Emma's douchebag move—by which Jamie meant her runaway bride impression and subsequent silence, not the actual kiss. Nothing like a road trip to give you time to sweat the small things, really.

The next time Emma stirred, Jamie said, "Hey." But softly because it had been her idea to leave Portland before the morning rush hour.

Emma yawned and sat up, tugging on her seat belt. "Hey." She reached for the bottle of Pepsi she'd gotten at Subway when they stopped for lunch and took a long gulp. "It's so weird to sit in the passenger seat in my own car."

"Totally," Jamie said, trying to think how to ease Emma into the conversation she'd been having inside her own head for the past ten minutes.

"What's up?" Emma asked.

"Who says anything's up?"

"That little furrow between your eyebrows," Emma said, taking another sip of soda. "Although technically it's down, I guess."

"It's nothing. Just, you said something earlier that reminded me of our first kiss, that's all."

"I did? Well, in that case, I'm sorry."

"For what?"

"All of it," Emma said. "Then and now."

"That's a total cop-out, and you know it."

"And your point?" As Jamie shot her a frown, Emma sighed. "Fine, let's talk about ancient terrible history while we're stuck in a car for the next—" she paused and checked the time on the dash—"three, possibly four hours."

Jamie considered arguing with her calculation, but Emma was probably close enough, especially if they didn't stop again.

"You know," she said instead, "for an internationally renowned defender, you're kind of a chicken shit."

"You say that as if you're just figuring it out now."

Jamie snickered despite herself. God damn Emma, making her laugh when she wanted to stay pissy about something that had happened when they were both barely old enough to drive.

"All right, all right," Emma said. "What do you want to ask me about the kiss that would be better off never speaking its name?"

"Jackass," Jamie muttered as she pulled into the passing lane. The Prius in front of them was going so slowly she might have crashed into it if she'd been more distracted by Emma's oddly cheerful profession of cowardice. Then again, her girlfriend's cheerfulness upon awakening from a mid-day nap shouldn't come as that much of a surprise. Most professional athletes were adept at power napping, in her experience.

And there it was again: *In her experience.*

"I guess I always wondered what was going through your mind when you dropped off the face of the earth," she said.

"You mean after I kissed you and literally ran away? Guilt, mostly. I felt awful because I wasn't sure you wanted me to kiss you."

"Seriously?" Jamie checked the Prius's status in her rearview mirror before easing the Subaru back into the right lane. "You couldn't tell I'd been daydreaming about kissing you that entire week?"

"I had my suspicions. But as I recall, you didn't exactly respond with enthusiasm."

"I was surprised! Besides, I won't say I'd *never* been kissed, but, well, I'd never been kissed by a girl before."

Emma blinked at her. "Really?"

"Really."

"I didn't know that," Emma admitted, and then groaned melodramatically, sliding lower in her seat. "Great. That just makes the fact that I jumped you even worse."

"Trust me, you didn't jump me." She left unspoken that she knew the difference.

"I know, but the last thing I wanted to do was take something from you that you didn't want to give."

"Funny," Jamie said, reaching over to hold Emma's hand in hers. "I felt the same way about you."

"What do you mean?"

"Your father had just died and I had all these feelings for you. When you kissed me, I thought maybe you were just confused."

"I *was* confused. But not about you. I knew how I felt about you." She paused, her palm warm and solid against Jamie's. "You weren't exactly in the best place, either, if you'll recall."

"No," Jamie agreed. Neither of them had been in what could remotely be called a good place, let alone the best. "I hope you can hear me, though, when I say you didn't do anything wrong by kissing me. Absconding afterward like Mt. Rainier was erupting, on the other hand…"

Emma laughed. "Obviously not my best moment."

"Good thing you're cute," Jamie said. "Otherwise…"

"Good thing," Emma replied sassily, sticking her tongue out as Jamie shook her head.

Now that the conversation had taken a turn for the past, it stayed there. The gap in their friendship had lasted nearly a decade, and they were still catching each other up on the years they'd spent apart in different sections of the country—and world. Many of their stories involved exes, which was fine with Jamie. But Emma seemed less enamored with tales that featured Clare or Laurie, so Jamie occasionally edited her stories of the past. That didn't stop Emma from saying things like, "Clare was with you, wasn't she?" Usually, Jamie had to admit that she had been, and Emma would purse her lips and temporarily clam up.

That was why Jamie hesitated before saying, "Speaking of New York, I was wondering—would you maybe want to go out for coffee with Laurie and her partner?"

They were in Southern Oregon now, and her road trip playlist was still going strong. In the background, Halsey was singing about ghosts, and as Emma stared straight ahead, her eyes unreadable behind her sunglasses, Jamie turned the sound down.

"I mean, obviously we don't have to see them," she said. "It's just, she asked, so…"

"No, that's fine," Emma said. "We should go. Totally."

"You sure?" Jamie asked. "Because if you'd rather focus on soccer and skip the social thing, we can see them another time. We'll be in New York again, no doubt."

Four years earlier, the day after losing to Japan in the World Cup final, the US team had flown back to New York and immediately made the rounds of assorted talk shows. Usually it was Ellie and Phoebe Banks who were hot commodities after a major tournament, but Jamie remembered intimately how Emma's face and voice had been splashed across her and Britt's television in the North London flat they'd shared with two other Arsenal players at the time.

"No," Emma repeated, shooting her a slightly apologetic smile, "we don't have to wait. I just—you know how I am. Turns out I don't really like that many people."

Eyes back on the road, Jamie suppressed a sigh, because the way Emma saw herself often seemed fundamentally opposed to the way Jamie and others saw her.

"But I like *you*, obviously," Emma added, "and I'm sure I'll like what's-her-name and her partner."

It was funny, Jamie reflected as she turned the music back up and hummed along with the chorus to "Ghost," that Emma was the jealous one. Although, possibly, there had been hints. Occasionally when they were teenagers, Jamie had thought she'd detected a note of discomfort in Emma's voice whenever Jamie mentioned her latest crush. That slight disquiet had helped convince Jamie that maybe Emma wasn't straight; that maybe, even, she harbored non-friend feelings for Jamie.

Smiling a little, she reached for Emma's hand again.

Emma glanced over at her. "What's that look?"

"Nothing. You're just cute when you're jealous."

"I'm not jealous."

"Right. *Totally*."

Emma laughed under her breath and squeezed Jamie's hand, and they drove on through the early summer day with gently rolling mountains edging the road, the freeway wide open before them.

#

Their view the following evening was considerably different.

"Welcome back, athletes," Jo said, smiling out at them from the front of the hotel conference room.

"Canada or bust!" Angie called out, and the rest of the team joined in with whoops and cheers of their own.

Jamie smiled sideways at Emma, who was seated beside her in the third row of chairs near Maddie and

Angie. Emma smiled back, her eyes happy, and Jamie elbowed her a little before glancing back at the front of the room.

"All right," Jo was saying, "a little business to take care of at the outset. Bear with me. I'll get to the fun stuff as soon as I can."

As Jo launched into a logistical overview of the upcoming training camp, Jamie looked down at her shorts-clad thigh practically touching Emma's on the neighboring chair. They had spent the past 48 hours together nearly non-stop, and Jamie still felt a small thrill at being this close to her. The only blemish on their road trip had been Jamie's anger with her mother about Lyon. On the way there, she'd decided she needed more time to process before confronting her mom. Instead, she'd pulled what Emma called "a Minnesotan" and avoided being alone with her mother during their stay. This wasn't all that difficult given they were in Berkeley for a total of 16 hours.

The visit had gone well, other than Jamie's latent hostility. They'd arrived in time for dinner and spent the rest of the evening in the hammock in Jamie's parents' back yard, seated side by side with their feet on the ground while her mom and dad sipped glasses of wine on the nearby patio. Naturally, her parents had wanted to know all about her new apartment, and had perked up noticeably as Emma described the extra storage and built-ins. Jamie had been a bit suspicious at their reaction—until her father said that since she was settled, they were hoping to box up some of her old things and send them to her.

Now Jamie frowned and tapped her foot as Jo ceded the floor briefly to Lacey. Why the sudden urge to clean out her room? Were her parents planning to sell the house? They'd assured her they weren't when she'd asked point blank, but she wasn't sure she believed them. She would have to text Meg about it. Maybe her sister knew something she didn't.

From the front row, Ellie glanced over her shoulder and narrowed her eyes at Jamie. And, *right*. She should probably pay more attention to the national team coaching staff's pre-World Cup speech.

Once Lacey finished her tortur—*fitness* update and various assistants put in plugs for the days ahead, Jo took over again.

"Look at the people sitting around you," she said. "These are the teammates who are going to have your back in Canada this summer. Not your family, not your friends on your club team, not the fans, and certainly not the media. The people in this room—they are your family for the duration. We, the coaching staff, are your family. Every single one of you is where you're supposed to be. You all belong here.

"So right now, I want you to shut down that voice of doubt in the back of your head. Ignore the naysayers. Don't engage with the reporters who are going to question our readiness and our formation and our abilities. That's their job. Your job is to keep all of that negative energy outside the bubble. Your job is to exist inside the bubble with the rest of us in this room. Your job is to believe that we can win the World Cup this summer. Because in order to win, we have to believe—every single one of us.

"So what do you think, athletes," she added, smiling calmly around the room. "Are you ready?"

"Yes!" Jamie said, hearing Emma's voice echoing hers.

"Hell yeah!" Maddie said.

"Fuck yeah!" Angie all but shouted.

At the front of the room, Ellie slapped hands with Phoebe and glanced over her shoulder again, eyes crinkling this time in a smile. *Hell yes,* Jamie imagined her saying. Because if anyone was ready to shake the monkey off her back and finally win a World Cup, it was Ellie.

Family, Jamie thought, smiling back at her friend and mentor. That summed it up nicely.

CHAPTER FIVE

Within the week, Emma and Jamie were retracing their steps from Carson back to the Bay Area for the first match of the send-off series: Ireland. Only this time, the entire team was along for the ride. As usual, US Soccer sent them first by flight and then, once they'd settled into the team hotel, by coach. And what a coach it was: newly painted red, white, and blue and adorned with two stars to signify the team's two previous World Cup wins. Painted prominently in bold letters across the length of the bus was the tagline of the current year's tournament: "ONE NATION. ONE TEAM." Or, as the Twittersphere put it: "#1N1T."

On Saturday morning, twenty-four hours before the Ireland match, the team practiced on the game field as was their pre-Game Day tradition. After a light training session that included set pieces and various walk-throughs, the coaches ended practice early. Emma didn't question the timing, only followed Jamie back onto the team bus, where they claimed their usual row directly across from Maddie and Angie.

"'Sup, Blakewell," Angie said, grinning. And then,

predictably but no less cringeworthy: "Welcome to the lesbian lovers row."

Emma gave Maddie a pointed look, who turned the same look on her girlfriend.

"Oh, sorry, I mean the women-loving-women lovers row," Angie amended.

Emma regarded Angie through narrowed eyes, but she didn't detect any sarcasm. Maddie must be making progress in her attempts to reform her girlfriend.

According to Emma's best friend on the team, Angie's habitual swagger was a mask she'd developed to deal with her previous girlfriend's rejection and her family's crappy attitude. Not only were the Wangs categorically uninterested in women's professional sports, they possessed an apparently common first-generation immigrant attitude toward careers. They had not left China so that their youngest daughter could make a living playing a game. Rather, they'd expected all five of their children to pursue careers in science or law, fields they perceived as being less vulnerable to discrimination against minorities. But their disapproval of Angie's pro soccer career paled in comparison to their disgust regarding her "perverted lifestyle," Maddie had told Emma. As devout Catholics, they could not condone what they saw as her "immoral tendencies."

"Then maybe you shouldn't have moved to America," Angie had reportedly shot back at her parents a few months earlier after yet another disparaging remark about her sexual orientation. "Because in case you missed it, homos have civil rights here."

She'd walked out practically on the spot and called Maddie from the airport to ask if she would mind if Angie arrived in Palm Springs for their planned vacation a few days early. Maddie didn't. In fact, she'd flown out the same day to meet Angie. Cutting short her visit with her own family hadn't bothered Maddie. After all, she'd told Emma, her parents were practicing Catholics, too.

Normally, parents weren't all that involved with national team friendlies. But this weekend, with the US playing Ireland on Mother's Day, at least a few moms were bound to be present. Jamie's, obviously, since she was local, and Lisa Wall's and Ryan Dierdorf's, since their families lived in Southern California. But Maddie's and Angie's shouldn't be around until the actual World Cup.

Shouldn't was the key word. Unfortunately, the publicity arm of US Soccer sometimes had different ideas.

Back at the hotel, the team assembled in a conference room for a meeting over lunch. They were chatting amongst themselves when the double doors opened and Caroline, the team's PR rep, strolled in followed by—

"Mom?" Ellie said, her tone disbelieving as she started to rise.

Emma followed her friend's gaze to the doorway, only to stifle a gasp as, one after another, the mothers of the national team streamed into the room. Emma glanced at Jamie, seated at a nearby table with her U-23 mates, and noted the way her expression hardened. Then Emma's own mother was stepping into the room, and Emma was moving to intercept her.

"What are you doing here?" she asked, laughing as they met in a warm hug.

"Your marketing team saw the obvious opportunity in a match on Mother's Day," her mother answered, stepping back with a smile. "Not that I'm complaining."

Emma wasn't, either. And with the cameras rolling, as they almost always were, most players—and their moms—were smiling as if delighted to be reunited. Except Taylor O'Brien, whose mother had died of breast cancer a few years earlier. She was holding tightly to her grandmother, both in tears at the unexpected reunion.

Certain other players appeared less than thrilled with the turn of events, though. Emma could tell Jamie's smile was forced as she listened to her mother prattle on about something, and while Ellie and her mother had hugged initially, now they were standing awkwardly near the door, Ellie's shoulders drooping slightly as her mother looked at everyone and everything except her. Angie's mother's embrace was almost nonexistent, and Emma watched the pair interact even as she chatted with her own mom about the team hotel. Angie was trying, but her mother only patted her arm and turned away to greet Rebecca Perry's mom. Angie's face fell momentarily before her self-assured mask slipped into place. That less-than-touching scene wouldn't be making the send-off series marketing video, that was for sure.

"What's wrong?" Emma's mother asked quietly.

"Nothing." Emma glanced at Maddie in time to see the cool smile and colder hug Mrs. Novak bestowed on her daughter. Like Angie, Maddie appeared outwardly unfazed by her mother's unimpressed greeting, but Emma knew better. "It's just, not everyone is as lucky as I am."

"I'm sorry to hear that," her mom said sincerely.

"Me, too. Now come on, spill. How long can you stay?"

Not long, it turned out. As soon as the game ended, she would be back on a plane to Minnesota in order to be at work first thing Monday morning.

"I wish I could stay longer," she told Emma.

"It's fine," Emma said, and meant it. With a caring mother who supported her life choices—and had never once betrayed her intimate confidences, as far as Emma knew—she really was lucky.

Some of the players' mothers looked more like their older sisters, and those, of course, were the stories the PR team honed in on. They interviewed all the mother-daughter tandems that afternoon, but Emma could easily predict which pairs would be immortalized in the official video: Rebecca and her mother, with their matching blonde ponytails and their mutual insistence that they were best friends forever; queer Gabe and her ultra-feminine mom, because they were opposites but loved each other deeply; Lisa and her mother, not only because of the usual cynical US Soccer representation but also because they routinely finished each other's sentences. Emma and her mom were close like that, too, but Emma had a feeling they would be considered too boring for the federation's promotional bent.

At least, until Caroline asked her on camera about what it was like to have such a strong female role model in her life. US Soccer, it appeared, had gotten the memo about her mother's promotion to Chief Nursing Officer of Pediatric Surgery at the University of Minnesota Masonic Children's Hospital.

"My mom is amazing," Emma said, smiling at her mother through the camera lights. "She and my dad both dedicated their careers to supporting families in crisis. I couldn't be prouder of the work she's done to help sick kids and their families through what are often the most stressful periods of their lives."

Her mom smiled back from the other side of the hotel couch. "The admiration is entirely mutual," she said. "I help repair bodies, but you inspire kids to work hard and reach for their dreams. I'd say you're continuing the family legacy, only with your own spin."

Emma hadn't thought of it that way before. While she didn't worry that her mom was hiding Wang-level disapproval of her athletic career, she did often wonder if her mother was secretly disappointed in her for not choosing a different, more intellectually challenging path. Nice to receive confirmation that she wasn't.

"You mentioned your father, Emma," Caroline put in. "I understand the two of you met while working at Boston Children's Hospital?" She directed the question at Emma's mother, who shifted slightly and blinked under the bright lighting.

"Yes, that's right," she started.

But Emma touched her mother's hand and tilted her head at Caroline. "What are you doing? You know he's off-limits."

The team's PR rep glanced down at her note cards and shuffled them in place. "Normally, yes, but you brought him up—"

"I mentioned him in passing," Emma said, tamping down her irritation. Sometimes it was like Caroline saw the players as participants in one giant theater production. Which, to be fair, in a way they were. "This is Mother's Day. Can we please keep the focus on my mom?"

"Of course," Caroline said, and guided the conversation back to the care of sick children in Minnesota.

"What was that about?" Emma's mom asked a little while later as they left the hotel room to make way for the next mother-daughter pair.

"It was nothing."

"It didn't sound like nothing."

Emma expelled a breath. "They're just always trying to sell the fatherless daughter story, you know?"

Her mother shook her head. "What's wrong with talking about him? His life—and death—are very much a part of who you are. Your brother, too."

"That's not what this is about," Emma said. "The federation wants to package all of us into these neat little boxes so that we're somehow more relatable to the average fan. They don't actually care about what Dad may or may not have meant to me. And frankly, I refuse to be marketed as part of *his* story."

A few months earlier, when the PR team had produced the individual player videos—"One Nation, One Team, 23 Stories"—that had been released only after the final roster was named, more than one bright-eyed intern had suggested Emma talk about how losing her father had shaped her soccer story. In reality, her father's death had barely impacted her career trajectory. She'd already been well-ensconced in the junior national team pool before his heart attack, and his surgical work had kept him so busy that he'd barely been around in those last few years. That wasn't the story the powers that be would want to hear, though, and she didn't trust the federation not to twist her words to suit a different, more sympathetic narrative.

Now, to her surprise, her mother laughed. "Oh, honey, you are the star of your own story, I promise you, just as your father was the star of his. Your brother and I, though? Sometimes I think we're simply along for the ride."

Emma stopped in the middle of the hotel corridor. "What are you talking about?"

Before her mother could answer, a voice sounded from down the hall. "Emma! Hey!"

She glanced over her shoulder to see Jamie striding toward her, her own mother in tow. And just for a minute, Emma felt the floor shift under her feet as memory overlaid the present. The sensation faded quickly, though, and she moved to meet Jamie.

"Are you done with your interview?" Jamie asked.

"Yes, thank god. What are you up to?"

"We were thinking of going out for coffee. Want to come?" Jamie's smile held an edge, as if she was desperately hoping that Emma and her mother would join them so that she and *her* mom wouldn't have to be alone together.

"I don't know. What do you think, Mom?" Emma asked, unable to resist teasing her girlfriend.

"Eh, twist my arm," her mother said, smiling.

They fell into step together, Emma and Jamie leading the way, their mothers behind them talking about last-minute flights and art installations and work commutes. As they neared the Starbucks at the end of the block, the conversation shifted to family. Once they'd ordered and were seated, Emma and Jamie exchanged furtive smiles as their mothers interrogated each other about their non-soccer-playing children.

"They're getting along well," Jamie commented, her voice low.

"Did you have any doubts?"

"Not really. Thanks for coming, though. Seriously."

"Of course," Emma said.

She was gazing at Jamie, appreciating the leftover glam of her styled hair and light make-up when she heard her mother utter the momentous words, "The wedding venue is confirmed."

"Wait—Ty and Bridget set a date?" she asked, staring at her mother.

She nodded. "They decided to get married on January second at a venue in DC called Top of the Town. It overlooks the Mall and is supposed to be one of the best wedding sites in the city, and they were both thrilled when a slot opened up last minute. I think that's why they waited so long to set a date. They wanted it to be perfect."

That meant Emma would have two weddings to appear in: Dani and Derek's in early October at the Space Needle, where they'd had their first official, non-casual-hookup date; and Ty and Bridget's on the day after New Year's at Top of the Town. As a bridesmaid in her brother's wedding, shouldn't Emma be one of the first to know the details?

"Ty asked me to pass along the news," her mother explained. "He knew I would be seeing you this weekend."

Jamie's mother put in, "My older daughter and her husband actually have news as well. But I think they'll want to tell you themselves, Jamie."

"Mom! You can't just dangle something like that," Jamie said.

Her mother's eyebrows rose. "Apparently I can."

Emma shared a look with Jamie. *What the hell?* But they didn't have long to bristle. Emma was facing the door to the coffee shop, so she was the first to notice Meg, clad in a bright pink windbreaker, her hair streaked with matching color. Jamie took one look at Emma's face and spun in her chair, already half-rising.

In seconds, Meg was at her side, enveloping her in a hug. "Hey, kiddo!"

"Hey, shorty!" Jamie responded, laughing down at her older sister.

Meg's husband Todd approached the table at a more sedate pace, offering Emma and the Maxwells hugs and Emma's mom a handshake. But Emma's mother pulled him in.

"I'm the odd Minnesotan out," she told him. "I don't shy away from hugs."

Jamie was practically buzzing with impatience. "So?" she said as soon as the greetings had been concluded.

"So I think I could do with some coffee," Meg said, glancing at her husband. "What about you?"

"Meg!" Jamie all but shouted. "What's your news? Oh my god—are you *pregnant?*"

The entire group stilled. Emma looked between Todd and Meg. Was that even a possibility? Of course, they were straight, so baby-making was always a possibility. But Jamie hadn't mentioned they were trying, had she? Emma *had* been a bit focused on the World Cup lately, so it was possible she had tuned out during an important conversation…

"No, you dork," Meg said, smacking her younger sister's arm. "We got *jobs*. At the same university. We landed a spousal hire."

"A spousal hire—that's amazing!" Jamie said, seemingly just as amped as she'd been at the idea of becoming an aunt. "Where?"

"University of British Columbia, in Vancouver."

"Vancouver?" Jamie repeated. Then she laughed and hauled her sister and brother-in-law into a joint hug. "Nice! We won't be that far away from each other."

"Driving distance. Every move, we get closer and closer," Meg said, her tone affectionate as she mussed Jamie's hair. "No more Europe, *capiche*?"

Jamie only shrugged noncommittally and offered Emma a secretive smile. *Let's retire to Europe*, Emma remembered saying during their London vacation the previous year. Before they left soccer permanently, before they settled down with a house and a family—it could happen. Probably it wouldn't, but it was a nice daydream nonetheless.

"Tim and I are feeling exceedingly lucky," Pam, Jamie's mother, told Emma's mom. "At least for now, all of our kids will be on the West Coast." She gestured toward the younger generation, the movement including Emma.

Emma blinked. Did she mean…? Was she actually…? As Pam smiled kindly at her, Emma gulped at the sudden tightness in her throat. Well, crap. How was she supposed to stay mad at the woman now?

Jamie slipped her arm around Emma's shoulder and

gave her a brief squeeze before they settled back into their seats. Her bright-eyed smile told Emma she was suddenly struggling with the same question.

Mothers. Geez.

"That leaves only Ty and Bridget back east," Emma's mom commented.

Jamie filled her sister in on Emma's brother's wedding news, and for a few minutes the conversation revolved around wedding food and which was better: iPod playlists or real live DJs.

Um, playlists, obviously.

"Speaking of," Meg drawled, elbowing Jamie from her position at the corner of the table, "when are we going to hear wedding bells from the two of you?"

Emma nearly spit out her coffee. Jamie did choke on a mouthful of tea.

"Ha ha, just kidding!" Meg gleefully clapped Jamie on the back. "Better grab some extra napkins, Todd."

While Meg's husband ordered their coffees—and procured additional napkins—the conversation returned to US Soccer's machinations to get all of the mothers to San Jose at roughly the same time.

"It's a pretty good event, as far as PR events go," Emma allowed.

Jamie, who still hadn't made eye contact with her since Meg's teasing, nodded.

"Plus it gave Todd and me an excuse to surprise you guys," Meg put in. "Best surprise ever territory, am I right?"

"I don't know about *that*," Jamie said, her blush finally starting to recede. "Emma showing up in London last year sort of has that covered."

"I don't know, Jamie," Emma said. "Your surprise visit at Christmas is a strong contender."

"That was totally my idea," Meg insisted.

Jamie gave her a scornful glance. "The great Christmas caper? Please."

Before the sisters could start bickering in earnest, Emma said, "Actually, a caper is a sub-genre of mystery fiction where the crime takes place in full view of the reader, so it's not so much of a *surprise* as it is—"

Jamie groaned. "Oh my god, you're such a nerd."

"Whatever. I like to read," Emma defended herself.

"I know," Jamie said, giving her a soft look that—given they were in public—Emma knew was meant to substitute for a kiss. "You're my little book nerd."

Their mothers looked on, smiling, while Meg coughed out, "Whipped."

And seriously, it was shocking how much Jamie's music professor sister could sometimes resemble Angie Wang.

#

The game against Ireland provided a welcome break from the enforced family time, Emma thought the following morning as she warmed up for the match. More than a few of her teammates seemed more pumped than usual as they prepared to take the field against a team they had beaten 10 times in 10 previous tries. In fact, Ireland had only ever scored a single goal against the US—a full decade earlier—which meant they weren't a real test. Not that Mexico or South Korea should present a significant challenge in the coming weeks, either. That wasn't the goal of the send-off series. These last few games on home territory were supposed to build the team's confidence and give the American fans an opportunity to cheer on their team in an almost guaranteed victory.

It was a perfect soccer day. The sun was out, the breeze was cool, and the stands were packed with 18,000 fans—an official sell-out—clad in red, white, and blue.

Emma caught sight of more than a few banners and posters bearing her face, which wasn't her favorite, but whatever. If it got their supporters psyched for the World Cup, so be it.

Walking out onto the field holding hands with their mothers at the beginning of the game was a little cheesy, too, but Emma smiled and kept her head high as they emerged from the tunnel, the crowd cheering them on. She was leery of public spectacle and so, she knew, was her mom, but this tribute to the women who had made all of their careers as professional athletes possible—driving them to practices and games, feeding them well so they had fuel and focus, kissing their bruises and soothing their hurt feelings when they failed to rise to their own or others' expectations—was actually really nice.

Emma hugged her mom when the announcer called their names, and after she'd waved at the fans, her mom leaned in to murmur, "I knew you would earn your spot back."

"Thanks, Mom," Emma said, arm around her mother's shoulders.

"Thank *you*," her mom replied, and squeezed her waist.

Definitely one of the better marketing stunts the federation had sprung on them, that was for sure.

And yet, the team was off from the moment the game began. Gone was the energy and connection of the match against New Zealand the previous month. Almost everyone had been playing with their club teams throughout April, and it showed. Individual players performed well and the defense was solid, but once again, just like at the Algarve, the chemistry on attack was lacking. Every once in a while there would be a surge of creativity, but then a pass would fail to find its mark or no one would fill the open space, and the attack would fizzle. Again.

And then, after forty frustrating minutes, something

incredible happened. Jamie lofted a corner kick into Ireland's box, and Maddie struck the ball low and hard to the far corner of the goal. The post player cleared it off the goal line—directly into Ellie's path. She tucked it neatly past the Irish keeper, and all hell broke loose.

Ellie had just tied Mia Hamm's international scoring record.

The crowd erupted immediately, and Emma and Jamie and the rest of their teammates swarmed Ellie. The US captain smiled and slapped hands and tossed the ball to Mel on the sidelines to keep safe, but then she waved everyone back into position, clearly prioritizing the team's World Cup preparation over her own individual glory. That was one of the reasons Emma—and everyone else with half a heart—loved her.

The energy in the stadium had done a 180, and the shift was reflected on the field. Suddenly, the US players seemed to be everywhere, communicating clearly, sprinting to get open off the ball, and winning practically every 50-50 ball they challenged for. Emma wasn't even surprised when, during injury time, Gabe dribbled deep into Ireland's defensive end and crossed a perfectly weighted ball to Ellie on the 12. She wasn't surprised, and yet she was stunned when Ellie rose into the air and snapped her head forward in one of her signature headers, burying the ball in the back of the net and becoming, just like that, the leading scorer in the world. Mia Hamm, a household name in soccer-savvy families, had scored 158 international goals, more than any other person in history—until now. Now Rachel Ellison held the title at 159.

As the stands erupted again and the non-starters streamed off the bench, Emma sprinted halfway up the field and launched herself into Ellie's arms.

"You did it!" she shouted as Ellie whirled her around. "You fucking did it!"

Then Jamie was there hugging them both, and so were the subs from the bench, and Emma couldn't help thinking how perfect this one moment in time was.

Ellie let the celebration last a little longer, and then the ref was blowing the whistle for half time and congratulating Ellie on their way off the field. The coaches followed suit, as did various federation employees lurking around the bench, and of course their teammates again. As they headed for the tunnel to the locker room, Emma noticed Ellie scanning the stands until she saw Jodie and her mom waving at her from behind the American bench. Ellie waved back, her smile huge, and Emma remembered what she'd said one night the previous winter in a hotel room in Brazil: *My dad said of all his children, I would always be his biggest disappointment.*

"In your face, Mr. Ellison," Emma muttered as she ducked into the tunnel.

"What?" Maddie asked over the sound of cleats crunching over concrete.

"Nothing."

Emma pushed the gloomy memory away. Today was a day for celebration, not for dwelling on stupid people and things that couldn't be changed. Good thing international scoring records didn't fall into that category.

In the home team locker room, Jo led a resounding cheer for Ellie, who ducked her head and redid the pre-wrap she used to keep her hair off her face. For an international soccer star, she wasn't a fan of the limelight.

"I believe you broke the record," Angie chanted, and soon the entire locker room was repeating the cheer, until finally Ellie stood up and took a bow.

"Speech, speech!" Gabe cried, and soon that cheer was taken up, too.

"Fine," Ellie said, sounding exasperated but smiling beatifically at them. "You were all here to see soccer history made. You're welcome."

Her friends and teammates whistled and booed, and then it was time for the coaches to chat about how, despite the momentous nature of the day, the team wasn't exactly where it needed to be. Two goals didn't feel like nearly enough given the lack of chemistry between the midfield and front line. Other than Ellie's five minute burst of scoring, the attack had faltered frequently in the first half.

Same old, same old, Emma thought. But at least their set pieces were on point, as Angie would say, thanks in no small part to the addition of a certain midfielder to the permanent roster.

The third and final goal of the match came in the fifty-fourth minute off of one of Jamie's perfectly placed corner kicks. Just as they'd practiced all week, Taylor O'Brien received the ball at the near post and volleyed it past Ireland's diving keeper. Taylor, the soccer pundits were saying, was going to have a break-out World Cup. Those were things the US team could usually rely on: set pieces saving their butts, and someone new stepping up at an important moment in the cycle.

That the Americans beat Ireland was a sign they weren't completely off track. That Emma refrained from breaking the jaw of the woman who had crushed Jamie's ankle two years earlier was, she thought as they signed autographs afterward, another excellent outcome on the day.

For once, the crowd waiting for Ryan and Jamie nearly exceeded the reception Jenny and Ellie regularly received. The small stadium had sold out a few days earlier partially because Jamie, a hometown girl, Britt, an Arizonan who had played with Jamie at Stanford, and Ryan, a California girl who had played her college ball at Cal, had dozens of friends, former coaches, and one-time teammates in the stands to cheer them on.

Shoshanna, Jamie's old therapist, was there too, waving excitedly at them from halfway up the stands, impossible to miss with her orange, oversized San Francisco Giants foam hand.

"I didn't know she was a baseball fan," Emma said to Jamie out of the corner of her mouth as they waved back.

"Neither did I," Jamie admitted, smiling broadly at the woman she credited with saving her life—in a super non-melodramatic way.

Speaking of high school, Jamie's older sister's best friend Becca and her wife Rhea had sat with Jamie's family behind the US bench, each of them wearing one of their twin daughters in a baby carrier. They were gone by the time the game ended, but Meg assured Jamie and Emma they hadn't seen the last of the duo. Becca, Rhea, and the senior Thompsons would be joining Jamie's family for dinner later.

Jo had released the players from team requirements for the rest of the day, which Emma would have been more excited about if her mother hadn't already left the stadium to catch her flight back to Minnesota. Jamie's parents had invited them out to dinner at one of their favorite Berkeley establishments, and while Emma normally would have loved the idea, she wasn't sure it was the best way to spend one of the 28 nights—28 NIGHTS—they had left before their first World Cup match. Not with Jamie barely keeping her anger at her mother in check.

But it wasn't like they had any choice. Family was family.

"You ready?" Jamie asked a little while later as they emerged from the locker room freshly showered and dressed in street clothes.

"The question is, are you?" Emma replied, squashing the urge to take Jamie's hand in hers. Technically, they were still on team time, though not for much longer.

"Yo, Jamba Juice!" Angie called from behind them. "Wait for us."

Angie and Maddie were joining them too, along with their mothers, Mary and Mary Pat, respectively—their very Catholic, blatantly homophobic mothers who would have probably preferred never to meet. Fortunately, in addition to Jamie's family and friends, Britt would be there too, along with her laidback, slightly hippyish social worker mom. The plan was for Leah, Britt's mom, to distract Angie's mother if necessary, since they went way back to youth national team days. Leah had actually offered to stage an intervention with her old friend, but Britt had assured her it wouldn't be necessary. Meanwhile, Angie had only squinted into the distance at the offer, her mouth slightly askew, causing Britt to amend that it wouldn't be necessary *tonight*, at least.

In a way, Emma thought as they made their way to the restaurant, she couldn't wait for the World Cup to suck them up because then they would be in their federation-enforced bubble, with carefully restricted media access and limited family time. Too bad the send-off series didn't qualify for the bubble. Because honestly? Emma wasn't sure anyone in the Berkeley city limits was ready for this particular dinner party.

CHAPTER SIX

It was a little surreal, to be honest.

Jamie gazed around the large table on the patio at Jupiter, the brew pub where she'd been coming to celebrate victory—and rail at defeat—for most of her life, from her AYSO days in elementary school to her club and high school teams. She'd even brought her college teammates here, which meant that this was not Britt's first time sitting around the outdoor fire pit in the historic building in downtown Berkeley.

Britt glanced up and caught her eye, and they shared a smile. Jamie had a feeling her oldest friend was thinking the same thing she was: *Holy SHIT. We're actually at Jupiter after playing for the national team!* A year and a half earlier, they'd been in London prepping for Champions League and hoping their dreams of making the USWNT weren't permanently squelched. Now look at them. Britt may not have started today's match, but she had come in at the sixtieth minute. Probably her playing time had more to do with Phoebe's sore shoulder and Avery's sprained ankle than Britt's connection to the region. But Jamie was pretty sure her friend would take every minute, even if she hadn't had to defend a single shot.

Dinner had gone well, too, which probably shouldn't be a surprise. What had they expected, that the Marys Pat would stand up and denounce their daughters' relationship in the middle of a crowded restaurant on Mother's Day? Well, actually... Both women had sent more than a few dark looks at Angie and Maddie huddled together laughing or exchanging sweet smiles like the newly in love girlfriends they were. If anything, it might have done some good for the two to see Jamie's parents being supportive of her and Emma. Similarly, Britt's mom had gone out of her way to comment positively on Britt's relationship with her girlfriend, Allie, in an attempt to lead by example. Maybe the Marys Pat would see that the world didn't end and the family didn't have to break apart just because a child turned out to be less than straight.

Becca and Rhea had driven that point home even further. They and their twin daughters stole the show, naturally. The babies were tiny still, only 10 weeks old and small even for that age according to their proud, exhausted moms. They had worn the babies into the restaurant—apparently they were fans of "attachment parenting," which Emma had explained meant they almost never put the babies down—but once there, Becca's parents and the elder Maxwells had been passing the twins around on a steady rotation. They weren't the only members of their generation to fawn over the babies, either. Each of the parents present seemed entranced by every burp and cry the tiny humans emitted.

Mary Pat in particular seemed fascinated by the story of the twins' conception, which Becca was more than happy to share along with certain details of the birth that made Rhea, for one, wince. Jamie had already heard the twins' birth story a couple of times now. Otherwise, she might have lost her appetite when Becca gleefully described the actions the doctor had taken when Rhea had retained one of the placentas, which may or may not have included upping her spinal block and reaching a hand up inside Rhea's uterus to remove the placenta manually.

Spoiler alert: That was absolutely what had happened.

As assorted table occupants made faces and pushed their plates away, Jamie picked up a slice of her wood-fired pizza and took a huge bite. Even if she hadn't already heard the story, she could always eat.

"And then," Becca continued, "our doctor asked if we wanted to keep the placenta so we could sauté it for dinner, which, I'm serious, people, some women actually do!"

Britt squealed in that high-pitched tone Jamie never expected to hear from her while other people around the table (the Marys Pat, once again in cultural synch) gasped and appeared to be swallowing down possible bile.

Emma, who had also heard this story multiple times, chose that moment to lean in and murmur, "Do you remember the first time you brought me here?"

Jamie looked at her. "You mean after that game where you told my hecklers they had tiny penises?"

Emma bit her lip. "That's right. I totally did that."

"See? Even then you loved me."

Emma held her gaze, eyes glowing in the flickering firelight. "Absolutely."

Jamie paused for a second, remembering the last time they'd sat at an outdoor restaurant near an open fire. That time, they'd been eight floors up over St. Louis in the shadow of the Gateway Arch, and while Emma's eyes might have glowed, it certainly hadn't been in happiness.

Yeah. Jamie would take this night over that one anytime.

"And you loved me back then, too," Emma prompted expectantly.

Jamie pretended to think it over. "Did I, though?"

"Jerk." Emma smacked her arm and reached for her glass of beer, a beautiful amber color that made Jamie think maybe even she would like the taste.

Eh, probably not. At least, not without a generous amount of lemonade to sweeten it.

"You know I did," she said softly so that only Emma would hear her. "I've always loved you, and I always will."

Emma's gaze softened again as it found hers. "I'll always love you, too, Jamie."

Jamie believed her. Emma might struggle with somewhat flexible truth-telling when it came to the day-to-day details of life, but as for the really important things? She was solid, an unchanging rock in the river of human vicissitudes. Or, you know, maybe an anchor in the storm of life. Both clichés, Jamie thought, worked equally well.

So yeah, dinner was good despite the potential for drama. It wasn't until they retired to her family's house later that shit got real.

At first, everything seemed fine. Jamie's parents brought out a couple of bottles of wine, and everyone hung around the living room. Meg and Todd were there, and the elder Thompsons and Emma, of course, and with such a buffer, Jamie could overlook the anger she still felt at the back of her mind knowing her mother had told even more people about the assault. On the one hand, Jamie had been a kid when everything went down. Her mother shouldn't have had to ask her permission to talk about it. But by not informing Jamie that Pete knew, her mom had let her navigate the soccer world for years believing that what had happened was her story to tell—or not. Mostly she chose *not* because why talk about it if she didn't have to? To find out that two of the most influential coaches in her soccer career had known all along—well, it was disconcerting, obviously.

At least Pete hadn't been at the game today. Jamie had heard he'd moved to the East Coast a few years earlier, where he was coaching a women's team at a Division II school.

As the conversation went on around her, she clutched her glass of wine and tried to get control of her spiraling thoughts. This Mother's Day was an anomaly—a beautiful, amazing, brief moment when they could all be together. She and Emma would have to be up early to catch their flight out, and she wanted to enjoy this time while they had it. With an effort, she pushed away memories of secrets and lies and tried to be fully present: to laugh at her father's silly dad jokes; to appear interested in her mother's latest art news; to ask pertinent questions of Becca's parents; to listen closely to Meg and Todd's description of their new campus and the reams of paperwork they would have to fill out to live and work in a foreign country that didn't feel foreign at all. But it wasn't easy to push down the simmering anger she felt every time she gazed at her mother for more than a few seconds.

Apparently she wasn't entirely successful because every once in a while Emma, who was curled into her side on one length of the living room sectional, squeezed her hand or poked her in the ribs or nudged her shoulder to bring her out of her head and back to the conversation.

Turned out being in the moment with her family wasn't as easy as it sounded.

"Do you want to talk about it?" Emma whispered later that night as they lay together in Jamie's childhood bedroom.

"No, thanks," she said, listening to the faint sound of familiar voices murmuring through the walls. Meg and Todd were in her old room, now the official guest bedroom, and beyond that were her parents, getting ready for bed the same as they always had. Only nothing was the same, was it?

"Okay," Emma said, her tone reluctant as she rested her chin on Jamie's shoulder. "But if you change your mind…"

"I know where to find you," Jamie said, and kissed her, rolling her eyes inwardly at the illicit thrill that shot through her body. There was nothing illicit about their relationship, but this was the same bed where she had spent hours fantasizing about Emma as a teenager. And as a college student. And as an adult. She couldn't imagine being with Emma in real life ever getting old.

By midnight, Emma was asleep beside her, golden hair spilling over Jamie's pillow in the precise way she used to picture it. She wished she could go back to her teenage self and tell her not to worry, that everything would work out. But of course she couldn't. Instead, she got up and went downstairs to find a late-night snack, another post-game tradition from her childhood.

Her parents usually left the light on over the stove, so she didn't think anything of the house not being completely dark. The voice that spoke her name, though—that was unexpected. She turned to see her mother seated at the kitchen table, stirring a spoon of honey into a cup of tea.

"Mom? What are you doing up?"

"I couldn't sleep. Nice to see that some things never change," her mother said, and slid the pan of homemade pound cake—one of Jamie's favorite desserts—toward her.

Jamie hesitated. She wasn't really in the mood to talk, cake or no cake.

"Please?" her mom added, her voice uncharacteristically vulnerable.

That wasn't fair. Jamie couldn't exactly say no, especially not on Mother's Day. She released a breath and moved toward the table, only to stop short at her mother's next words: "What happened? I can tell there's something."

Jamie regarded her for a moment, her banked anger immediately flaring. But, just as she'd done all day, she tried to rein it in. "Nothing happened."

"Come on, Jamie. You've had that pinched look around your mouth every time you've looked at me this weekend."

Her mother's knowing tone reminded Jamie of Emma when they were arguing, and not in a good way. She shook her head. "Fine. You really want to know?"

Her mother nodded, but she looked less and less certain the longer their eyes held.

Jamie could lie. She could obfuscate and invent, deny and avoid. That was what she'd long done with her mother on the topic of Lyon. But something had changed during her recent trip to France, and frankly, she was tired of protecting her mother's feelings. Shouldn't it have been the other way around, anyway?

"What happened," she said, "is that I found out that Jo Nichols has known for years that I was raped." She picked her words intentionally, going for the combination that would inflict the most damage.

Sure enough, her mother flinched as if Jamie had slapped her. She supposed, verbally, she had.

"I didn't—what would—how?" her mother finally settled on.

"How do you think? Pete Tyrell. Courtesy of you."

Her mom lifted a hand to her mouth. "Oh, Jamie, I'm so sorry—"

"What, for sharing private information with my coach without asking me first?" Jamie shot back, taking a step closer. She had been taller than both of her parents for years, and now she loomed over her mother. "Or for not telling me you'd told him? What exactly are you sorry for, Mom?"

"Stop it, Jamie," her mother said, her hand dropping again. "I won't be spoken to that way, not by you."

"Are you kidding me? That's what you're going to come back with?"

"When you're calmer," her mom said, rising to her feet and folding her arms across the front of her robe, "we can talk about all of this. But I won't deal with you when you're like this."

"Like what? When I'm angry with you?" Jamie retorted, crossing her own arms across the front of her sweatshirt. "Well, tough, Mom, because I am pissed at you, and justifiably so. You betrayed my confidence ten years ago and didn't even have the balls to, I don't know, maybe mention it somewhere along the way?"

Her mother held up both hands. "I only wanted to help. Can't you see it from my perspective?"

Jamie stared at her. "What the actual fuck? The only perspective you've ever wanted me to see it from is yours. I'm the one who was raped, not you."

"What are you talking about?" Her mother looked stricken, her face pale and lined with worry, eyes glinting behind her glasses. Was she going to cry? The thought almost stopped Jamie. Almost.

"I'm talking about the fact that you never asked me about what happened, not even once. You fobbed me off on Shoshanna and then it was like you pretended it never happened. Except that for years, I could see it in your face every time you looked at me. For *years*! You looked at me like I was this damaged, ruined version of the child you had once loved."

"Jamie!" her mother said, her voice rising. "That's not true!"

"Don't tell me that how I feel isn't true," Jamie

practically bellowed. "You don't get to do that. They're *my* feelings. They're not right or wrong. They just are, and you can't change them."

Thank god her parents *had* fobbed her off on Shoshanna. Without a caring stranger's help, Jamie wouldn't have been able to stand before her mother now and hold firmly to her own truth.

"Please, lower your voice," her mother hissed.

Jamie snorted. "Oh, what, you're afraid the rest of the family will hear us? What a shock that you're more concerned with what other people think than with how I actually feel."

At that, her mother sighed and looked away, visibly deflating. "I didn't mean to imply that your feelings aren't true," she said. "I only meant that I tried to talk to you about what happened. I tried so many times, but you shut me down every time."

Jamie blinked, her anger fizzling slightly. "I don't remember that."

"You don't?" When Jamie shook her head, her mother frowned. "I guess that's not entirely surprising. Trauma does different things to different people. But… does that mean you don't remember what you said to me the last time we talked about it?"

"When?" Jamie asked warily.

"Right before you started your sophomore year of high school," her mom said, as if it were obvious.

Jamie stared at her, trying to remember any conversation with her mother during the summer in question. But there was nothing, just a smooth, dark wall inside her mind that didn't allow even a pinprick of light through.

"I don't," she admitted, her heartbeat kicking up a notch. "Not at all."

Her mother's face fell and she looked down at the floor, rubbing her hands along her forearms. "Oh. Well, it doesn't matter, anyway. It's just that—I—I'm just so sorry. I'm sorry I've made a mess of this whole thing. I wanted to be there for you, Jamie, I truly did, only you didn't seem to need my help. Or, I suppose, it was more that you didn't want it."

Jamie could see the pain on her mother's face, hear it in her voice, feel it reflected in her own chest. "What are you talking about? You're my mom. Of *course* I wanted your help."

Her mother's smile was sad, and she reached out and touched Jamie's hand where it was still cradled tightly against her torso. "I'm glad to hear you think that, but it simply wasn't true at the time. At least, it wasn't what you said," she amended.

Jamie still couldn't remember any conversation that came remotely close to what her mother was describing. Had her mother imagined it? Was she using a fake conversation as an excuse for her decade-old parental shortcomings? Or was it more likely that Jamie's memories from the period directly after the assault were suspect?

The latter, she had to admit, her anger deflating even more. She was known among her friends for her terrible memory. People's faces? Sure. But their names? Not so much. The question of whether or not it was possible she couldn't remember multiple conversations in the aftermath of France—it wasn't really a question, was it? That time had been especially fraught, for obvious reasons. It had taken months of work with Shoshanna to construct a plausible facsimile of the events in Lyon, and even now the memories seemed shimmery and unstable, as if they could make and remake themselves at will. Their own will, not hers.

She frowned slightly and rubbed her temple. She'd

managed to earn a mild concussion during her lone week of training with the Thorns. Not enough to sit out more than one practice, but the spot where Greta's fist had collided with her head still sometimes smarted, especially if she was feeling tense. Now definitely qualified on that front.

"Look," she said, her voice quieter. "My memories of that time are a little hazy. I'm not saying we didn't talk, only that I honestly don't remember if we did."

Her mother stared up at her for a long moment before nodding. "I understand that's not unusual for people in your situation."

"It's okay to say it out loud," Jamie said, her irritation immediately rising again.

"Is it? Because that's not what you said at the time."

She closed her eyes for a long moment. "And what exactly did I say?"

Her mother pinched the bridge of her nose and shook her head. "I told you, it's not important. You were hurting. I didn't take any of it personally."

The way she couldn't hold Jamie's gaze as she said this argued otherwise.

"Can we sit down?" Jamie asked, waving at her mother's vacated seat at the table.

Her mother hesitated before nodding. "I'll put the kettle back on."

It took patient probing and a significant amount of herbal tea as well as half the remaining pan of pound cake, but eventually Jamie convinced her mom that "letting the past stay in the past" only worked if it wasn't actively impacting the present.

"You were angry with me," her mother finally admitted, sweeping cake crumbs from the table and depositing them on a cloth napkin that was new since the last time Jamie had lived here. "You were angry with everyone, actually."

That much she remembered. It was why soccer had become such an important outlet—because it allowed her to focus her rage and pain onto a small leather sphere that she could strike with all her might without fear of repercussion. In fact, the harder she played, the more praise she received. That was why her parents so easily forced her into therapy. By threatening to take away soccer, they, albeit unknowingly, had threatened the one thing she knew for certain could help.

"I was angry," she admitted.

Her mother watched her for a long moment before nodding. "I understood why, of course. You were right when you said that what happened was partially my responsibility."

"Wait," Jamie said, and leaned forward across the dining table. "I said what?"

"You really don't remember?"

"I told you, I don't. I said that what happened to me was your fault?"

Her mother looked down at the table, pushing the crumbs around on top of the napkin. "It was so long ago. Do we really need to rehash it all now?"

"Yes," Jamie said. "I think we do. Please?"

Her mom glanced up. "I suppose I deserve that. Fine. Here's what happened: I tried to talk to you a few times, but you shut me out. Until, finally, you didn't." Her eyes narrowed and her face tightened. "And then I almost wished I hadn't pushed you so hard. No, I did wish that. No *almost* about it."

A glimmer of memory flickered in Jamie's mind. She remembered being angry with her mother, but not for trying to talk to her. No, she'd been angry about—"I was mad at you in Lyon, wasn't I?"

Her mother nodded. "You were upset with me for missing one of your games in order to go on a tour of the city's murals."

That was it! That was why Jamie hadn't seen the murals the first time around. For one thing, she'd been busy playing soccer. For another, she'd resented her mother for prioritizing Lyon's frescoes over her. "I said you were only there for the art, didn't I?"

"Yes. And you know, I've thought a lot about it, and you weren't wrong. I don't mean that I wasn't excited to go to France with you, but for a youth soccer tournament? I think we both know that was more your father's speed. I just couldn't pass up the chance to visit a city I had read so much about."

More memories came flickering back. Jamie had been lying in the hammock when her mother tried to talk to her after France, hadn't she? At least, it felt like maybe she had. The day had been warm and dry, and she had just come home from club practice when her mother cornered her to ask about her latest session with Shoshanna…

"Oh, god," she said, lifting her eyes to her mother.

"Do you remember?" her mom asked.

"I think so. I told you…" She stopped, because the words seemed too cruel to repeat now. Assuming she even remembered them correctly?

"You told me it was my fault you'd been hurt," her mother said. "That I'd only come to France for the art; that I hadn't paid enough attention to you and that was why you snuck out with your friends."

What an awful thing to say. Jamie swallowed against the tightness in her throat, squinting against the pain throbbing in her temple. "I'm sorry," she said, her voice low and tight. "I shouldn't have—"

Her mother reached across the table and took her hand, holding it tightly. "No," she said, her voice fierce.

"No. Don't you be sorry. You weren't wrong. You weren't right, either, but you weren't wrong, Jamie. I should have come to your game that morning. It was the final match, and I chose to be somewhere else. Your father never would have done that to you."

"Maybe not, but even if he'd been there, I still probably would have gone out that night," Jamie told her. "It was Goose and Frankie. They were a year older than me and from the city, and I thought they were so cool. I wouldn't have told them no, even if Dad had been there. I don't think I could have."

"But I *was* there," her mother said, her voice faltering. Tears stood out against her light brown lashes, making her blue eyes that were a mirror version of Jamie's shine in the dim light. "I was right there, and I couldn't stop it. I shouldn't have been sleeping. I should have known there was something wrong."

The phrasing stirred another memory. At one time, Jamie had thought the same thing. How had her mother not somehow sensed she was in danger? How had she not found her way to the bar to save Jamie? But a decade later, she knew exactly why: because her mother was human, and so was she. There was nothing magical about what had happened that night. Jamie had made a series of bad choices, and she would forever be stuck with the consequences. That was all.

"Mom," she said softly, and turned her hand up so that their palms were touching. "It wasn't your fault. It wasn't even my fault. Going to that bar was definitely my responsibility, but what happened there wasn't my fault. The only person responsible is the guy who did it. Not you, not me, not Goose or Frankie, not anyone except him."

Her mother shook her head, staring down at the table. "But I should have—"

"Mom. It wasn't your fault," Jamie repeated. "It

wasn't. I promise."

Her mom looked up at her, hand clenching in her grasp. "Do you mean that? Do you really believe that's true?"

"I really do," she said. "I'm sorry I ever made you think I didn't."

Her mother waved away the apology and dabbed at her overflowing eyes. "You were young and you were in pain. I just—I guess I always thought that you blamed me, probably because I blame myself. Even if it wasn't my fault, I won't ever forgive myself for not being there for you when you needed me. I should have tried again to talk to you. I should have kept trying. But I suppose after that, I was afraid of what I would hear, so instead I pushed it all down and convinced myself that I couldn't help you. That Shoshanna was the only person who could reach you."

In a way, she hadn't been wrong. Shoshanna had the experience—and the emotional distance—that made the difference. Jamie's parents could have tried identical tactics and she would probably have rejected them simply because they were family.

"I'm not going to lie," Jamie said, because she was done with that. "I do wish you had tried again. But I understand why you didn't. One of the things Shoshanna taught me is that rape affects more than just the victim. Collateral damage, she called it. I'm just sorry it's taken us this long to figure it out."

"No, I'm the one who's sorry," her mother said, chin jutting out in that typically stubborn manner she had.

And Jamie laughed, because it was nearly one in the morning on Mother's Day and she was hopped up on sugar and blueberry tea and her mother was half-smiling, half-crying across the table from her. And because, for now, everything made sense in a way it hadn't in much, much too long. Still painful, but far more comprehendible.

When she went back to bed a little while later, Emma sighed deeply and pressed her lips to the side of Jamie's head.

"Love you, Maxi," she murmured sleepily.

And Jamie laughed again, softly, even as she cursed Angie and her ridiculous nicknames.

Her laughter soon faded, though, and she lay awake in the bed beside Emma, staring up at the dark ceiling where she knew the constellations she and her father had mapped out in painstaking, glow-in-the-dark plastic detail still resided. Bits and pieces of her conversation with her mother flashed through her consciousness, and she couldn't help wondering what else lay inside her mind, hidden and unyielding. Forgetting was a technique the brain used to protect against traumatic memories, but as a strategic tool, it was imprecise at best and catastrophic at worst. She didn't remember saying terrible things to her mother, but she knew she probably had. She had been so battered and bruised that she didn't doubt she'd lashed out at those closest to her.

God, it was so fucked up. All this time Jamie had thought her mother was making what had happened about herself when in reality she, too, had been traumatized. And Jamie, in her pain, had only made her mother's trauma worse. Her throat tightened and an ache lodged inside her chest, and for a brief moment she wondered if she might be having a heart attack. It happened sometimes to athletes—a congenital defect went unnoticed until too late. Maybe she was going to die here in her childhood bedroom with Emma sleeping beside her… But no, this pain was familiar. She knew exactly what this feeling was.

Jamie squeezed her eyes shut and focused on her breathing. She picked one of her mantras, the phrase about all beings everywhere being happy and free, and went through it slowly, picturing her mother first and then herself. But not herself as she was now. Rather, she concentrated on the memory of herself as she had been right before she left for Lyon. She sent waves of love and support to that old, vulnerable version of herself, and it must have worked because her breathing steadied and the ache in her chest eased. It worked, and the tingling in her hands and feet and the dizziness swimming at the edge of her vision gradually subsided.

Her eyes were open again when a car's headlights swept across the room, momentarily revealing the universe of stars studding her ceiling. Down the hall, a bed creaked, followed by the sibilant sound of her parents murmuring to each other in the dark quiet of the room they'd occupied ever since she could remember.

At last, when she was certain it would never happen, Jamie slept.

CHAPTER SEVEN

Emma glanced around the restaurant. It had been a while since she'd been here—the previous year's January camp, maybe? Now that they were back, she wasn't sure why they'd stayed away so long.

When she was first on the team, rarely had a residency camp passed without a visit to Manhattan Beach Post, a former post office turned social house. At five on a Friday night, they hadn't had to wait long to be seated. Initially they were shown to a table near the front windows that was big enough to accommodate the lot of them: Emma, Maddie, Ellie, Gabe, Ryan, and Jenny. But before they could settle in, Ellie had pulled the host aside, and the next thing Emma knew they were being led to one of the larger group tables farther inside.

"I didn't want to be so close to the windows," Ellie had said by way of explanation. "It's getting chilly." Then she'd looked down at her phone and typed what Emma had assumed was a text.

Five minutes later, Tina Baker and Steph Miller had filed into the restaurant, followed by Jodie and an older couple dressed in brightly colored clothes and speaking in unmistakable Midwestern accents. The two USWNT mainstays had been hanging around the National Training Center for the past few days, but Jodie's parents were a new addition. Emma always forgot that sophisticated, fashionista Jodie was from Wisconsin. When exactly had her parents arrived? And what were all of these seemingly random and yet not random at all people doing here, anyway?

Emma had quickly texted Jamie: "Something's up. You guys should get here ASAP."

Despite Ellie's strong encouragement to come along, Jamie had stayed back at the team hotel to finish watching *Pitch Perfect* with her U-23 buddies. They had tickets to the sequel, *Pitch Perfect 2*, later that night, and Jamie and the others wanted the first installment to be fresh in their minds.

"On our way," Jamie had replied with a running woman emoji.

Now Emma took a sip of her fancy cocktail and exchanged a raised-eyebrow look with Maddie, who appeared to have sent a similar text to her girlfriend. Maddie shrugged subtly and went back to her conversation with Ryan about the newly released USWNT World Cup kit. Nike had invited Maddie, Jenny, and Ellie to attend the official unveiling, where they had modeled the new environmentally friendly uniforms—each kit had been made from a dozen recycled plastic bottles—and answered questions from the sports press.

The following night, Jenny and Ellie had appeared on *American Idol*, where they'd presented Ryan Seacrest with his own custom jersey and put in a plug for supporting the World Cup. It was just the start of the pre-World Cup marketing frenzy, which Emma was so not looking forward to. She didn't mind public speaking, but talking politically expediently about herself and her teammates?

Not her strong suit.

"I heard you said at the unveiling that players who look good perform better," Ryan said, smirking at Maddie. "Did you come up with that, or were you just toeing the party line?"

"What do you think?" Maddie answered, and rolled her eyes at Emma.

Maddie and Ryan might have each other's backs on the field, but they had never gotten along all that well off of it. Maddie claimed it was because Ryan was bitter that UNC had ruined Cal's chances of winning the College Cup too many times to count, while Ryan said Maddie simply didn't have a sense of humor. Emma had never forgotten—and neither had Maddie, obviously—Ryan's crack her first year on the team about how bisexuals should freaking make up their minds already. Emma didn't think Ryan really believed that, but the damage had been done. Maybe if Emma's mother had said that same thing to her on repeat for the past decade, she would hold the monumental grudge Maddie had carried all these years, too.

Then again, maybe they simply didn't like each other, and Ryan's crappy joke had only made their natural enmity worse. There was always that.

Fortunately, Emma didn't have to get involved in their enduring feud because at that moment, Jamie and Angie waltzed in. Even though it had only been an hour since they'd seen each other, Emma felt her mood lift instantly. Although, admittedly, her cocktail on an empty stomach already had her feeling fairly good. Jamie scanned the restaurant until her gaze fell on Emma, her face lighting up. What a life, to be dorks in love. And, you know, elite athletes with Nike contracts and the opportunity to win a World Cup.

Angie quickly claimed the spot beside Maddie while Jamie slid an extra chair in beside Emma's.

"Hey," she said, smiling.

"Hey." Emma smiled back and took another sip of her drink, trying not to feel too giddy at Jamie's appearance. It was dinner out, but technically they were on team time. Actually, they would be on team time basically from now until the World Cup final on July 5. Assuming they made the final, which Emma was definitely assuming.

Jamie drummed her fingers on the table and eyed Emma's glass. "What are you drinking?"

"A Dementor's Kiss."

Jamie's laugh took the form of a short huff. "A what?"

"It's an Old Fashioned made with Fidencio mezcal, Amaro Nonino, cocoa, and chili powder," Emma explained. They didn't have practice the following day, so she—and everyone else at the table—was taking advantage.

Jamie stared at her. "I don't recognize half of those ingredients, and the other half sound disgusting together."

"They're not," Emma protested, laughing. "Here, want to try a sip?"

"Um." She hesitated briefly. "Okay, why not."

Emma slid the glass over. When their hands connected, Emma told herself that she was a grown-ass woman with a successful career and her own condo to boot, but her mini lecture to self didn't stop her breath from catching as Jamie's fingers brushed against hers. She watched Jamie lift the glass to her mouth, eyes closing as she first inhaled the drink's scent and then tested the taste by drawing a tiny bit of alcohol into her mouth, swallowing it, and then licking her lips afterward. *Daaaamn.* Jamie made sipping whiskey look sexy as hell.

Then again, Jamie looked good even without the Old Fashioned. Her hair and make-up were on point, just like it had been on Mother's Day weekend. But this time around, her outfit was more sophisticated than the jeans and crewneck sweatshirt she'd worn to coffee with their moms.

Lightweight gray pants hugged her thighs and calves, while her sky-blue collared shirt matched her eyes almost perfectly. The sleeves were rolled above her elbows, revealing a chunky watch that emphasized her forearm muscles. Emma couldn't help but stare at the fine hair on her arms, bleached golden by the California sun. She wanted to run her hands up those arms, wanted to trace Jamie's tattoos with her fingertips…

Okay, then. With difficulty, Emma tore her gaze away from her girlfriend. Apparently her drink was more aptly named than she had realized.

Their server brought more menus, and soon the new arrivals were debating their drink orders. Jamie decided on a virgin Golden Hind, a passion fruit mojito topped with a maraschino cherry. Angie's drink was similarly adorned—though definitely not virginal—and as soon as their cocktails were delivered to the table, the two were racing to see who could tie her cherry stem faster with her tongue.

Emma couldn't help glancing at Maddie. Her similarly enamored friend bit back a smile and waggled her eyebrows, and Emma shook her head. Honestly, these two. Did they know how hard they made it to stick to team time rules?

After they'd ordered a dozen or so tapas-style dishes for the table, Jamie leaned closer. "I like your dress."

Taking advantage of the warm Southern California weather, Emma had brought along her favorite dress, a subtle paisley print maxi in muted greens and blues with a V-neck in front and dual straps that crossed in the back. Not only was it comfortable, but it made her shoulders and back look good.

"You can borrow it anytime," she said, and flipped her loose hair over the opposite shoulder.

"I might just take you up on that."

"Really?"

"Why not? I've been known to do drag before."

Across the table, Gabe's eyes widened. "Did you just say you've done drag?"

Jamie hesitated, glancing at Emma before answering. "I might have dressed up once or twice in college."

"Me, too. Drag king champs, baby!" Angie said, holding her hand over Maddie and Emma's heads for Jamie to slap.

As Jamie's palm collided with Angie's, Emma conjured an image of her girlfriend in a tailored shirt and dress pants, a tie knotted loosely at her throat. Were there photos somewhere? She hoped so. She would have to remember to ask Jamie later.

The first tapas dishes to arrive were plates of giant potato wedges also known as Fee Fi Fo Fum Fries, followed by several orders of green beans, bacon cheddar buttermilk biscuits, and grilled naan. Lastly, cheese plates from Italy and Vermont arrived with pomegranate cous cous, cured meat, and truffle honey-laced chicken—Maddie's favorite. Conversation briefly paused around the table as they all dug in, the ensuing quiet punctured mainly by requests for plates to be passed and the happy moans Maddie insisted on (over)sharing.

When Angie began feeding Maddie cheese and pastrami, her fingers lingering on her girlfriend's lips, Gabe made a slightly disgusted sound.

"Whatever," Maddie said. "I was there when you and Ellie were doing your thing, remember?" She had the decency to keep her voice down, though, so that Ellie and Jodie and, more importantly, Jodie's parents, all currently engaged in conversation with Steph and Tina at the opposite end of the table, wouldn't hear the reference to Ellie's Sapphic past.

Gabe blushed, as well she should. The team had all but caught the two with their hands down each other's shorts in a hallway outside a locker room in Texas a few hours before a match. The self-appointed nerd squad—Emma, Ryan, Avery, and Kristie, a now retired goalkeeper—had taken considerable delight in puns on the word "friendly" for months afterward.

Actually, maybe the team time policy was a good idea, after all.

"I do not know of what you speak," Gabe said primly, pushing her hair away from her face.

Emma joined in the group laughter, but as Gabe's gaze settled on her, she immediately wished she hadn't.

"Really, Blake?" She lifted an eyebrow. "Should the pot actually be calling the kettle black?"

Emma could feel Jamie's eyes on her. "I didn't say anything."

"Uh-huh, that's what I thought." Just as Emma was sure she'd dodged the bullet, Gabe fake-coughed, two words carrying clearly through the sound: "Tori Parker."

Beside her, Emma felt Jamie tense. *Freaking Gabe.* She couldn't bear being the brunt of the joke, could she? Emma wasn't usually much for rubber-necking, but she couldn't help glancing at Jamie, noting the slight crease in her brow as her mouth settled into a thin line.

"Yeah, but haven't most of us hooked up with a teammate at some point or another?" Angie asked. "Like you, Max. You're not exactly Miss Innocent yourself, are you?"

Jamie's head shot up and the look she sent Angie was a thousand times more intense than the glare she'd leveled at Emma on the deck of the St. Louis team hotel. So that was what Jamie's mother's Death Glare looked like. Good to know.

"Come on, Max," Angie said, apparently comfortable with taking her life in her hands, "you know you and Brooke were adorable."

"Brooke Cantwell?" Gabe asked. "You hooked up with Brooke Cantwell?"

"In Chile at the Under-20 World Cup," Angie confirmed. "They were quite the couple for a while, Maxwell and Cantwell. Although, really, Brooke's last name should have been Can Well if you ask me."

Everyone groaned and Jamie whipped a cheese cube at her former youth pool teammate. "No one asked you, jackass."

"Rude," Angie said, and popped the cheese in her mouth.

Emma vaguely recalled Brooke Cantwell, a petite blonde striker with a wide smile and a surprisingly powerful shot. She and Jamie would have been adorable together, Emma had to admit. What had ever happened to Brooke? Emma couldn't remember. So many people had rotated through the national team program in the past decade that it was impossible to keep track of where they all ended up.

At that moment, Ellie tapped her glass. Emma glanced up in time to see Jodie nod reassuringly at the team captain, who took a deep breath before looking around the crowded table. Maybe they'd finally set a date and the longest engagement in the history of humankind—including Emma's brother's—would at last come to a close.

Maddie apparently thought so as well: "Finally," she murmured to Emma while offering a practiced smile to the group at large.

"So," Ellie said, her voice tight with an emotion Emma couldn't quite identify, "we have some news." She reached for Jodie's hand and held it on top of the table. "Jodie and I got married earlier today."

Beside her, Jamie choked on air. Emma knew the feeling as she gaped at her longtime teammate and friend.

"You *what?*" Angie asked, voicing the question that was clearly on everyone's mind.

"Don't worry, there'll still be a big party at some point after the World Cup," Ellie said, smiling at Jodie who nodded vigorously, "but we realized we're probably not going to be back in Oregon anytime soon, and Jodie's parents had this trip planned for a while. Since I have a place in Tahoe, I'm considered a California resident, so here we are."

Something about the reasoning—and the super googily eyes Ellie was giving Jodie—made Emma pause.

"Do you think they're pregnant?" Maddie whispered.

"That's exactly what I was thinking," Emma whispered back.

Almost on cue, Jodie's hand dropped to her belly and stayed there as Ellie leaned in to kiss her cheek. Emma had known they were thinking of trying, but *now?* The baby would be born between the World Cup and the Olympics, which meant Ellie would be the parent of a newborn at the Olympics next year. Of course, given that Jodie was apparently the one carrying the baby, Ellie wouldn't have a huge physical hill to climb back up before Rio. One good thing about being involved with a woman was that you always had a spare womb in the family. That, and you never had to worry about accidentally getting pregnant.

Thank god.

Voices around the table chattered excitedly, asking the same questions currently circling Emma's mind: *Where?* The county court house. *When?* That afternoon. *Who had been their witnesses?* Jodie's parents plus Steph and Tina. *Why now?*

As Ellie hesitated, Gabe's voice cut across the background restaurant noise. "Rachel Ellison, you better not be pregnant!"

Her words hung over the party while Ellie glanced at

her fiancée—*wife*—with a look that clearly said, *I'm sorry I invited my ex.* Jodie gazed back at her with an expression that seemed to simultaneously communicate both *I told you so* and *What can you do? Lesbians.* Meanwhile, Jodie's parents looked on with half-horrified, half-fascinated gazes. Midwesterners weren't accustomed to lesbian ex-girlfriend displays, it seemed.

"In fact, Gabriel, I'm not currently with child," Ellie said, her voice stern and eyes chilly. "But thanks for asking. Any other questions?"

Emma didn't doubt that there were, given who was seated around the table, but for the moment everyone contented themselves with hugs, laughter, and vociferous congratulations.

"No wonder you're here without the rest of your trio," Emma said to Steph as she waited for her turn to hug the happy brides. "I can't believe you didn't tell me!"

"It was pretty sudden," Steph said, smiling.

And why was that, again? The timing still didn't make sense unless…

"Jodie is totally preggers," Emma heard Angie say to Jamie as they returned to their seats a few minutes later.

Apparently Emma wasn't the only one who'd come up with that particular conspiracy theory. Again, at least it wasn't Ellie. Because Emma really couldn't imagine the coaching staff's reaction if their captain and leading scorer, the woman who had just set the new international scoring record, revealed that she might not be able to play in the World Cup. Or, possibly, the 2016 Olympics.

"Gay marriage is legal in Oregon, though, right?" Gabe asked as conversation at their end of the table resumed. "They could have done this up there at any point?"

"Totally," Jamie answered. "Since last year."

Angie shook her head. "It's so irritating trying to

remember where it's legal and where it isn't. What are we up to, thirty-something states now? Shocker that most of the ones where it's still not allowed are in the Bible Belt."

"Did you hear about Alabama?" Gabe asked. "They were so pissed when that federal judge said their gay marriage ban was unconstitutional."

"That asshole Roy Moore actually ordered the counties not to issue licenses." Angie exhaled noisily. "I can't believe he's a real judge."

"That's the Deep South for you," Gabe said. "Only place in the country where no one blinks when a proselytizing pedophile is elected to the state's highest court."

Proselytizing pedophile, Emma repeated inside her head as she sipped her drink. Yay, alliteration.

"Hopefully same-sex marriage will be legal everywhere soon," Jamie put in.

"Are you talking about the Supreme Court case?" Gabe asked.

"Totally. I think there's a good chance SCOTUS will rule in our favor."

Angie snorted. "Dream on, James. Twenty bucks says they punt again, just like they did with Windsor."

The Supreme Court had announced in January that it would hear a case that revolved around a central question in the ongoing gay marriage debate: whether or not individual states had the constitutional right to ban same-sex marriage for their residents. The court had heard two and a half hours of oral arguments in April, and claimed they planned to issue a ruling before the term ended in late June. In mid-May, though, all that had been heard was arguing back and forth on both sides about whether SCOTUS would issue a sweeping decision for the entire country or offer a limited ruling that applied only to the four states named in the complaint.

Emma rested her hand on Jamie's back. "I'm with Jamie," she announced. She'd been surprised two years earlier when Justice Kennedy—a practicing Catholic—had written the majority opinion on US vs. Windsor, which had struck down the federal Defense of Marriage Act, the smarmy legislation Emma's mother had always said would be more accurately titled the Defense against Gay Marriage Act. Why America needed defending against an institution based on love had never been suitably articulated, in the Blakeley family's opinion.

"Um, yeah, Em," Gabe said. "I think we all know that by now."

Emma rolled her eyes and looked for something to throw at the midfielder, but as she reached for the nearest dish—a Fee Fi Fo Fum Fry plate, as it happened—Jamie grabbed her hand.

"Don't even think about it, Blake."

Emma responded by holding out a single fry in her palm as a peace offering. She'd nearly forgotten that Jamie regarded fries as food of the gods. As Jamie received the lone fry reverently, their friends laughed, and so did they, smiling into each other's eyes.

What a good night, Emma thought. She and Jamie were out at an excellent restaurant with their closest friends from the team, two of whom had just gotten married and may or may not be expecting their first child. Not only that but in a couple of hours, they would be meeting the rest of the team at *Pitch Perfect 2*, which was sure to provide at least some queer subtext for those so inclined even if it didn't offer an actual Bechloe kiss. Jamie insisted the kiss between Beca and Chloe was all but guaranteed, but while Emma could appreciate her girlfriend's optimism when it came to the fate of same-sex marriage in America, the chances of two stars of a Hollywood franchise engaging in a same-sex kiss on screen seemed much less likely.

All in all, though, tonight was a welcome break from the hurry up and wait malaise of their final pre-World Cup camp. They'd spent the week since San Jose training, working out, and training some more all while trying not to read the press. Emma had watched more game film of their upcoming opponents than she could ever remember doing. There had also been massive amounts of team bonding over the past few weeks, which was why this rare afternoon off—a round of soccer tennis after lunch didn't really count as a training session—was so appreciated. Jamie and Angie and their U-23 buddies had no idea what was about to happen to them. It wasn't like Emma or Maddie could warn them, either. The World Cup was something you had to experience for yourself.

"Anyone up for a stroll on the boardwalk?" Jodie asked as they split the bill among so many parties that Emma felt sorry for their server.

Jamie and Angie both checked their phones and then nodded in cautious acquiescence. They wanted to get to the theater near the 405 early to find good seats, but there was still plenty of time before the movie started. Emma exchanged a look with Maddie, and they snagged their girlfriends' arms, tugging them out into the summer evening. The restaurant was only a few blocks from the Manhattan Beach Pier, and soon Emma and Jamie were strolling along the boardwalk with their friends, hips and shoulders brushing occasionally.

The scene was familiar—the smell of salt in the air, the grit of sand against pavement beneath their shoes, the shrill cry of seagulls and the rhythmic roll of the tide in the background as they walked. Somehow, it seemed as if she and Jamie were always drawn back to a sunlit California beach. As a diehard Pacific Northwesterner, Emma preferred the less crowded Oregon coast, especially Cannon Beach. Haystock Rock wasn't that far from

Portland. Maybe she should lure Jamie there after the World Cup, or maybe after the NWSL championship, or maybe after the post-World Cup victory (non-victory?) tour, or maybe after, *after*, AFTER…

Jamie nudged her and they shared a smile. Honestly, this was the most relaxed she'd seen Jamie since her big Mother's Day talk with her mom. Emma couldn't quite believe she'd slept through the whole thing, but on the return flight to LA, Jamie had distracted her from the perverse notion of human flight by filling her in on what had gone down over pound cake. While her relationship with her mother hadn't been magically fixed in a single conversation, Jamie had seemed noticeably less angry when they'd said goodbye to her parents at the airport. To Emma, that seemed like a solid step in the right direction.

Jamie's arm brushed Emma's again, and she only barely resisted the urge to wend their arms together. Ahead of them, Maddie and Angie had no such qualms. They walked with their arms firmly entwined, bodies touching with every step as the group paced the crowded boardwalk, the reflection of sunlight off the breaking waves a shimmering band of light in the distance. This was why Wangvak and Madgeline had higher stats on Tumblr than Blakewell—because Maddie and Angie were more comfortable with public displays of affection. Not that Emma was keeping track of their shipping name stats. That was a competition she and Maddie left to their younger girlfriends.

They passed a volleyball game in action and then a giant log where a handful of people sat drinking from cans of beer, Bluetooth speakers blasting hip-hop. The scene reminded Emma of her trip to San Francisco in high school, when she and Jamie had gone for a run that took them to the beach at Golden Gate Park. They had sat on a log near the ocean, and Jamie had said something about the cliché "what doesn't kill you makes you stronger." Last year, right before they got together, Jamie had called that same cliché crap.

"Sometimes," she'd told Emma over the phone one night shortly before Craig cut her, "there are things that take so much out of you that you need time on your own to recover."

Jamie's hand brushed hers now, their palms touching for a brief moment, and as a wave of familiar peace washed over her, Emma reflected that the things that made you stronger were more often the ones that *didn't* involve trauma. People, relationships, moments in time that included love and trust and connection didn't, in fact, leech your energy. Rather they replenished it, easing old hurts and allowing joy to grow in their place.

Or something like that, anyway, Emma thought, enjoying the comfort of Jamie's companionship as they walked on side by side, accompanied by the murmur of their friends' voices and the sound of the waves rushing the shore, the sun casting a river of light that stretched from the nearby beach to the far-off horizon.

CHAPTER EIGHT

Jamie entered the coffee shop and blinked in the sudden dimness. She'd forgotten how sunlight—even the morning variety—could be amplified in New York, bouncing between tall buildings made of glass and steel. As her eyes adjusted, she realized Laurie and Beth hadn't arrived yet. Which made sense. Unless her ex-girlfriend had changed dramatically, she was probably running late.

"They're not here," she told Emma, who was staring down at her phone.

"'Kay." Emma tucked her phone back in her purse and glanced around. "This place is cute."

It was, all hippy and rustic with colorful Central American table cloths and posters on the walls that advertised a variety of social justice opportunities. Also typical Laurie.

Shortly after Jamie had broken up with Brooke Cantwell, Meg had introduced her to Laurie, the pitch of her a capella singing group at Stanford. A senior with her post-college path all planned out, Laurie had not only helped Jamie heal, she'd also provided a window onto a life outside soccer. They'd dated for almost a year, and then

Laurie had graduated and joined the Peace Corps, just as she'd been planning all long. They broke up right before she left the country because neither was interested in a long distance relationship, not because they didn't care about each other. That had made it easier to stay friends, and in the years since, they'd managed to meet up semi-regularly. At this point, Laurie was a stable fixture in Jamie's life.

"Do you want to grab coffee?" Jamie asked. "They could be a while."

Emma frowned slightly—Jamie knew she disapproved of people who were chronically late—but nodded. Soon they were in line, and Emma was making a capella puns Jamie was sure she never would have thought of without the *Pitch Perfect* franchise.

They'd seen the sequel a week earlier, and it was everything Jamie had hoped for even without any actual girl-on-girl action. Jamie wasn't as naïve as certain people (Emma, Angie, Maddie, etc.) seemed to believe, so while she had held out hope for a kiss between Beca and Chloe, she hadn't expected it. Mostly she was just happy that Chloe, who should have graduated three years ahead of Beca, was somehow still around to make eyes at her across the campfire. When Chloe confessed that her one regret from college was that she hadn't experimented enough, Jamie had nearly squealed aloud. She was already anticipating the awesome fan fiction that the suggestive line would no doubt inspire from the loyal Bechloe fandom.

It was a good thing they'd watched the movie the night it came out. Since then, their schedule had been excessively hectic. Borderline crazed, even. Two days after Ellie shell-shocked the lot of them with her marriage announcement, the team had defeated Mexico, their biggest CONCACAF rival, 5-1 at Stub Hub in front of 27,000 fans. For once, the offense had clicked. Ellie and Jenny had scored two goals apiece in a performance that gave Jamie hope for their World Cup campaign. She'd actually scored a goal herself and assisted on another, and her sister had texted her links to articles on assorted sports outlets that were suggesting she would be one of the players to watch in Canada.

Awesome. Super helpful, really.

The day after the game, the team had flown to the East Coast for the third and final match of the send-off series. Not only would they be playing South Korea on Saturday in front of another sold-out crowd, but the players and coaches would also be doing a media tour of New York City—whatever that meant. At this point, Jamie was looking forward more to the two days of R&R they'd been promised before heading up to Winnipeg for the opening match of the group stage. The World Cup wasn't far off now at all.

"Hey, you," a voice called from behind her, and Jamie turned to see her ex-girlfriend striding toward her, dark eyes hidden behind sunglasses, warm smile familiar. In a moment, Laurie had reached her and was pulling her into one of her classic hugs—tight but not too tight, her body vibrating with enthusiasm.

"I can't believe you're on the World Cup team, Jamie!" Laurie said into her ear.

Jamie blinked through the hair tickling her nose and laughed. "I can't believe it, either."

Laurie pulled back and pushed her sunglasses to the top of her head. "You totally deserve it, though. I'm really happy for you."

"Thanks, Laur," Jamie said, gazing affectionately at her ex. She looked good, her eyes clear and happy, her hair shorter but just as uncooperative as usual. With a white mother and a black father, Laurie used to bemoan her hair's unruly nature. Now it was styled in a cloud of curls that suited her bone structure and made her eyes seem even larger.

"Hi," Emma said from Jamie's elbow, her tone slightly amused.

"Oh! Right, sorry," Jamie said, suddenly flustered. "Emma, this is Laurie Moore. Laurie, this is Emma Blakeley."

"I know who she is," Laurie said cheerfully, eyeing Emma's proffered hand for a moment before shaking it. "And this is Beth, my partner."

"In crime," Beth added, her eyes mischievous as she stepped forward to hug Jamie. Her embrace was brief but just as warm as Laurie's. "It's great to see you again, Jamie."

"You, too, Beth."

They chatted about New York and the send-off series as they waited in line, the conversation focused on casual topics. Like dinner at Jupiter, this scene felt a little surreal to Jamie, too. She was here with Laurie and Emma, two women she'd loved but had thought were lost to her, both of whom were back in her life in completely different roles. This was one of those times when she appreciated the lesbian cultural requirement of staying friends with your exes.

Once they'd found a table in a corner near the window, the polite chit-chat turned more personal.

"How are your parents?" Jamie opened with.

"Oh, you know Victor and Victoria," Laurie said breezily. "He's always at the lab and she rarely leaves her greenhouse, but they seem happy enough."

Beside Jamie, Emma choked a bit on her chocolate croissant.

"Those really are their names," Laurie said, and glanced at Jamie. "You didn't mention that?"

"No," Jamie said, shrugging. "I guess it didn't come

up."

The truth was, Emma hadn't even been sure she would come along this morning. She'd considered staying at the hotel in Harrison to get a massage—her right quad, which she'd injured a couple of years earlier, had been nagging her lately, and Jamie knew she was worried about a costly injury at the worst possible time. They were all worried about that, really.

Beth smoothed over the semi-awkward moment with an anecdote that had taken place a few weeks earlier at the Moore family home in Greenbelt, Maryland, where Laurie's father worked for NASA.

"Do you guys get down there a lot?" Jamie asked, trying to ignore the way Emma kept glancing at a nearby table.

"A bit, but not as often as my parents want," Laurie admitted.

"Sounds familiar," Jamie said. "Do any adult children ever visit their parents enough?"

"There are the ones who still live at home," Beth commented, "like my little brother. But our parents complain they see him too much. Probably there's a healthier balance out there somewhere."

"Speaking of siblings, how's Meg? Last I heard, she and Todd were in grad school in Utah." Laurie shuddered, as if the thought of Utah was unpleasant.

Jamie felt the same way. Utah was not known for its kindness toward queers or people of color. Neither were most of its neighboring states, either.

As she filled Laurie in on Maxwell family developments, Jamie noticed again that Emma's gaze had returned to the table near the window where a pair of teenage girls had their phones unsubtly pointed in their direction. Jamie didn't much care if some rando captured photos of their coffee double-date. Good for them, and good—in theory—for the USWNT and the World Cup. Emma, however, chewed her lip and tapped her foot frenetically. Obviously, she didn't feel the same.

Jamie started to reach for her hand to squeeze it in what she intended to be a comforting gesture, but Emma moved it away and stared at her, expression transmitting a clear *What the hell?* As Laurie glanced between them, her gaze narrowing, Jamie smiled tightly, trying to pretend that Emma's reaction in front of her ex-girlfriend wasn't completely mortifying.

"Anyway," she said brightly, "how's work at the UN?"

"You know we don't actually work for the UN, right?" Laurie said.

"Yes, but you still work *at* the UN, right?" Jamie snarked back, falling easily into the familiar banter.

Laurie and Beth, who had met in the Peace Corps in Morocco, now worked for a non-profit that consulted with the UN's Economic and Social Council on the status of women in North Africa. Emma had asked for details on their walk to the coffee shop, but Jamie had only shrugged helplessly. She'd always meant to read up on Laurie's NGO, but somehow she still hadn't. Fortunately, Laurie and Beth didn't mind filling them in on their organization's mission to promote economic independence among the women of rural Africa.

Their pastries were long gone and their caffeinated beverages dwindling when Emma excused herself. She said she needed a restroom, but Jamie suspected she mostly wanted a break from the boundary-pushing teenagers. The two girls turned away, giggling slightly as Emma passed them, and Jamie watched for an anxious moment as Emma seemed to pause.

Keep walking, she thought at her girlfriend. Not like Emma could hear her.

Fortunately, Emma moved past, and Jamie released a

breath. Of course Emma wouldn't antagonize their young fans. She had been doing the patient, occasionally frustrating work of promoting the women's game in the US far longer than Jamie had been. It was only since the scene with Jenny's stalker in St. Louis that Jamie had begun to worry about Emma's reactions. While Jamie had been the one to literally tackle the guy, she knew that Emma was still spooked by the fan's decision to approach them in real life. When Jamie had asked her about her jumpiness after an open training session in LA, Emma had replied that if Jenny's stalker could do it, what was there to prevent other Internet crazies from appearing at a public USWNT event? Or, worse, at their team hotel or even their private homes?

Nothing was the answer, and they both knew it. There was nothing to stop anyone from approaching them, just as there was nothing to prevent any person in the world from transgressing against another if they wanted to badly enough. New York City with its sheer mass of human beings all in constant, often tense proximity was just another reminder that people were not always good to each other. Jamie had grown up in a city, but Emma was a child of the suburbs. That particular difference from their childhoods sometimes crystallized in Jamie's mind. This current trip—like their trip to London last year—was one of those moments.

"Everything okay?" Laurie asked.

"Totally," Jamie said, channeling more false cheer. "I think we're both just a little jittery. We leave for Canada in less than a week, and even though this is my first World Cup, it's Emma's third. There's this sense among the veterans that it's now or never. For them, it really could be."

"She's what, my age?"

"Yeah, but that means she'll be almost thirty-three during the next World Cup. That's practically ancient in soccer circles."

"In plenty of places around the world, thirty-three actually is ancient thanks to lack of access to healthcare and other resources you and I take for granted," Laurie said, giving her the look that reminded Jamie of college whenever she'd said something unintentionally offensive. Laurie used to criticize—justifiably, Jamie could admit—the culture of elite sports in America, where men in particular made enough in a year to feed, clothe, and educate thousands of impoverished families in the US and beyond.

"I know," Jamie said, only just resisting the urge to apologize. She was hardly the sheltered college kid she'd been when she first met Laurie. Just like her ex, she had worked hard to get to where she was in her career. Not only that, but she had lived in a foreign country for nearly three years all on her own. Well, with Britt. And, admittedly, she hadn't had to learn a foreign language to live in London, even if Welsh accents could be challenging. Either way, it was irritating that Laurie still had that way of making her feel young and not quite up to snuff.

"You do seem happy, though," Laurie said unexpectedly. "I always thought you would end up with a soccer player."

Jamie frowned slightly. "You did? Why?" Oh, god, had she talked about Emma to Laurie while they were together, too? Did every single one of her ex-girlfriends know about the torch she'd carried long and far for Emma Blakeley?

"I just thought you would be happier with someone who shares your passion."

That made sense, actually. "You, too, huh?" Jamie said, her smile encapsulating both her ex and her current partner.

"Yep," Laurie said, and reached for Beth's hand. "Plus you used to talk about Emma all the time."

"No, I didn't," Jamie said, groaning slightly.

Laurie only shrugged, but Beth grinned and said, "It's true. She told me that forever ago."

And there it was. Still, she could only shake her head because Emma was Emma, and Laurie wasn't wrong about Jamie's seeming happiness. She was happy, for so many good reasons.

"Blakewell, huh?" Laurie added teasingly, and Jamie threw her napkin at her.

Laurie and Beth had been affectionate throughout the coffee date, and now as Jamie watched them smile easily into each other's eyes, she felt a flash of envy, a momentary pang of regret. Her parents had loved Laurie. For years after they broke up, her mother and father had asked after her as if they hoped Jamie and Laurie would somehow find their way back to each other. When Jamie had finally asked what made them recall her first serious girlfriend so fondly, her mother had told her that Laurie had single-handedly opened Jamie up. Once they'd started dating, she'd apparently begun expressing her emotions more freely, smiling more and hugging her family the way she used to when she was "younger," which Jamie knew was code for "before Lyon."

"You were a different person after you met Laurie," her mother had explained. "A much warmer, more affectionate person. She helped you learn to love yourself and others, and that's something every parent wants for their child."

Her parents would be excited to hear the latest update on Laurie's life, but their interest was different now, more tempered now that Jamie and Emma were back together. Finally together? Whatever. They were a couple, and Jamie's parents seemed nearly as pleased with that turn of events as Jamie and Emma were.

When Emma returned to the table, it was,

unfortunately, time to head back to New Jersey. They had a morning VR session scheduled at the team hotel before lunch, which would be followed by afternoon training at the stadium. And this was a semi-relaxed day. Tomorrow was the team's official Media Day event at the Marriott Marquis on Times Square, where close to 200 members of the media would grill them about their World Cup preparations. As if that wasn't enough reporters to last a lifetime, the morning after that they would be up before dawn to have their hair and make-up done for their appearance on *Good Morning America*, the number one morning newscast in America with millions upon millions of viewers.

Jamie's iron stomach felt a little less metallic and a lot queasier at the thought.

"Ah, the life of an international soccer star," Laurie teased as they hugged goodbye. "Again, I'm so happy for you, Jamie. You've achieved everything you wanted, which is no small thing."

"Not quite everything," Jamie said, moving on to hug Beth. "We still have to get to Canada and win the whole she-bang, you know."

"Wait, which she are you banging?" Laurie asked, grinning.

Out of the corner of her eye, Jamie saw Emma wince. "Shut it," she said to her ex, laughing to take the sting out of her words.

They walked out together and parted ways on the sidewalk in front of the coffee shop, Jamie and Emma headed west toward Penn Station and the PATH train, Laurie and Beth north toward the UN.

"Good luck in Canada," Beth told them, waving over her shoulder with one hand, the other clasped around Laurie's.

"Kick some grass!" Laurie called out.

"You, too!" Jamie returned as the distance between them widened. And then Laurie and Beth were obscured from sight behind a building that anywhere else would have been classified as tall but here in NYC was considered on the small side.

As she and Emma headed back to the train station, Jamie tried to tamp down a renewed pang of envy. Laurie and Beth had held hands in the coffee shop, on the sidewalk, wherever they wanted, broadcasting their relationship to anyone and everyone. Jamie wished she and Emma could swing hands as they strolled along the city sidewalk strewn with cigarette butts and other detritus, but there was a time and a place for public displays of affection and this was not one of them. Big dreams often required sacrifice, and Jo Nichols and the federation had made the rules—of their involvement with each other and their participation on the national team—perfectly clear. But the restrictions were only temporary, only applicable while they were both under contract with US Soccer.

Emma was quiet beside her, and Jamie tried to picture a future where they might walk down this same street hand-in-hand. Would Emma ever be comfortable showing affection in public? Jamie wasn't sure, particularly given the extenuating circumstances her girlfriend had only recently revealed. Jamie couldn't forget Emma's description of the Boston police station she and Sam had visited after her online stalking situation had taken a particularly frightening turn. She couldn't forget how Emma's voice had shaken as they sat in the Roman ruins above Lyon discussing her experience with delusional fans. She couldn't forget her own flash of fear, either, when Emma shared the police officer's suggestion that she and Sam have a gun on hand "just in case." Guns scared the crap out of Jamie, and to think that Emma and Sam had been told that buying one might be the only way to stay safe…

Emma and Sam had suffered a fairly intense trauma even if the man had never made physical contact, and Jamie understood that meant that Emma saw risks in being together that she simply didn't. She hadn't known about Emma's history with Sam until Lyon, but it wasn't like not being able to hold hands or otherwise be affectionate in public was a deal breaker. She loved Emma, and as long as Emma loved her back to the best of her ability, that was enough. Well, not *enough*. But, moving forward, Jamie trusted Emma to respect her boundaries and to treat her with love and compassion. And honesty. She definitely wasn't about to forget that one.

If future Emma consistently failed to do any of those things? Then that would be grounds for a conversation Jamie was hoping they wouldn't ever need to have.

"Thanks for coming to coffee," she said, nudging Emma slightly with her shoulder.

Emma glanced up, startled. "Of course. Thanks for inviting me."

"Of course," she echoed. After a moment, she added, "You okay?"

"Totally."

"Okay."

Emma looked at her again. "What?"

"I said okay."

"Yeah, but it was *how* you said okay."

"That's funny, because I was thinking it was how *you* said totally," Jamie returned.

They walked a few more paces and reached a red light. She always forgot how many traffic lights there were in New York until she was trying to get from one Manhattan location to another. With the city's crazy cab drivers and the plethora of insane bike commuters and delivery people, it wasn't a good idea to jaywalk, either.

"Laurie's great," Emma said. "Maybe a little too great… I mean, you said you broke up because of the distance, not because your feelings changed, right?"

Jamie blinked. Was Emma insecure? She was, wasn't she? "I'm pretty sure you wouldn't be thinking like that if you knew what Laurie and Beth said while you were in the bathroom."

"Thinking like what?" Emma asked defensively. As Jamie just looked at her, one eyebrow lifted, she sighed. "Fine. What did they say?"

Jamie told her, and soon Emma was smiling, but quizzically like she didn't quite believe it. And Jamie remembered that the outwardly confident perfectionist that Emma projected to the rest of the world was a mask that hid the girl whose father had made her doubt her lovability.

"No way," Emma said.

"Yes way," Jamie insisted. "Apparently, Clare wasn't the only one who picked up on my preoccupation with a certain soccer player from my past."

Emma looked down and bumped her shoulder into Jamie's. "Obviously, I'm not that easy to forget."

"No," Jamie agreed. "That, you are not."

Emma was quiet again while they waited at another corner, yellow cabs and shiny SUVs honking and cutting each other off at high rates of speed only a few feet away. Then she said, "Did you see those girls at the next table?"

Jamie nodded. "I thought you were going to yell at them for a second."

"I almost did. I mean, it's like they don't realize we're actual people who might not be in the mood to have our private conversations recorded."

"I know, but…" Jamie trailed off as the light changed. She checked to the left before starting across the street. She'd seen enough movies to know that drivers didn't always stop at red lights.

"But what?" Emma prodded.

"I guess I'm wondering why a couple of kids with a poor grasp on social boundaries upset you so much," Jamie said carefully. As Emma looked at her, face taut, she immediately regretted her word choice. "I mean, I think I get it. It's because of what happened with Sam, right?"

After a moment, Emma nodded, her face relaxing. "Yeah. And I'm sorry. I know you deserve someone who's out and proud and can't stop talking about how lucky they are to be with you. But even without the federation breathing down our necks, I probably won't ever be able to give you the kind of relationship Laurie and her girlfriend—"

Jamie stopped suddenly, her hand on Emma's elbow. "Emma. I don't need you to tell the whole world that you love me, okay? I get how difficult that is for you, and you don't have to worry about it. You're not going to lose me because we don't hold hands in public."

"It's not that easy, Jamie, and you know it. You've literally said that you think I should come out. Remember your speech a couple of months ago about all the bi and pan kids I could help?"

Jamie released her arm. "I wouldn't call it a speech, but yes, I did say that. And I still think you could help a lot of kids by coming out. But I said that before you told me about Boston, before I knew why you and Sam broke up. I mean, I would love it if you were okay with us being more public, I'm not going to lie. But I don't need it. It doesn't have to be an issue between us, Emma. That's what I'm saying."

Emma squinted at her, and then she sighed a little, her shoulders visibly relaxing. "Really? Because I saw the way you looked at them today…"

"So I'm a little jealous that they're not world famous

athletes with restrictive relationship clauses in their employment contracts. Can you blame me?"

Emma smiled and shook her head. "No. Nope, I can't."

"Good," Jamie said. "Now come on. Don't want to be late for virtual reality, do we?"

They were almost back to Penn Station when Emma glanced over at her and said, "So Laurie was a senior when you were a sophomore?"

Jamie nodded.

"Just like me."

"Just like you."

"Huh," Emma said, and her voice dropped. "Do you perchance have a thing for older women, Maxwell?"

"Apparently," Jamie replied, sliding her hand across Emma's back and letting it rest briefly against the curve of her waist. From experience, Jamie knew that the skin there was soft and supple, and yet just beneath the surface Emma's abs were as strong as steel. Or rocks. Or whatever other abdominal-defying simile was currently most popular on the Interwebs.

"Why," Emma teased, "because you need someone to look after you?"

Jamie shifted her caress into a light squeeze. "No, because I'm more mature than the average person my age."

"Right." Emma coughed into her elbow, the words she muttered clearly audible: *"Skateboarding while stoned."*

"You know I don't do that anymore!"

"Oh, yeah? When was the last time? We're talking ballpark. The year will do."

Jamie sighed, her eyes seeking the train station only a block away now. "2012."

Emma burst out laughing.

"What?" Jamie went for the easy guilt trip. "It was

hard watching some of my closest friends win a gold medal without me."

Emma's smile faded into something softer. "Aw, I know."

"You don't, though." She stopped and bit her lip, realizing that the joke had somehow turned sour. She'd been about to say that Emma had never really suffered, that she'd been handed everything. That she was, maybe, *spoiled*. But that wasn't fair. While Emma may have come from a place of privilege—as did Jamie; as did most American soccer players, especially of the white, female variety—she had risen to where she was now by working her ass off. You couldn't play at their level without sacrificing friendships, relationships, family events. Not everyone understood being chucked over for a soccer tournament, even if it was to qualify for the World Cup or the Olympics.

Then there was the constant work to keep your body at an elite level. You could take a day or two off here and there, even a week every once in a while. But the older you got, the harder it was to come back. That was why most of the athletes Jamie knew subsisted on a steady diet of carbs, protein, and exercise; why routine ruled the life of even the most gym-averse professional soccer player. The level of focus required—on diet, sleep habits, exercise regimes—to maintain supremacy in a sport where there was always someone younger, faster, hungrier aching for a shot at your spot ensured that Emma and Jamie and everyone else on the national team was about as far from spoiled as a person could get.

"You're right," Emma admitted, her hand brushing Jamie's. "I don't know what that felt like. But you're here now, and I, for one, am thrilled you made the roster. Even if you occasionally still show the decision-making skills of, say, a fourteen-year-old boy."

Jamie tilted her head. "That's fair." She wished she could kiss Emma's cheek, wished she could let her lips linger on the warm skin that would likely smell faintly of foundation and an earthier scent that was all Emma. But she contented herself with a return smile. "I'm glad I made the roster, too—even though that means I now have to suffer through Media Day."

A sign on a stone building they were passing caught her eye: The Church of St. Francis of Assisi. She glanced into a courtyard, and sure enough, there was the church named for the patron saint of animals and nature, a corner of quiet in the most unquiet city Jamie had ever known. It seemed like a sign. It was a sign, wasn't it?

"It'll be fine," Emma assured her as they reached the station.

Jamie pulled open the door and held it for Emma. "How do you know?"

"Because this isn't my first rodeo, remember?" They crossed the station, following signs to the PATH train back to New Jersey. "And even if it's not, it isn't like video and audio recordings are forever."

Jamie only just stopped herself from smacking Emma in the ass. Instead, she contented herself with a flick to her girlfriend's shoulder. "I hate you."

"No, you don't," Emma said, smirking at her as they found the correct stairwell. "Last one to the platform has to do the other one's laundry!" she added, and sprinted ahead.

Technically, the team's laundry was done by unlucky federation interns. But that didn't prevent Jamie from sprinting after her. Emma's quad was sore, after all, a weakness Jamie fully intended to exploit. Emma, she knew, would have done the same.

As she gained on her laughing girlfriend, Jamie remembered what Laurie had said: "I thought you would be happier with someone who shares your passion." Her ex had been completely right about that.

She passed Emma at the very last stair and blew past her onto the train platform, still laughing as waiting passengers glanced up from their phones disapprovingly.

"Jerk!" Emma said, and stuck her tongue out.

Jamie glanced around to make sure they no one was in earshot before saying, "That's what you get for getting involved with someone younger, old lady." And then she was off down the platform, Emma's indignant laughter echoing in her ears.

They could do this, she thought as Emma caught up to her and they found a spot to wait. With Emma at her side, even facing down 200 sports reporters at Media Day didn't seem as daunting.

Or did it? The jury was still out on that one.

CHAPTER NINE

As the opening chords of "The Star-Spangled Banner" rang out across Red Bull Arena, Jamie stood on the field with her teammates and surveyed the sold-out crowd, sweat pooling at the small of her back in the early summer heat. As a West Coaster, she had never been a fan of this kind of heat and humidity, but this was a good warm-up for the World Cup. Canada might be north of the border, but summer temperatures for many of the tournament sites averaged in the 90s.

The anthem ended and the starters gathered for a photo, arms around each other's shoulders, smiles wide. Jamie could feel the anticipation rising in the stadium, both among the fans and among her teammates. Finally, they were playing an actual match. The game against Korea—the last match of the send-off series—was supposedly the reason they'd come to New Jersey. But while the past few days had been filled with the usual training sessions on the field and in the classroom, multiple formation walk-throughs, and individual and team video analysis, they had also been chock full of media appearances. Fortunately, the PR team provided training on public speaking at most national team camps, and since they'd arrived on the East

Coast, Caroline and her staff had spent time after dinner each night coaching them up. Jamie was pretty sure their tutelage was the only reason she had survived Media Day.

First on the docket at the hotel on Times Square had been a surprise lunch visit from Robin Roberts, during which the *Good Morning America* anchor had delivered an inspirational speech about overcoming breast cancer and leukemia. Her talk, during which she thanked the players for taking the Title IX baton and "just running with it," had rightfully gotten the team buzzing about character and perspective, two of the life lessons Roberts had highlighted. Her visit had been the perfect lead-in to what had easily been the most nerve-wracking experience of Jamie's life. But each time she had felt herself close to floundering during the individual sessions, when each player was given their own microphone to respond to questions from reporters, she had channeled an image of Roberts speaking a few hours earlier. After all, being on the proverbial hot seat wasn't anything like sitting in a chair for hours on end while life-saving medicine poured through your veins, setting your nerve endings aflame.

After Media Day, the team appearance on stage at *Good Morning America* the following day had felt like a breeze to Jamie, mostly because she hadn't been tasked with holding a microphone or responding to Robin Roberts's questions. Being on camera wasn't one of her strengths. She'd been interviewed like everyone else for her individual player profile on US Soccer's YouTube site, and she'd appeared in a few promo videos, but usually not with a speaking part. She felt fairly confident standing in the group with her tattooed arms folded and her game face showing, but anything else? Not so much. She couldn't even bear to watch her "23 Stories" video once she'd approved the demo.

Emma, on the other hand, was accustomed to center

stage in US Soccer's many promo videos. Along with Ellie and Jenny, she'd volunteered to handle one of the mics on *GMA*. They'd all done beautifully, of course. They had seemed comfortable chatting with Ed Sheeran backstage, too, another feat that had proved beyond Jamie's abilities. She'd been too tongue-tied to even think of trying to request a selfie with him. Celebrity interactions with anyone other than her famous girlfriend and their teammates was not really her thing.

During their two minutes of on-camera fame, Robin Roberts had given a shout-out to Angie's birthday. Jamie and Britt had elbowed their friend as a band of American Outlaw supporters in the crowd cranked up their instruments and sang the birthday song to a blushing Angie. Only half an hour from where she'd grown up, Angie was in her element in the New York metro area. Jo had even given her the start today against South Korea, and her name had drawn an even larger roar from the crowd than Ellie's. Or maybe an equivalent one. It had only been three weeks since Ellie had broken the international scoring record, and the crowd was clearly pumped to see history made.

As the team gathered for its final pre-match cheer, Jamie was just pumped to finally play.

The game started well enough, with an American goal opportunity almost immediately after kickoff. But Jenny clanged the ball off the crossbar, and as the Korean keeper grabbed the rebound and motioned her team upfield, Jamie could feel it: The doldrums were settling in.

It happened like that sometimes. One missed shot, one foul call, one yellow card, and a team's energy would crash for no discernible reason. Warm-up had felt a bit tight, in Jamie's opinion, but not tight enough for what followed. The US team couldn't seem to find their footing. Not literally because Red Bull Arena offered a beautiful, natural grass surface. The field was in excellent shape, so it couldn't be blamed for their poor passing or sluggish shape. The blame lay squarely on the players because soccer was a players' game.

Coaching decisions could also take a toll. Like most of her teammates, Jamie believed that tasking Ellie and Rebecca with serving as the lone strikers up top while Jenny played outside midfielder was not the best use of personnel. Ellie might be the leading scorer in the world, but she was no spring chicken, as she herself would be the first to admit. Making her responsible for pressuring half the offensive quadrant meant she spent more time chasing down the ball than capitalizing on scoring opportunities. What was wrong with the formation from the previous two matches, with Maddie playing the ten and Jamie the six beside Gabe, with Ellie, Jenny, and Rebecca sharing striker honors? Honestly, the final game of the send-off series was hardly the time to be experimenting with the line-up, Jamie had heard more than one player complain. While she understood that they had to be ready to switch things up in Canada in case of injury or fouls, she suspected that today's personnel changes had translated into a lack of confidence across the board.

Whatever the cause, Jo suggested strongly at halftime that they figure it out and FIX IT. The stadium was full of fans looking to send them off in style with a solid victory under their belts.

They didn't fix it. The lethargy continued in the second half, and Jamie could almost feel the disappointment pressing down on the crowd as the minutes ticked steadily away without a score on either side. When the final whistle blew with the score tied 0-0, the crowd applause was more polite than passionate. The team shook hands with their heads down. They'd played to a scoreless draw against South Korea, a team they'd beaten on seven previous tries. Jamie could imagine what the press would say about what could essentially be considered a loss on the eve of the World Cup. It didn't help that she'd played poorly, either. She had only just earned her starting spot. She couldn't afford to blow it this close to Canada.

The day wasn't a total soccer bust, though. The 2015 FA Cup final that morning at Wembley Stadium had seen Arsenal defeat Aston Villa for a record 12th title. Not only that, but Arsenal had finished the season ahead of Manchester United, as Jamie delighted in reminding Emma over dinner that night.

"Whatever," Emma said. "At least we both made Champions League."

"Your boys barely made it," Jamie said. Only the top four teams in the Premier League advanced to the group stage of Champions League, and their teams had come in third and fourth, respectively.

"Winning ugly counts just as much as winning pretty," Emma said primly.

"I guess Man U would know about winning ugly." As Emma narrowed her eyes, Jamie laughed. "You said it, not me!"

Their match against Korea had ended an hour earlier, and now they were stuffing food into their mouths as fast as they could, chatting about anything and everything—except the game. Usually after a friendly, everyone wanted to dissect the match. Tonight, though, that wasn't the case.

"Maxwell."

Jamie glanced up from her plate, her smile fading as she realized Jo was standing at the end of the table. "Yeah, Coach?" she asked, swallowing in what she hoped was a subtle manner rather than one that revealed her sudden abject fear.

"Visit me later, will you?"

"In your room?" Jamie asked, her mind not firing on

its usual cylinders.

Jo's eyebrows rose. "Yes, in my room. Twenty minutes, okay?"

"Yes, m'a—sure thing."

"Ooooh," Angie murmured once their head coach was out of earshot. "Someone's in trouble. Were you out of your room again, Max?"

Jamie was pretty sure this was a reference to their youth days. Specifically, to the night she found out about Tori Parker and snuck out of her room to call Emma. Thank god those days were over, never—she hoped—to return.

"Nah," she said casually. "She probably just wants to talk about you."

"Jamie's in tr—wait, what?" Angie frowned.

"You know, about the thing that happened on *GMA* with the Outlaws."

Angie stared at her, the wheels turning inside her head almost audible.

Jamie couldn't help it—she cracked up. "Oh my god, you should see your face."

"Hey, that wasn't funny," Angie complained.

"It was totally funny," Britt said, and held out her fist for Jamie to bump.

Emma caught her eye, her expression encouraging. Jamie nodded, trying to project confidence. *Fake it 'til you make it*, a lesson she'd learned in therapy, was a useful tool in manifold situations.

Any semblance of humor fled as soon as she started the short walk to the elevator. *Oh god oh god oh god, please don't let her bench me.* She repeated the words over and over like a mantra, even though she understood at some level that doing so was as ineffective as most such prayers. Jamie had no control over the coach's decisions regarding playing time. All she could do was show up and try her hardest, and hope that was enough.

The USWNT coach was alone in her suite, reading glasses propped on top of her head, trusty laptop on the coffee table. "Jamie," she said, closing the computer. "How are you doing?"

Jamie perched on the other end of the sofa, trying to keep her jumpy legs still. "Fine, thanks. How are you?"

Jo smiled slightly. "I'm well. You know, not many people ask me that."

"Probably because they're scared of you," Jamie posited, and then immediately backtracked. "Not that there's anything to be afraid of."

"Thanks," Jo said. "I think. So, this will be your first World Cup with the senior side. Are you feeling prepared?"

"I think so. At least, as much as I can be. Emma and Ellie say you can't really anticipate what it will be like until you've done it, so…" She shrugged, unsure what Jo was looking for.

"How did you feel about the game today?"

"Oh. Um, not so good, I guess?"

"Which part? Or parts. It doesn't have to be just one thing."

"Well, the team wasn't really clicking," Jamie said. "I mean, obviously."

"Okay. Why do you think that is?"

Jamie frowned, regarding the woman before her. She had watched Jo play for the national team when she was younger, and then she'd played for Jo on the under-16 and under-23 sides. Jo had been her role model, her mentor, her leader. Was she really asking Jamie to share her thoughts about the team, or was there something else going on?

"I think the scoring struggle is real," she said, her tone

cautious.

"Yes, but why? In your opinion."

Jo had always valued direct communication, so Jamie took a breath and said, "It seems like our midfielders and strikers aren't making the kinds of connections we need. The 4-4-2 feels a little old fashioned, to be honest."

"What would you do to change things up? You must have some ideas."

"Maybe," Jamie allowed. "I kind of like Chelsea's take on the 4-5-1. I know people say it's all about defense, but it seems like a modified version of Gardiola's 4-3-3 to me, with the striker on top free to create without having to worry as much about defensive responsibilities."

At that, Jo laughed a little and shook her head.

"What?" Jamie asked.

"Are you sure you haven't been a fly on the wall at our coaches meetings? Because that's one option we've been discussing. You may have a future in managing, kiddo."

Managing? Jamie tested the idea, picturing herself in Melanie's role as an assistant with the national team or even, someday, Jo's. Huh. She could almost see it.

"What about you personally?" Jo asked. "How did you feel out there?"

"Slow," Jamie admitted, sure her leaden legs had shown.

"Too much soccer lately, or not enough?"

Jamie thought about the question. "Neither. More like too much thinking. Usually when I play, everything else fades away. But not today. I couldn't get my mind to stop spiraling."

"Spiraling, huh. You do tai chi, don't you?"

"Usually, but it's been hard to work it in lately. Our schedule's been so wonky."

"Wonky is the perfect word, and unfortunately, it's not

about to change anytime soon. So what can we do to make sure you don't miss your self-care routine moving forward?"

The phrase "self-care routine" was so reminiscent of trauma recovery doctrine that Jamie startled slightly. Jo was watching her as calmly as ever, her eyes and face warm and engaged. Was this an opening? Did she know that Jamie knew that she knew? Had Emma…? But no, Emma would have said something if she'd spoken to Jo again. Wouldn't she?

Jamie glanced down at her phone and smoothed her thumb across the power button. "I have an exercise app I use most days. I guess I could add an entry for tai chi right after I brush my teeth at night."

"That sounds like a good plan. Let me know if you need help. Lacey, I'm sure, could always be convinced to develop a team-wide model for habit development and retention."

Her tone was dry, and Jamie smiled. "No doubt."

"Well, if there's nothing else…" Jo said, lifting an eyebrow.

Jamie paused, chewing her lip. The other woman seemed to be waiting for something. Was this about Lyon? Only one way to find out.

"Emma told me you knew," she blurted, entirely unrehearsed. "About Lyon—from Pete, I mean."

"Ah," Jo said, nodding. "And you have questions for me?"

"Not really. Or, I mean, maybe just one?" As Jo gazed her at encouragingly, she added, "I guess I just wonder—would I even be here without, you know, what happened?"

"I don't know," Jo said. "Only you can answer that question."

Jamie frowned. "What does that mean?"

"It means that you are who you are now because of your history. Would you have persevered through injury after injury if you didn't already know how strong you were? If you didn't already understand what it means to be a survivor?"

Jamie toyed with the hem of her shorts while she thought back to the year that had followed the worst night of her life. In the immediate aftermath, she had struggled. *Hard.* She'd even considered ending her life when the pain and fear had seemed too much to live with. But then her parents introduced her to Shoshanna, and Jamie had slowly begun to emerge from the darkness. One of the many useful things Shoshanna had taught her was that pain exists both as a learning tool and as a motivation to heal and repair whatever has been injured. If you burn your arm on the door of a wood stove, you'll remember the next time you load the stove to be careful of the hot door. You'll also want to treat the burn because if you don't, it might become infected, which could lead to increased suffering.

Shoshanna approached psychological injury from a similar vantage point. Under her tutelage, Jamie had learned to heal her emotional wounds by reconditioning her outlook to match who she wanted to be, not who she had been during and immediately after her assault. Shoshanna had encouraged her to use the pain of the attack as a motivator to heal and improve rather than sinking under the weight of her shame and anger. Part of that improvement had included focusing on what she loved most—soccer—and becoming as good at it as she possibly could. Flourishing in the aftermath of psychological injury was one of Shoshanna's central goals for the sexual assault survivors she counseled.

Jo was right: What had happened in France was part of Jamie, as was the difficult and rewarding work she'd done afterward on the road to recovery.

"I don't know if you remember the pre-game talk I gave in Brazil," Jo said when Jamie remained silent. "It's one of my favorites, based on the premise that what doesn't kill us makes us stronger. I genuinely believe that we're all shaped by our experiences. Sometimes we're led by love, and other times we're forged by fire. But metal that's heated isn't only more pliable; it's also stronger. And yes, I know, I'm getting all inspirational speaker-ish here. But one of the things I appreciate most about you, Jamie, is your ability to fight. You fought through Lyon and its aftermath. You fought back from your ACL injury and then again from a broken ankle. You know what that stubborn persistence tells me about you? That you're a warrior. And I need a team of warriors because the World Cup is serious business, and I need serious people to help me bring that title back to this country."

Jamie was already smiling by the time Jo finished. "You stole that line from a movie, didn't you?"

Jo smiled back. "Only the last part." She hesitated and then held her arms open. "You're here because you earned your spot, Jamie. I promise."

Jamie scooted forward and let herself be hugged. "Thanks, Coach."

"You're more than welcome." Jo patted her back and then pushed her away in a typical jock move. "Now get out of here and rest up. R&R takes a surprising amount of energy."

"At least we get to sleep in."

"True. Have a good night, kiddo."

"You, too," Jamie said, and gave Jo a two-fingered salute before slipping out of the suite.

At the end of the corridor, which looked like every other hotel hallway she'd ever been in, Jamie bypassed the elevator and headed down the stairs to her own floor. The talk with Jo hadn't gone at all how she'd expected, but it had been good. With every step, she felt her muscles flex, felt how, if she wanted, she could run a 5K right now, even after playing a full match earlier in the day. The listlessness that had plagued her during the game was gone, and her head felt clear. Jo, she was beginning to think, was a genius at assessing her players and their needs. That was why she got the big bucks, Jamie supposed. Though nowhere near the big bucks the US Men's National Team coach received, of course.

Later, after brushing her teeth and tying chi, as Angie liked to call it, for a solid fifteen minutes, Jamie lay in her hotel bed and stared up at the ceiling. *Back to basics*, she reminded herself. *Control the things you can—attitude, work ethic, and effort—and let go of the things you can't.*

She had this. Or, she would after team vacation, anyway.

#

It wasn't an actual vacation, more like a 48-hour break from pre-World Cup scrutiny. Jamie and Emma took advantage of the free time by booking a hotel suite on the Upper West Side not far from the Museum of Natural History, just the two of them for two whole nights.

During the day, they dined on their favorite Cheat Day foods—pizza, cheeseburgers, and fries—and hung out with their friends on the team. "The national team takes Manhattan!" Jamie, Britt, and Angie took inordinate pleasure in shouting randomly as they rollerbladed through Central Park or surveyed the city skyline from the top of the Empire State Building. At night, Jamie and Emma retired to their quiet room in an ornate older building whose gargoyles reminded Jamie of *Ghostbusters*. Emma had stayed there the previous year during a trip to meet with one of the medical foundations her family was involved with, and Jamie fell in love with the room's Victorian feel and the view of the San Remo and Central Park in the distance. But what she loved most of all was the plush king-size bed that she and Emma could stretch out on, or roll across, or even (it was only *once*) tumble off of during a particularly passionate moment.

They weren't hurt, fortunately. Otherwise, Ellie and Jo would have killed them. Jamie didn't really think she would blame them, either. If the news got out that two USWNT starters managed to injure themselves days before the start of the World Cup while engaging in spirited lesbian sexcapades? Yeah, that wouldn't be completely embarrassing or anything. Not to mention, likely a violation of US Soccer's personal conduct clause.

But 48 hours off the federation clock was always going to go too fast, and soon it was their last morning drinking coffee and tea in the hotel restaurant and dining on the flakiest croissants Jamie had ever had the pleasure to taste. Soon, very soon, they would have to catch a cab to JFK to meet the rest of the team for their flight to Winnipeg. While Jamie was beyond ready for the World Cup to start, she would miss being off the team clock with Emma. At least they were going to Canada together. Other players were about to embark on an extended absence from their partners, except for Phoebe, whose college soccer coach husband had the summer off and would be following the US team around Canada for the next five weeks.

Across the breakfast table, Emma had her phone out and kept showing Jamie her favorite photos from their tour of NYC. She had uploaded a few to her private Facebook page, as had Jamie, but in general they refrained from sharing anything too personal. Facebook and Instagram weren't the most secure platforms, and even if they had been, passwords could always be hacked. That was one reason Jamie had never posed for a naked pic of any kind. Well, that and she was at heart a giant prude. Pictures that showed off her tattoos were one thing, but boobs or other body parts? No, thanks.

"What about this one?" Emma asked, holding up her phone.

"Aw, I love that one," Jamie said.

Maddie had taken the shot of them on the Empire State Building's observation deck. The photo was from behind, and Emma had her arm around Jamie's waist and her lips pressed to her cheek in a stolen kiss. Jamie was turned toward her slightly, and with her Sanskrit bicep tattoo and part of her Phoenix tattoo visible under her racing back tank top, it was obvious just whom Emma was kissing.

Emma stared down at her phone, lips pursed. "Maddie always takes the best shots of us, doesn't she?"

"I know. I really feel like we should return the favor, but I think our picture-taking skills might be crap."

"Mine are, but you're the artist in this relationship."

Jamie smiled into her tea. So many things about that sentence and the soft tone Emma had delivered it in made her happy.

"All right then," Emma announced, suddenly businesslike. "I'm putting it on Instagram."

"Cool," Jamie said, and took another bite of her croissant, the buttery dough instantly melting on her tongue.

"My public Instagram," Emma clarified, her fingers moving over her phone screen.

Jamie looked up. "Your public—but that's linked to your Twitter feed, isn't it?"

"Exactly."

"But you're kissing me!"

"Yes. Yes, I am." She winked exaggeratedly at Jamie. "Get it? Like the Melissa Etheridge album?"

"I am a lesbian, Emma. But what exactly are you trying

to do here?"

"As a lesbian, shouldn't you understand the concept of coming out?"

Jamie felt her jaw drop. "Wait, *what*?"

Emma shrugged. "I thought about what you said, and you're right. I could help a lot of people. Plus we're under a social media blackout, so you know, this is the perfect time to do it." As Jamie continued to stare at her, she added, "Honestly, in a few days, no one's going to care who's kissing who."

Her reasoning made sense, but was this really the time to call attention to their relationship? Would they end up being a distraction to the team? Given the way they'd played on Saturday, they probably couldn't be blamed for any future poor showing. The offense had been struggling since long before Jamie had joined the team. If anything, their stats had improved since she'd been on the scene.

"I don't know, Em," she said, "I thought—I mean, I didn't think you wanted people to know about us."

Emma sighed quietly. "I know, and I'm sorry I made you feel that way. I love you, Jamie, and I'm not afraid for people to know that."

Jamie blinked and exhaled long and slow. "Okay. If you're sure."

"I'm sure of you. Everyone else, not so much." But Emma hit the post button anyway, sending their photo out into the Interwebs along with the caption, "It's been real, New York! See you on the flip side. GO USA!!!"

"Should we have warned Caroline?" Jamie asked half an hour later as their cab driver took them across the city, flying over slight hills and banking around corners as if they were in a chase scene from a movie. Her phone had lit up with so many notifications that she'd had to turn off her social media feed, but her text messages weren't as easy to silence. The team's PR manager had informed her that her presence was requested in a meeting as soon as they landed in Winnipeg.

Emma showed her a matching message on her screen. "What are they going to do, kick us off the team right before the World Cup starts? We're riding the wave, babe, and they can't risk knocking us off the board."

"Ooh, nice analogy," Jamie said. "That's why you decided to do it now, isn't it? Because the world's eyes are literally upon us?" It was so clever, perfectly befitting the captain of the national team's nerd squad.

"Maybe. Anyway, it's not like we broke the terms of our contract. We weren't on team time, and a kiss on the cheek is hardly a violation of the relationship clause."

"Have I told you lately that you're a genius and I love you?" Jamie asked, grinning at her girlfriend.

"Keep it coming," Emma joked.

"No, I'm serious. I'm really proud of you," she said, squeezing Emma's hand.

"Thanks," Emma said softly, intertwining their fingers and holding on tight. "The feeling is completely mutual."

They didn't let go until they reached the airport where their teammates mobbed them and congratulated Emma on sort of, pretty much coming out. And then they were boarding the plane that would take them to Canada, where the title of World Cup champion was on the line. As Emma had predicted, that would no doubt overshadow everything—even #Blakewell's first official public (cheek) kiss.

As the plane taxied down the runway, Jamie thought of Jessica North, one of the last players cut before the World Cup. She hoped North saw the photo and was forced to recognize once again that Jamie and Emma were headed to Canada together to represent the stars and stripes while *she* would be stuck at home, watching the World Cup on television knowing that almost could have been her.

    Karma really is a bitch sometimes. Even for those who don't believe in it.

CHAPTER TEN

"Hold the elevator," Emma called, jogging down the hotel corridor. She'd gone back to her room before dinner to grab her purse, even though she didn't really need it. But after what had happened in St. Louis, she didn't like to be far from her mace. So here she was, racing to catch the elevator she had heard ding from halfway down the hall.

She skidded to a stop in the elevator alcove, her words of thanks freezing on her tongue as she came face-to-face with Taylor O'Brien standing beside three women Emma immediately recognized as Australian national team members. This wasn't awkward or anything, given the US and Australia would be opening up their World Cup group play in just a few hours. Against each other.

"Emma," Taylor said, the relief in her voice palpable. "Hi."

Emma hid a smile and stepped into the elevator car. "Hey, Taylor." As the doors slid closed behind her, she slipped past Taylor and pulled Elizabeth Trent into a firm hug, smacking her on the back. "Lizzie!"

"Blakie!" Elizabeth crowed back, and they pulled away, laughing.

"I can't believe I haven't run into you yet," Emma said, giving Trent's teammates a jock nod—silent eye contact with a quick upward jerk of the chin. They returned the gesture as Taylor looked on, mouth slightly open. Emma only just resisted teasing her about catching flies.

"Same," her Aussie friend said. "I mean, we got here the same day you did."

"I think our federations have been trying to keep us apart," Emma confided.

"Whatever," Elizabeth said, rolling her eyes. "It's not like we're guys. You'd think they would know by now how small the women's football world is."

"Right? I bet the only reason they didn't stagger the meal schedule today is because it's Game Day." As the elevator arrived on the ground floor, she added, "By the way, this is Taylor O'Brien. Taylor, this is Elizabeth Trent. We played together in Boston back in the day."

The door opened, depositing them in the hotel lobby, and all five women filed out, heading for the hall where the team meal rooms were situated. Along the way, Trent introduced her teammates, two of the "whippersnappers," as she called them fondly, who had recently "invaded" the Aussie national team. Emma smiled at the newbies, but the Australian pair merely eyed her suspiciously and sped away as soon as they reached the meal rooms. Taylor waved awkwardly and also skedaddled.

"Oh my god, did you see their faces?" Trent asked as she lingered beside Emma in the corridor.

"Totally. Newbies. What can you do?"

"They are so going to have their minds blown." Trent's expression grew sly. "Speaking of fresh blood, I understand you're dating a newcomer yourself."

Emma nodded. "I am."

"Well, it looks good on you. Actually, so does she,"

Trent added, and then laughed as Emma examined her fingernails before buffing them on her US Soccer warm-up top.

"What about you? How's Henry?"

Henry Van Wyck was Trent's husband, a sportswriter who had worked with Emma's ex back in Boston.

"Really good," Trent said. "He says a writer can work from anywhere, so he pretty much follows me around, which is so much better than spending weeks or months apart. Although, I mean, it's not as convenient as having him as a teammate would be," she added, grinning.

"You'd be surprised how inconvenient the federation can make it, actually."

"Huh. I hadn't thought of that," Trent admitted. "Though I can't imagine why I didn't. I swear, federation execs love coming up with new ways to torture us."

"It feels like that sometimes, doesn't it?"

A couple of other Aussie players passed them, nodding politely at Emma and giving Trent a significant look, which she rolled her eyes at. But as soon as they were out of earshot, she nodded at the Aussie team's meal room. "Guess I should get in there."

"Me too. Good luck tonight," Emma said, tugging her old friend into another hug. As she pulled away, she added jauntily, "You're going to need it."

"You're the ones who are gonna need luck," Trent said.

"Dream on."

"Back at ya." As they started into the neighboring event rooms, Trent paused in the doorway. "Hey—you hear the news about Blatter?"

"Totally," Emma said, her smile wide. "His bullshit finally caught up to him. Couldn't happen to a nicer dickweed."

Trent laughed. "You said it. Later, Blake."

"Later, Lizzie," she replied, and headed inside to load up for the night's main event: USA vs. Australia in their opening match of World Cup group play.

The team had left New Jersey on June 2 in a thunder storm and arrived in Winnipeg to the news that Sepp Blatter, head of FIFA, had resigned over corruption and bribery allegations. Blatter, who had just been reelected to lead football's international governing body, had few supporters in the women's game. Not only was he in charge of an organization that literally scoffed at the idea of equal treatment of male and female players, but he had also made demeaning statements in the press about how women's football could be improved by instituting more feminine clothes—for example, "tighter shorts. Female players are pretty, if you excuse me for saying so."

Emma didn't excuse him in the least. In fact, his abrupt resignation on the very day many of the World Cup teams arrived in Canada seemed like an excellent omen for the tournament.

Another good sign had been the cooler than average temperatures they'd encountered. Not only could heat exhaustion decimate a team's ranks, but playing on synthetic turf in high temperatures could be dangerous. Without water to keep it cool, an artificial turf field could be up to *100 degrees* hotter than natural grass, which was why Jenny and Phoebe had photos of melted cleats from the Kansas City turf. Cooler temperatures in Winnipeg meant they didn't have to wait to practice until after dark, when the turf was as its coolest.

The morning they'd arrived, the US coaches had eased them into training, starting with a weight room circuit before moving outdoors in the afternoon. They'd even given the players most of the second day off to explore the city. Day three, Friday, had seen them meeting with FIFA reps to receive their player credentials and have their head shots taken before a low-key training session in the afternoon.

Emma didn't feel like the lack of training was a bad thing, though. By now, Lacey had honed them into lean, mean fighting machines, and they were beyond ready to play. Emma felt confident saying that Australia felt the same. When you stayed at the same hotel, it was hard not to have a sense of your opponents' preparations. Like having your pre-game meal in adjoining conference rooms—just another awkward moment in women's football, one that Emma was fairly certain had never happened (and *would* never happen) on the men's side.

Jamie caught her eye from a table near the buffet, because of course she and Ellie had set up as close to the food as possible. Emma waved before focusing on the spread the team nutritionist had requested ahead of their first match. She had no doubt it would be good. At least food was one area where US Soccer didn't discriminate between the women's and men's programs.

Two hours later, she was still burping up garlic chicken as she stood in the tunnel at Winnipeg Stadium, waiting to take the field. It wasn't the food making her feel nauseated but rather the occasion: The 2015 World Cup was about to begin. If the US didn't win the whole thing this time, they would have to wait four more years for another shot. That would mean Ellie and Phoebe—arguably the greatest striker and goalkeeper tandem in US Soccer history—might end their national team careers without winning a single World Cup title.

No one in an American uniform wanted that to happen.

"Holy crowd, Batman," she heard Jamie murmur as the walls of the stadium around them reverberated with chants of *U-S-A! U-S-A! U-S-A!* "It's seriously just like in

Miracle."

Given their jersey numbers, Emma was just behind Jamie in the line-up. Now she nudged her girlfriend to get her attention.

"Don't worry," she said, injecting her voice with more confidence than she currently felt. Being aware of Emma's fears at her third World Cup might make Jamie even more panicky at her first. "As soon as the whistle blows, it gets better. I promise."

Jamie smiled slightly, probably at the reference to the LGBTQIA+ youth support organization she'd recently agreed to endorse. "Yeah, okay. Thanks, Em."

"Of course," Emma said.

Their eyes held for a long, wordless moment, emotions like fear and excitement and love and fear again flitting between them, and then the head match official received word that the broadcast was ready. It was time.

Also, it really was like *Miracle*. Or it would have been if the crowd in Lake Placid had been made up of screaming schoolgirls and middle-aged soccer moms and dads. Interspersed among the cries of "U-S-A," Emma could hear rhythmic iterations of the US Soccer slogan, "I believe that we will win!" Then the referee lifted the game ball off its stand, and the two teams streamed out of the tunnel and into the light and sound.

And it was so much sound! Winnipeg Stadium, like Red Bull Arena in New Jersey, was a soccer-specific arena that seated around 30,000. The American Outlaws supporters' group was out in force, along with tens of thousands of their countrymen and women clad in USWNT replica jerseys and various other red, white, and blue garb. Most of the seats in the stadium were filled, and American flags and banners covered nearly every open space. Emma almost felt sorry for Australia. The home team advantage the US players had been told to expect had materialized in force. She would have bet her left foot that the only other team that had drawn a crowd this size was Canada, the actual home team, who had played the opening match of the World Cup two days earlier before a sell-out crowd.

Even after the success of the send-off series, the American contingent in Winnipeg was louder, more passionate, and just generally bigger than Emma had expected. During the past few days, the players had talked amongst themselves about not letting down the people who believed in them—people who somehow, incredibly, numbered in the millions.

But not Emma's father.

The thought occurred to her as the team gathered at the edge of the field for their traditional pre-game, post-anthem huddle. She didn't usually miss her dad's presence at national team matches, not even the big ones. Maybe she did today because Canada was so close to home. Here at the World Cup surrounded by a sea of red, white, and blue, his absence stood out in a way she wasn't accustomed to.

Shaking her head to herself, she pushed away the momentary pang and focused on Ellie's speech. There would be time to think about feelings later. Right now it was Game Time.

"Guys, this is everything we've ever dreamed of." Ellie waved around at the cheering crowd, dotted with American flags; at the stadium lights flickering to life overhead in the early summer evening; at their opponents in their colorful yellow jerseys huddled together not far away. "For all the players who came before and dreamed of this, we have to fucking bring it. *Bring it* on three. One, two, three, BRING IT!"

"It has already been broughten," Jenny Latham declared as the starters headed onto the field.

Emma felt a laugh rise, taut and punchy, and for once

at the beginning of a game, she let it come. Game one of the World Cup vs. Australia was starting now, finally, after months upon months—*years*, even—of planning and preparation. Years of beep tests and GPS monitoring, VO2 max testing and power lifting; years of obsessing over dietary requirements and travel arrangements; years of sacrifice and separation from the people they loved most. Finally, *finally*, they had made it to this field at the outskirts of Winnipeg where tens of thousands of mostly American fans had gathered to cheer them on in the first game of their World Cup campaign.

Three stars, here we come, she thought, and followed a sprinting Jamie out onto the field.

#

Admittedly, the game wasn't quite the start they were looking for. In the fifth minute, one of Australia's talented young strikers nailed a shot from the top of the eighteen that Phoebe had to lay out fully to deflect, and even then it crashed off the crossbar and narrowly avoided the back of the net. Phoebe sprang up afterward clapping her hands and barking orders at the team, and Emma knew that she, for one, was psyched to have gotten her first save of the tournament out of the way. That it had been one for the highlights reel would only help Phoebe's confidence moving forward.

Seven minutes later, the US team's good luck continued when Maddie took a potentially ill-advised, long-range shot through traffic that clipped an Australian player on its way toward the goal. The wrong-footed keeper didn't have a chance to correct her approach, and the crowd erupted as the ball found the net and Maddie leapt into the air, swinging her fist in triumph.

The team, naturally, went crazy, too, swarming Maddie who grinned a tad sheepishly at the lucky goal.

"Never met a shot I didn't like," she joked as they

jogged back to their end of the field.

"You miss a hundred percent of the shots you don't take," Ellie countered, clapping her on the back.

The breathing room felt almost as good as their luck, but Australia continued to play better than Emma had anticipated, with quick forays and counterattacks into US territory that left the defense scrambling to catch up. A team was always most vulnerable in the first few minutes after they scored, but Phoebe lived up to her reputation, making key save after key save—all in the first 25 minutes. Team USA's luck finally ran out in the 27th minute, when Bella Chapman, Australia's veteran striker known for her speed, slammed the ball into the corner of the US goal just out of Phoebe's reach. The few non-American fans in the stands cheered, but the quiet before the kickoff—yeah, that didn't feel so good.

At halftime, with the score tied 1-1, the US team filed into the locker room and dropped onto benches. While the training staff re-taped ankles and massaged sore muscles, Jo went through the stats. Australia had more shots on goal currently as well as more corner kicks and longer time of possession. In other words, they were out-playing the Americans.

"I know how you feel," she said, turning away from the white board to level her gaze at the fidgeting players. "I've been where you are now, felt that same pressure on my shoulders, the eyes of the world on me and my teammates to see if we had what it takes. Those fans out there are wondering the same thing. They're wondering if you're going to show up.

"The good news is, the first half is over, and we aren't losing thanks to Maddie's confidence and Phoebe's general unstoppability." A hoot went up around the room, and Jo let it go for a moment. Then she raised her hand, gazing at each of them in turn. "But now you need to tell yourselves *that's it.* You've allowed your nerves to dictate play for forty-five minutes, and now it's time to play the way I know you can. Those fans out there traveled hundreds, possibly even thousands of miles just to be here, right now. Don't you think they deserve to see you play at the top of your game?"

Emma nodded with the rest of the team, feeling a pulse of determination surge through her. Jo was right. Those fans out there deserved to see the best US team possible, as did the fans watching at home. With Fox broadcasting every American game live, the number of people watching today's match would probably number in the hundreds of thousands. Possibly, even, in the millions.

"Soccer is a game of two halves," Jo said, her voice picking up in urgency. "Now, let's go out there and show the world that we're better than that first half!"

"Boo-yah!" Ellie said commandingly, rising to her feet.

"Boo-yah!" the team repeated, the chorus echoing against the concrete walls of the locker room.

Less than a minute later, Emma emerged from the dim tunnel into the stadium lights as the crowd began to chant, "I believe that we will win!"

She nodded over at Maddie, the next closest player. Maddie nodded back, her features set. They weren't going to let their fans down. Not today, and not on Friday when they would face Sweden in this same stadium. Definitely not next week when they played Nigeria for the final group match all the way over in Vancouver. They might have landed in the Group of Death, but for the US, there would be no early exit, only a steady progression to the final match three weeks and six days from now.

I believe that we will win, Emma thought as she warmed up for the second half. **I believe that we will win.** I BELIEVE THAT WE WILL WIN.

I BELIEVE.

#

They beat Australia on another goal from Maddie and a classic finish by Ellie, but the win definitely didn't count as pretty. Phoebe saved their asses, as the stats sheet showed—Australia placed more shots on goal than the US, and without Phoebe's acrobatics, the game may well have turned out differently. But as everyone who plays soccer knows, ugly earns just as many points as pretty. This result was important, especially given that Sweden and Nigeria had played earlier in the day and tied 3-3. With the only win so far in Group D, the US was in first place.

The following day, the players who'd seen significant minutes spent the day recovering with the training staff while the rest of the team trained on the pitch. In yet another awkward turn of events, the Australian starters were in the pool when the US players arrived, engaged in their own post-match recovery. Although *awkward* might be the wrong word. Emma didn't mind the tattoo porn or Maddie's jokes about the view down under while they waited their turn. But when she caught one of the Aussie team's strikers sending Jamie a particularly bright smile, she had to force herself to breathe deeply and turn away. It didn't help that her girlfriend caught her eye as she did so, clearly biting back a smile.

Whatever. Emma was almost thirty. She was mature, damn it. Besides, they'd won the night before and Emma was the last person Jamie had kissed.

"My raspberry is better than yours," Jamie said a little while later as they paced through the pool workout Lacey had drawn up.

"I don't know," Emma said, lifting the edge of her compression shorts to show off her own gruesome abrasion caused by the artificial turf. As Jamie blinked and looked away, her ears turning red, Emma felt mildly mollified. At least she wasn't the only one who was human.

"You know what's irritating about this?" Maddie asked, gesturing toward the raw flesh on her elbow.

"That it stings like a bitch in chlorine?" Angie offered. She'd come in and played the second half after Gabe had earned a yellow card just before half time. The coaches weren't taking any risks with cards and ejections at this stage of the tournament.

"Well, yes," Maddie admitted. "But I was referring to how the under-20 boys' World Cup is going on right now in New Zealand, but on GRASS."

Typical, they all agreed. The good ole boys at FIFA had made it abundantly clear over the years that they cared more about the boys' junior international championship—which, incidentally, was being played to miniscule crowds while the women's tournament was receiving historic levels of fan engagement—than they did about the "pinnacle event of women's football," as FIFA's own marketing team called it.

But focusing on crappy FIFA and their crappy crappiness was not worth their time or energy, the players decided. Mary Kate had them under strict instructions to spend their off-the-field energy on positive things like eating their favorite healthy foods, spending time with friends and family, and visualizing themselves on the podium in Vancouver. Their frustration over the turf issue was justified, Ellie pointed out. Just, maybe not particularly useful at this juncture.

For a while, the conversation shifted to the latest season of *Game of Thrones*, everyone's favorite series currently—except Jamie and Britt, who had both refused to watch past the first beheading in the first episode of the first season. Which, the group agreed, wasn't even that bad of a beheading for *GoT*, all things considered. For example, there was—

"Seriously, you guys, can we not talk about

beheadings?" Jamie interrupted.

"Seriously," Emma echoed, glaring around at their friends, who had the grace to look abashed.

They exercised in silence for a few minutes, and then Angie asked, "Did you guys hear about Ecuador?"

The players in the wading pool gave a collective wince. Cameroon—not exactly a global powerhouse themselves—had demolished Ecuador 6-0. But that wasn't even the worst scoring discrepancy so far. Germany, the odds-on favorite behind the Americans to win the whole thing, had defeated Ivory Coast 10-0 on the second day of the tournament.

"I heard Jo telling Mel that it's FIFA's responsibility for expanding the World Cup field without ensuring parity," Ryan said.

Which, yes, completely true. But in Emma's view, the German coaches and players could have shown compassion to their competitors if they'd wanted to. Scoring in the double digits against an inferior side like Ivory Coast, who hadn't even been expected to qualify for Canada, felt gauche to Emma. She was a defender, though, so that probably explained her perspective.

"Speaking of inferior opponents," Jenny Latham said as she did squats and lunges in the waist-high water, "anyone want to bet on whether or not we get a day off before Sweden? I've got twenty bucks that says we will."

Several people splashed water at Jenny, who protested even as she tried to defend herself. "What? I'm only trying to make things interesting!"

Emma exchanged a look with Maddie that clearly indicated how little they needed Jenny to "make things interesting."

"Betting is illegal," Ellie said irritably.

Jenny threw up her arms. "Oh my god, I obviously do not mean the illegal kind! Lighten up, you guys."

"I know I'm new here, but isn't the World Cup already pretty interesting?" Jamie asked, half-smiling at her former FC Gold Pride teammate.

Jenny relented, a reluctant smile replacing her defensive frown. "Good point, Rook," she said, and sent a palmful of water in Jamie's direction.

Momentarily, the workout session devolved into a water fight. Then Lacey and her team separated them into smaller groups for stations, and the in-fighting abated. Mostly. When you spent day in and day out with the same people in the pressure cooker of the World Cup, there was bound to be tension. But most of the players were either too experienced to let the tension get to them or, like Jamie, too new to the pressure to recognize its full effects.

When this was over, they needed to go on an island getaway, Emma thought as she jogged in place in the pool, visualizing Jamie beside her in a shady hammock swinging gently in the breeze at the edge of a sunny beach. They would swim in saltwater pools and walk on pristine sand and relax at night in an in-room hot tub. More importantly, they would eat and drink whatever they wanted and not talk about soccer or working out even once—unless they felt like checking out the resort's exercise room, of course. Endorphins were addictive for a reason.

As Lacey's assistant blew her whistle to switch stations, Emma sighed and pushed the fantasy away. One day, that would be them. But for now, they had so much more soccer ass to kick.

CHAPTER ELEVEN

"We're downstairs," the text read. "See you soon?"

"Down in ten," Jamie texted back, and then ducked into the bathroom to brush her teeth and spray down her bed head before breakfast with her sister and brother-in-law.

Meg and Todd had been at every game of the World Cup so far and claimed to have no intention of missing any future matches, either. With the summer off before they started their new professor gigs in Vancouver, Jamie's sister and her husband had decided to spend June crisscrossing Canada in their well-traveled Subaru Legacy. This way, they could get to know their newly adopted country, the one that had been willing to give them both jobs at a good university in what Meg insisted—and Jamie was well on her way to believing—was the best city in all of Canada.

Before their final group match against Nigeria a few days earlier, the coaches had given the American players the day off. Jamie and Emma had spent it sightseeing with Meg, Todd, Tyler, and Bridget, who had flown to Vancouver the day before to begin their World Cup vacation. Somehow, Tyler had managed to talk Emma into walking across the Capilano Suspension Bridge, a 460-foot long swinging bridge that hung 230 feet up over the Capilano River. Jamie still couldn't believe that Emma had agreed to make the crossing, though given that they were on a collision course with Germany in the semifinals, maybe there were scarier things than swaying suspension bridges.

Jamie had enjoyed exploring the cliffs near the bridge, but her favorite part of the day had been renting tandem bikes and riding around Stanley Park, an activity that met the lone recovery day requirement Lacey had assessed for their day off. The weather had been Pacific Northwest perfection, with abundant sunshine and temperatures in the low 70s. Stanley Park was known for its seawall, collection of totem poles, views of the city, and trees. So many huge trees—cedars and fir, hemlock and spruce—and the remains of old growth sentinels that had long since fallen.

There was something about evergreens that had always made Jamie feel calmer. Maybe it was simply the additional oxygen they generated, but a mid-day bike ride under the trees with lunch from a café near Lions Gate Bridge was the break she hadn't known she needed from all things World Cup.

Until now, Toronto had been Jamie's favorite urban area in Canada. But after their day off in Vancouver, the capital of BC had overtaken the largest city in the country, in her estimation. Toronto, in the throes of preparing to host the 2015 Pan American Games, hadn't been selected as a World Cup host city. Instead, the sixth WC venue was a small stadium in Moncton, New Brunswick, population 35,000. Which, really? Jamie was just relieved the US didn't have to play there. Not that there was anything wrong with Moncton or New Brunswick. It was just that the site was as far in Canada as you could get from Vancouver, other than

Prince Edward Island. But Jamie doubted PEI had a stadium, given that its largest city numbered in the low tens of thousands, according to one of her college buddies whose mother had been born there. A hockey rink, yes. But a football stadium that could host a World Cup match? Honestly, she was surprised that Moncton even had a stadium big enough.

Currently, the US team was in—she paused to think about it—Edmonton. Right. They were in Alberta, which was next door to British Columbia. They'd been in Edmonton for four days already preparing for their Round of 16 match. They hadn't known until after they arrived that they would be playing against Colombia, the third place finishers in Group F behind France and England. In fact, the charter flight had gotten them to Edmonton just in time to check into their hotel and watch the final group matches.

The following day had been about recovery, both from their match against Nigeria and from another travel day. That meant ice baths, workouts in the pool, time in compression therapy boots, yoga, and massage, to name a few. Each player had to pick at least three recovery options after a travel or game day to keep their bodies functioning at an optimum level throughout the tournament. At least Edmonton was only 700 miles from Vancouver, a distance that took a mere hour and a half by plane. If they'd had to travel to Moncton (or BFE, as Ellie and Phoebe referred to it), a direct flight would have taken seven hours.

She doubted Meg and Todd would have driven to New Brunswick. Not even for the World Cup.

When Jamie said as much a few minutes later as they drank coffee and tea in the hotel restaurant, Meg tilted her head to one side. "I don't know. It's not every day my little sister gets to play in the biggest soccer tournament in the world. Besides, you know I can't pass up free tickets."

"*Little* sister? Dream on," Jamie said dismissively. But she smiled at the warm, gooey feeling spreading through her. Meg was moving to Canada because of her career trajectory, but she was road-tripping all across her new home nation because she was and always had been someone Jamie could count on. And also, apparently, because each national team player was allotted a certain number of tickets to distribute to friends and family.

"Um, excuse me?" The words accompanied a tap on Jamie's shoulder, and she turned to see two girls in pony tails and USWNT home jerseys smiling at her nervously.

"Hi," she said, smiling back. "How are you?"

"Good," the older girl said. "Are you Jamie Maxwell?"

"I am. Are you soccer fans?" They nodded eagerly. "Cool. Where are you guys from?"

As she chatted with the star-struck girls, Jamie could feel her sister watching. She ignored Meg, though, as she signed an official World Cup program and thanked the young fans for coming all the way to Edmonton to root for the American team. Only after they'd skipped away did she turn back to her sister. "What?"

Meg gestured at the girls, who had returned to their parents a few tables away with glowing smiles. "They totally love you!"

"They totally love the team," Jamie corrected. Fans had approached her for selfies and signatures throughout the last few weeks, and it no longer seemed like such a big deal. Still, she couldn't help sitting up a little straighter at the admiration in her sister's gaze.

"Yes, you're famous, and girls and women everywhere look up to you," Todd said, leaning forward on his elbows. "Now, what's the skinny on Colombia?"

Her brother-in-law was a secret gossip queen. An avid reader of *People* magazine, he had been eager to hear whatever details Jamie could glean of the inevitable drama that lurked behind the scenes. He wasn't picky; it could be anything, politics or personal. But he lived for rivalries and relationship drama that remained hidden from the rest of the world.

"Actually," Jamie said, glancing over her shoulder to make sure no American or Colombian players were around (because, of course, the two teams were staying in the same Edmonton hotel), "Ellie dated one of the Colombian players when they both lived in Sweden a few years back."

"*No*," Todd said, looking happily scandalized.

"Yep."

"Does Jodie know?"

"Of course. It was public knowledge—at least in soccer circles. Besides, Ellie and Jodie talk about everything." Jamie knew this from personal experience, having overheard multiple conversations she'd wished she hadn't while living in the national team captain's guest room.

"Wait!" Todd lifted a hand to his mouth and whisper-shouted, "She didn't date the player who accused you guys of belittling Colombia and then promised you would lose, did she?"

"I mean, I would call it more of a boast than a promise," Jamie said, pushing her hair away from her face as she dodged the question.

He practically squealed. "That's why Salome Sanchez hates you guys, isn't it? Because things with Ellie ended badly?"

Damn it. She should have known he'd be following that particular storyline.

Meg gave Todd a look that clearly indicated gossip hour was over and proceeded to ask Jamie, as she had done before each of the previous matches, "Anyway, are you nervous about the game?"

"I don't think so," Jamie said, cupping her hands around her mug of pomegranate green tea. "It's good being here. It feels real. Most of us have been working toward this all our lives, and now that we're here, turns out it's just soccer. Obviously on a considerably larger stage, but still the same game, the same tactics, the same strategies. Only the pressure is different, really."

"Well, you've always been good at handling pressure," Meg said.

Jamie hoped so. Because this tournament had plenty of that, and they had only just finished the group stage. China had beaten Cameroon two days earlier and was waiting to meet the US-Colombia victor in the quarterfinals in Ottawa. Shit in Canada was definitely getting real.

"To be honest," she told her sister, "I'm more nervous about the officiating."

"What do you mean?"

"Do you remember that ref I told you about in Portugal who majorly effed up the Algarve Cup final?"

Meg's eyes widened. "No! You got stuck with *her*?"

Jamie nodded. "Once again FIFA demonstrates their commitment to screwing over the women's game."

"I can't believe Ellie dated Salome Sanchez," Todd murmured, his eyes focused on the middle distance as if he hadn't heard a word Jamie and Meg had said.

Jamie glanced at her sister, trying to bite back a smile. Meg only shrugged, her non-verbals clearly communicating that she loved the big dork in spite of his questionable obsessions. Jamie did, too. And not just because he had purchased a World Cup jersey embroidered with her name and number that he had worn for nearly the entirety of their road trip.

After the sibling coffee date, Jamie headed to the team's meal room to load up for the day. They would be playing Colombia at six that evening, which meant they would have to monitor their caloric intake carefully since the game was scheduled during—*ugh*—dinner time.

"You ready for Game Day, Jamester?" Angie asked when Jamie sat down at what had become their usual table.

"You know it." Jamie bumped her friend's extended fist and nodded at the table's other occupants, which included her lovely girlfriend who was on her second cup of coffee, judging from the bright smile she sent Jamie. Or maybe she was just excited because the "real" World Cup—i.e., the knockout rounds—was finally beginning. "Totally ready," she added, and began to shovel food into her mouth. Wouldn't do to bonk at the Round of 16.

The Round of 16. And yes, she knew she should be nervous, but more than anything she was enjoying the ride. She had played fine through the group stage—nothing spectacular, but solid if you didn't count the yellow card she'd picked up for a late tackle against Nigeria. As she'd told her sister, she'd learned over the past two weeks that at the end of the day, it really was just soccer.

Which wasn't to say she hadn't been nervous at all. Before the opening match against Australia, Jamie's answer to Meg's question had been HELL YES. As she stood in the tunnel at that first game—her first ever World Cup match—Jamie had actually worried that her heart was beating so fast it might explode. Or maybe, possibly, she might faint. She had really hoped she would lose consciousness in the tunnel rather than on the field to minimize the photographic evidence. But then Emma had offered up words of encouragement and flashed her that confident smile that told Jamie her girlfriend believed she was capable of amazing things, and her heartbeat had slowed—a little; enough for her to breathe more easily, anyway.

With Emma behind her (literally), she'd taken the field determined to lose herself in the sport she'd been playing since she was four years old and the Berkeley YMCA put on a clinic that Blair, her childhood best friend, was attending and would she maybe like to go, too? She had pretty much been a soccer player ever since that first day she stepped onto a grassy field and a coach told her to run after the black and white ball and kick it with her feet and for no reason whatsoever should she even think of picking it up with her hands. She wasn't one of those kids who struggled with the penultimate soccer rule, the ones who would randomly pick up the ball before dropping it like a hot potato. For some reason, not using her hands seemed perfectly normal to her.

Ironic that she'd turned out to be a lesbian, really.

She wasn't the only USWNT player who'd been nervous against Australia, either, but she was pretty sure the team had worked out their nerves between the first and second matches. Getting one game under their belts seemed to have settled her teammates as much as it did her, even the ones who had been to the show before. By the time they'd returned to Winnipeg Stadium for game two against Sweden, their highest-ranked opponent in Group D, the team had seemed more focused.

Still, they'd played Sweden to a scoreless draw, which made the fans and the press grumble about their lack of offensive prowess. The most dramatic moments of the Sweden game had revolved around defensive plays: the many last-minute saves by Phoebe and her Swedish counterpart Greta, Jamie's teammate on the Thorns; Emma and Lisa's tight control of the US team's defensive third; and Ryan's header off the goal line during one of Sweden's corner kicks. The Swedish fans had insisted that the ball had crossed the line, but the Hawk-Eye goal-line cam had proven that Ryan headed the ball out with room to spare. Goal-line technology meant that anytime the ball crossed the line fully and completely, the match official's watch vibrated to indicate a score.

Obviously, that hadn't happened against Sweden.

Their third and final group match against Nigeria hadn't fared much better, either, with only a single goal that came right before half time. Not for lack of trying, though. While the US had struggled to stay organized in the face of Nigeria's characteristic physical play, they had gotten off fourteen shots in total, with seven of those on goal. The Nigerian keeper had played well, with half a dozen saves compared to Phoebe's two. But what it really came down to was that the US players simply weren't finishing their opportunities—something they'd struggled with consistently the entire time Jamie had been around the team.

But now they were at the World Cup, and that struggle could no longer be set aside or excused as part of the preparation process. *This* was what they'd been preparing for. From here on out the tournament would be single elimination. No matter how great their defense was—and it had been exemplary so far—if they didn't figure out their offense, they would go home without the trophy, without the title, and, probably, without the number one ranking in the world.

Yet despite the US team's lack of firepower, the coaches and captains had outwardly projected an appearance of calm throughout the group stage. Melanie said it was a building process, and as long as they kept improving, they were in good shape. No one wanted to peak too soon at the World Cup. One of Jo's favorite adages was, "It's not where you start; it's where you finish." And Phoebe and Ellie had both said that while the US side may not have played their best soccer yet, they had done enough to win their group, which had been the plan all along. Now they just needed to keep doing enough to get to the podium in Vancouver.

One step at a time, one city at a time, one game at a time. One meal at a time. At least she'd have another meal in a few hours, and then a half-meal after that. Plus there were always Lacey's recovery shakes after the game, a blend of electrolytes, proteins, and other nutrients composed with each player's specific body chemistry in mind—as well as her taste buds. If all else failed, Jamie could always drink her shake at half-time and request a refill later.

In the meantime, there was actual bacon and eggs to pre-fill her glycogen window. Because even if Lacey had never said that was a thing, Jamie was pretty sure it must be.

#

That evening, Jamie sprinted onto the field, buoyed by the streaks of red, white, and blue, and the noisy chants of U-S-A in the stands. Despite what she had told her sister, there had been a good sixty seconds at the outset of every game so far in Canada where she felt light-headed. She was on the US Women's National Team playing for a World Cup title. It was unreal, but at the same time, as she'd told her sister, she had been working toward this moment, this one, single tournament, nearly all her life.

No pressure, obviously.

Emma slapped her back as she walked by, as had become their ritual before kickoff. The contact should have grounded her, but today for some reason, it didn't. As she stood in the center of the field waiting for the Romanian referee to start the game, she legitimately thought she might pass out. But then the whistle blew, and they were off. As soon as Ellie touched the ball back to her, Jamie's butterflies fled and, just like in the earlier matches, she settled into the flow of the game.

Colombia was a bit of an unknown. Ranked twenty-eighth in the world, they had qualified for the World Cup for the first time in 2011 after three previous failed attempts. The US had met the South American side only twice before, once in the 2011 World Cup and again in the 2012 Olympics, and had defeated Colombia both times by the same score, 3-0. But Salome Sanchez, their leading scorer as well as Ellie's problematic ex, was quick and unpredictable. Between Sanchez and a cadre of physical, creative midfielders, Colombia had overwhelmed France's defense in the second game of the group stage to upset the European side 2-0. That said, Colombia's first-string goalkeeper had been suspended for the Round of 16 because she'd accumulated two yellow cards during group play. This situation was an example of why most rosters had three goalkeepers. No one wanted to have a field player (Mia Hamm circa 1995, anyone?) be forced to play keeper in a World Cup match.

The US started fast, as was the game plan. Ellie scored in the fourth minute on a rebound off the backup keeper's glove, only to have the goal disallowed on an offsides call. They continued to threaten for the next ten minutes, until Gabe ran into Sanchez while chasing down an errant pass. The Colombian captain immediately hit the ground and rolled three times in a move that would have been impressive if it wasn't such obvious acting. Well, obvious to everyone except the head referee, who promptly whipped out a yellow card. Given it was Gabe's first foul of the match, a yellow card seemed extreme—except that Gabe was one of the players at the Algarve who had "accidentally" struck the officious (and incompetent, both teams had agreed) referee with the ball during the run of play.

Unfortunately, Gabe was one of several American players, including Jamie, sitting on a yellow from the group stage. By giving her a second card, the referee had just guaranteed that Gabe would have to sit out the quarterfinal match against China—assuming they made it that far.

Ellie surged forward, her eyes hard as the referee recorded Gabe's name in her match notes. Before she could make contact, Maddie stepped between them, her hand on the US captain's chest.

"Leave it," Jamie heard Maddie say, her voice low and commanding.

After a moment, Ellie stalked away. But Jamie didn't miss the searing look she sent Sanchez, who smirked back and even added in a slight, taunting wave. No wonder Ellie had married a non-soccer player. Playing against your ex could get ugly.

While the US had rebounded from having a goal called back, the yellow card was a different matter. Suddenly the American players seemed to be reacting to Colombia rather than dictating the pace themselves. Instead of maintaining possession and building patiently out of the back, they were ball-chasing and playing catch-up, unable to string together enough clean passes to settle into their own style of play. The US attack in the first half hinged on long balls and 50-50 passes that, more often than not, Colombia managed to snag or at least disrupt. Somehow, the Colombians seemed every bit the giant killers they'd claimed in the press to be.

And then, five minutes before halftime, it happened. Jamie was contesting with a Colombian midfielder for a chip pass when they smacked into each other. Jamie was taller and broader, so she only wavered slightly while her opponent crashed to the ground. Immediately Jamie held up her arms in an "I didn't do anything wrong" gesture, even though she knew—she *knew*, damn it—that to do so was to call attention to her complicity. Sure enough, the referee blew her whistle and reached for her pocket.

No, Jamie thought, staring at her. She couldn't do that! It hadn't been—Jamie had barely—

But even as the silent protests flashed through her mind, she could see as if from a distance the referee waving the card in the air almost triumphantly. Yellow. She'd given Jamie a yellow card, which meant that, like Gabe, Jamie would now have to sit out the next match. She had worked so hard for so long, and now this officious asshole was trying to take it all away? No way. *No fucking—*

She hadn't even realized she'd started toward the ref, who was looking down as she added Jamie's name and number into the match records, until Emma stepped between her and the navy-clad woman.

"Chill," Emma said softly. Her hands gripped Jamie's shoulders as she stared into her eyes. "Let it go. There's nothing you can do here except make it worse."

Jamie resisted the urge to shove Emma out of the way so that she could—what? Yell at the ref and get kicked out altogether? She closed her eyes briefly, took a deep breath, and reminded herself that while she may not be able to control the referee, she could still control herself. In fact, she had to not only for her own sake but for her team.

She nodded shortly at Emma. "Okay. Thanks."

Emma squeezed her shoulders and let go. "Of course."

Play resumed, but for Jamie, the last five minutes of the half felt like a dream sequence where her autonomic responses were slow and her body refused to cooperate the way it normally did. She felt like she was running with ankle weights on, her legs heavy and her feet unwieldy. The image of the referee waving the yellow card at her kept replaying in her head on a loop, making it difficult to concentrate on the game at hand. She couldn't play in the next game. She wouldn't be on the field for the quarterfinals. What if the team played better without her and Jo decided they didn't need her anymore? What if she had come this far only to be benched for the rest of the tournament for fucking up so egregiously?

Oh, god. She was going to throw up. She'd let everyone down—Ellie, Jo, Emma, her family. They had come to Canada to support her and she'd screwed everything up.

She barely heard the whistle that signaled halftime. In a daze, she followed her teammates off the field and back to their locker room beneath the stadium, where Ellie and Emma gave her a brief pep talk—*It wasn't a yellow card offense; that ref is terrible and we all know it; keep your head in the game*—before Jo cleared her throat from her position by the white board where her pre-game notes remained untouched: "Pressure. Patience. Probing. Progression. Possession. Play smart. Play to win, not to not lose."

And underlined three times: "Leave it all on the field."

"I told you the night we arrived in this country that we would be tested," she announced without preamble. "Well, athletes, this game is one of those tests. You did everything right in the first fifteen minutes and still Ellie's goal was disallowed and two of your teammates are facing suspension. Who are you going to be in the face of adversity? Who are you going to choose to be in the next forty-five minutes?"

She looked around the room, holding the eyes of the players who looked back. "Right now we are teetering on the brink of elimination. At this minute, our fans are wondering which path you're going to choose. Will you focus on the parts of the game you can't control, or will you start with the basics?" She gestured at the white board. "The 4 Ps. Playing smart. Playing to win, not to avoid losing. And most of all, leaving it all on the field. Everything you have. Because there is no going back, athletes. There is only moving forward. So let's see what you have."

And with that, she walked out of the room, the other coaches following.

For a moment, the locker room was silent. Then Phoebe and Ellie exchanged a look, and Ellie said, glancing around the room, "I'm not ready to go home yet. Are you guys?"

"Hell fucking no!" Jenny Latham shot back, and just like that, the tension was broken.

"All right, then," Ellie said. "You heard Jo. We've got forty-five minutes to turn the show around. Let's do it. Oosa on three. One, two, three, oosa-oosa-oosa-ah!"

The cheer was a reference to a USWNT that was no longer, a way of connecting to the team's storied history. Rumor had it that in 1985, when the team made its international debut against Italy, the Italian fans were so impressed by the American players that they started cheering for the USA, which they pronounced, "OOSA." The chant had become something of a ritual that the team invoked to signal the program's legacy. Today, Jamie took it as a reminder of everything they were playing for—everything they had to lose, yes, but everything they had to win, as well.

Ellie caught up with her on their way out of the tunnel and slipped her arm around Jamie's neck, giving her a brief side-hug. "Don't let it get to you, okay? Just focus on the now. The future will work itself out, one way or another."

Jamie nodded. This was good advice. She only hoped she could follow it.

As she sprinted onto the field, she had to force herself not to glare at the head referee, who was standing at the center circle with her whistle in her mouth and her eyes on her watch. How did that woman not know she was a menace? More importantly, how did FIFA not recognize her incompetence? Or maybe they did. Maybe assigning her to a big match like this—one in which a bad referee could make the difference between advancing or going home—was purposeful. Maybe this was their way of punishing the US team for daring to sue them in international court over artificial turf at the World Cup. Didn't take much of a stretch to believe that one.

Her conspiracy theories hit a wall two minutes into the second half when Emma served Jenny Latham a through ball that allowed her to drive into Colombia's penalty area. Jamie watched, initially elated and then horrified as Colombia's goalkeeper slide-tackled the US striker near the top of the box—and missed the ball entirely, only making contact with Jenny's trailing leg. Jenny went down hard, screeching out a curse as she fell. Unlike their South American opponents, she didn't roll half a dozen times to sell the foul. She didn't have to. The keeper had been the only person between her and a certain goal. There was no way Jenny would have gone down if she could possibly have stayed on her feet.

The partisan crowd barely had time to erupt in shouts and whistles before the referee blew her whistle and pointed to the penalty spot. Then she reached for her pocket, and instead of the yellow card Jamie expected, she pulled out red and practically flung it at the keeper, who stared at her for a moment, clearly stunned, before trailing after her with her hands spread out. But the referee ignored her and held up a warning hand to Colombia's captain, who came to plead her keeper's case.

Was it a red cardable offense? Jamie wasn't sure. But if her own incidental contact with a Colombian player in the mid third of the field had drawn yellow, then she supposed the keeper destroying Jenny's scoring opportunity on a clear foul was grounds for ejection. She couldn't help but feel sorry for the young player, though, who at only 20 years old was the youngest person on the pitch. She wouldn't have even played today if the starting keeper hadn't been suspended. Talk about a nightmare World Cup.

The backup keeper—the backup's backup, Jamie corrected herself—had next to no time to warm up as the Colombian coaches discussed their options and the player who had been sent off hugged her teammates and slowly made her way to the sideline. Ultimately, the Colombian coaches decided to sub out one of their two strikers, though not Sanchez but rather a younger, less experienced teammate. A red card meant the South American side would have to play down a woman for the rest of the game. Since they couldn't very well field a team without a keeper, the least dangerous player from a defensive standpoint—the striker—left the game.

If anything, Colombia's third-string keeper looked even younger and considerably more frightened than the player she was replacing. Jamie pictured Britt in the same situation. Would she look as shell-shocked? Maybe, but probably not. Britt was closer to 30 than 20 and had won a youth world championship. While that experience may not compare to the pressure and drama of this World Cup, it definitely gave Britt a leg up.

Soon the new Colombian keeper was jumping up and down in the goal mouth while Jenny lined up to take the penalty kick. She wasn't the best PK taker around. In fact, she rarely made the top five in practice when they were prepping for penalties. But the shot was hers if she wanted it, and she had made it clear to Ellie that she wanted it.

Maybe too much, Jamie thought a moment later, wincing as Jenny's shot pinged just wide of the goal. Or maybe she'd just had too much time to think. Most strikers didn't do well if you gave them extra time. The best scorers in the world, like Ellie, could handle additional time to consider their options. But most strikers, even phenomenal ones like Jenny, did better on instinct. Time gave your brain options, and scoring happened most frequently when the shooter had minimal options to choose from.

The energy that had surged through the crowd when the referee signaled the penalty kick dropped again—except for a small contingent of Colombian fans seated near their team's goal. They made more sound than Jamie would have expected at Jenny's miss, and continued to cheer loudly whenever their team made a defensive play. With only ten players facing off against the US side's eleven, Colombia had more than their share of opportunities to come up big on defense.

At a break in action, Jamie put her hands on her hips, closed her eyes, and lifted her face to the cloudy sky. The previous day had been the summer solstice, which meant that the sun wouldn't set for another few hours yet. The temperature had been close to 70 at kickoff, and it was a perfect summer soccer night. She'd been playing summer tournaments since she could remember, like Surf Cup in Southern California where she and Emma had met. This was just another game in a long line of games, she told herself, and with her eyes closed, she could even believe it. But then she heard the sound of a ball being struck cleanly, and Ellie was bellowing at her and she opened her eyes to see the ball sailing in her direction and... Right. Back to it.

She caught the ball on her right foot and managed to evade an oncoming Colombian. Head up, she dribbled toward the goal, mind efficiently cataloging angles and speeds. Jenny was ahead of her just outside the box, so she touched the ball to her. But Jenny's back was to the goal with pressure on in the form of a double team. She dropped the ball to Jordan Van Brueggen, who dribbled up the line before passing back to Taylor O'Brien, open in a supporting position.

"To me!" Jenny shouted, pointing in front of her with her left index finger the way she always did when she wanted the ball.

Taylor dribbled a few steps farther, just enough to

make one of Jenny's defenders step to her, and then she sent a pass directly to Jenny's feet. The striker neatly turned the ball past the remaining defender and into the penalty area, where Jamie was unsurprised to see her wind up for a shot. The only player between her and the goal was the keeper, but Jenny's angle was terrible. She should really pass off to—

Jamie's thought cut off as the ball rocketed toward the goal and Colombia's backup keeper bobbled Jenny's low, near-post shot. Wait, had she actually palmed it into the back of the goal? Was that an own goal? Did it even matter?

"Hell yes!" Jamie cried, sprinting madly toward Jenny, who raised her arms to the sky in triumph and, Jamie thought, probably more than a little relief. She had made up for her missed PK. In the 53rd minute, the US was finally on the board.

The flag stayed down (Jamie checked), and the team piled on for a group hug, laughing and cheering Jenny on. The goal had been lucky. Jamie wasn't sure the shot had even been on frame. But that didn't matter. What mattered was that they were up a goal and a player against an increasingly dispirited Colombian team. All of a sudden, the victory that had seemed out of reach in the first half now felt almost certain.

Which was why they needed to double down even harder, Jamie thought, nodding when Ellie shouted instructions to press after kickoff. The most dangerous time defensively was the first two minutes after you scored a goal. Wouldn't do to let Colombia back in the game now.

"Let's put this puppy to bed," Maddie said, nodding at Jamie, Gabe, and VB.

Jamie and the others nodded back. "Let's do it."

Colombia fought hard, Jamie had to give them that. But they were fighting an uphill battle, short-sided against the US, the favorites who not only were generally viewed as the fittest, most athletic team in the world (thanks to Lacey) but also possessed the home crowd advantage. The game had taken on an air of inevitability, in Jamie's estimation, and she found herself buoyed by the sense of certainty permeating the stadium. The crowd alternated chants of "U-S-A! U-S-A! U-S-A!" with "I believe that we will win!"

Jamie was with the fans because with thirty minutes left to play, she believed they were going to win, too.

Even the referee seemed to have settled in because Jamie barely noticed her. That is, until Ryan sent a perfect through ball into the box for Gabe to run onto only for Gabe to be taken out with a hefty hip check by the nearest Colombian defender. The referee, again, didn't hesitate. She pointed at the penalty mark and whipped out a yellow card for the defender, who shook her head in apparent disgust and walked away.

Jo called in from the sideline, "Ellie! It's yours."

Everyone looked around at her in surprise. Ellie was not one of the team's strongest penalty takers. But she only nodded once, stepped up to the spot, and, at the whistle, drove the ball past the diving keeper into the corner.

Her record was growing. With that shot, she had just moved into second place all time in World Cup goals: thirteen, one ahead of Germany's Mila Friedrich and two behind the Brazilian star Marisol's record-setting fifteen. Germany had beaten Sweden 4-1 two days earlier without scoring help from Friedrich, and Brazil had been upset by Australia 1-0 in a result that had left some US players complaining that they wouldn't get a chance to wreak revenge on Marisol's side. With three potential games still ahead of them and Brazil on their way home, Ellie and Friedrich would be battling each other to surpass Marisol's record.

Of course, the US needed to round this game out in order to provide Ellie with a chance at breaking the record. After piling onto the pile of players congratulating Ellie, Jamie jogged back to her position on their defensive end to await kickoff.

Except she never got the chance. The digital display board the fourth official was holding up had her number on it. Jo was subbing her out. Automatically Jamie glanced over at Emma, who gave her a subtle nod. She nodded back and jogged off the field, slapping hands with Emily Shorter, who had made the squad despite only recently coming back from a knee injury. Shorter took over right back and pushed Taylor O'Brien into the six—Jamie's position. She'd barely reached the sideline when Gabe's number flashed, with Angie's on the opposite side of the display board. Obviously the coaches weren't taking any chances with their yellow cards.

Jamie and Angie hugged as they passed. Hopefully, they'd get to be on the field at the same time again soon—although not if she wouldn't be allowed to play in the next match. *Fuck.* She'd really drawn a second yellow, hadn't she?

"Nice job out there, kiddo," Jo said, slapping Jamie's shoulder as she reached the bench. "Now take a break, yeah?"

"Yeah," Jamie grated out, even though she didn't want a break. Like, at all. But she caught herself as she found a spot on the bench beside Britt. Speaking of acting entitled… Apparently she was finally feeling comfortable on this team.

"Way to go, James," Britt said, and offered up her fist.

Jamie bumped it and reached for her recovery shake, stashed under the bench near her kit bag. "Thanks, man."

"I must say, I believe that we will win," Britt said in a cultured English accent, giving each word in the phrase a slightly different emphasis than Jamie was used to hearing.

"I must say, I agree," she replied in a suitably haughty accent.

They were right. The US held on to win easily, holding Colombia to another shutout. The victory was such a relief that Jamie temporarily let it overshadow everything else—including her stupid, ridiculous yellow card.

"Well done tonight, athletes," Jo said in their postgame team huddle as they stood at the edge of the field, arms around each other's shoulders. "You handled each challenge thrown at you and came out on top. Tomorrow morning we head to Ottawa to face China. But tonight, celebrate the win with your family and friends. As long as we keep moving forward, we get to keep playing. So here's to forward progression!"

"Boo-yah," the players called out in unison, laughing.

What wasn't funny was that their offense was still struggling to finish. Still, the win tonight gave them more chances to fix that aspect of their game. As Jamie overheard Ellie tell a TV reporter immediately after the match, "We keep telling you guys we haven't peaked yet. Give us time. We'll get there."

The same reporter commented to Maddie that the Americans had been lucky Colombia's starting keeper wasn't able to play. She'd replied, "Tournaments like this always come down to a bit of luck. So yeah, we'll take it."

Once again, luck had been on their side—if you didn't count the two yellow cards in the first half. Jamie definitely counted them. Gabe, she was pretty sure, did too.

"At least neither of us will be alone in the stands," Gabe commented as they walked to the waiting bus a little while later.

Jamie had been assessing the straggling fans, memories of St. Louis making it difficult to concentrate on much else. They'd had fans waiting for them at every hotel before and after matches; at various training facilities; even in hotel lobbies during their unofficial breaks from the team. Emma, she knew, was struggling with all the potential moments of stranger danger, as she sarcastically referred to them. But, typically, Emma didn't want to talk about her fears. She simply wanted to focus on the team. And winning, of course.

Now, as Gabe's words sank in, Jamie glanced at her quickly. "Wait, what do you mean 'in the stands?'"

"We're not going to be allowed to sit with the team," Gabe said. "You didn't realize?"

"No." Jamie shook her head. "I've never been suspended."

"Wow. That's impressive."

Jamie shrugged. What did it matter that she had never drawn a red card when she had managed to get herself suspended during the biggest tournament of her life? And now, to find out she would be exiled to the stands, away from the rest of the team?

She stalked toward the bus, her eyes resolutely forward. Friday was going to suck.

CHAPTER TWELVE

Jamie refreshed the browser on her tablet again, scrolling impatiently through the new additions to the SCOTUS live blog. She had spent the previous morning's training session checking her phone surreptitiously at breaks in the action, but today was Game Day, so she didn't have to be anywhere between breakfast and lunch. She didn't have any place special to be later, either, except in the stands with Gabe to watch as their teammates took on China in the World Cup quarterfinals.

Whatever. There wasn't anything she could do about that except get through it. Refreshing her tablet screen, on the other hand? That she could definitely do.

She wasn't supposed to be online, given the coach-imposed moratorium on reading the news, but she couldn't help it. She'd been waiting for the Supreme Court's ruling on same-sex marriage ever since oral arguments had been heard in April. So maybe she occasionally saw headlines about the World Cup while searching for an update on only the most important SCOTUS decision ever for American queers. It wasn't like she read (all of) the articles that mentioned the US team directly, just enough to know that the sports press was unimpressed with the team's performance so far.

From Jamie's perspective, the press was simply trying to drum up drama where there wasn't any. The most important thing was not getting sent home, and the US team had managed that objective every step of the way so far. If they hadn't, she wouldn't be sitting here now on yet another hotel bed in yet another Canadian city.

Where were they again? Not Edmonton anymore but Ottawa, the nation's capital located in uber-flat Ontario. They'd only been given three days between the Round of 16 against Colombia and their quarterfinals match against China—including a travel day. China, on the other hand, had played their Round of 16 match two full days before the US side faced Colombia. That meant China would have a slight leg up over the US in this evening's game. Those sorts of advantages tended to even out in the course of a month-long tournament. If the US won tonight—and of course they would, Jamie told herself fiercely—their semifinal match would be played in Montreal, only a couple of hours away by bus. Jamie was looking forward to the break from jet travel and, more importantly, jet lag.

But she was getting ahead of herself and the team, she thought, stretching slightly on the bed and glancing out the window. This hotel was one of the nicest she'd ever stayed in, a century old Gothic and Renaissance chateau—the French word for *castle*—with marble and granite accents, antique furnishings, and a view of Parliament directly across the main thoroughfare. The building felt like a real castle, with its marble staircase, an art deco swimming pool complete with a Greek fountain at one end, and Renaissance-style arches that reminded Jamie of the *traboule* she and Emma had explored in Lyon with her Arsenal teammates.

It almost seemed as if the farther the American side went in the tournament, the nicer the accommodations got. Not that she minded. Canada was even broader across than the US, and the grind of travel had definitely set in by now. Having a comfortable space where they could rest and recover was nearly as important as balanced meals and daily training time. The veterans had been complaining the most about Canada's sheer enormity, reminiscing nostalgically about the comparative ease they'd enjoyed getting around Germany in 2011. Not to mention playing in the UK during the London Olympics—so many football stadiums in such close proximity!

Ah, well. Jamie imagined they would survive Canada, though she didn't say as much. Personally, she had found the reality of maneuvering the national team from location to location fascinating. The size of the dedicated support crew it took to load their boxes of gear in an enormous tractor trailer and transport it from one team hotel to another was mind-boggling. From the players' boots and kits to the coaches' video projectors and the team's athletic treatment tables, the amount of money required to fund the national teams was ridiculous, especially on the men's side. Rumor had it that the men's head coach was paid *ten times* what the women's head coach made, though the federation was secretive about actual figures. Jamie had even heard that the under-20 boys' coach made more than Jo, but whatever. Worry about what you could control, right?

In addition to all the travel, Jamie had struggled to manage the feeling of being under a microscope. The veteran players didn't seem to mind or even notice the number of cameras following them, but Jamie did. Not only were there fans with phones and digital cameras waiting at all hours of the day and night at the stadiums, hotels, and airports the team navigated, but US Soccer staff and members of the international sports media were constantly lurking in both expected and unexpected places, telephoto lenses attached to their DSLRs, video cameras perched on their shoulders. Jamie suspected there had been more photos and video taken of her in the past few weeks in Canada than in the totality of her life to date. Well, maybe not more. But possibly an equal amount.

The unlocked door opened, and Jamie smiled when Emma poked her head into her and Rebecca's room.

"Everyone decent?" her girlfriend asked with a cheesy dad wink.

"Pretty much," Rebecca said without looking up from her phone.

"Come on in," Jamie said, still smiling. She couldn't help it. Emma looked cute with her hair loose around her shoulders, the damp ends leaving wet marks on the team sweatshirt she was rarely without, even in the middle of the summer in Eastern Ontario.

"Any Supreme Court news yet?" Emma asked, and dropped onto the bed beside her. Rebecca side-eyed them from the other bed but didn't comment. She and Gabe had been doing their own hanging out, so to Jamie's mind, it would be a case of the pot calling the kettle black if her current roommate ratted them out for holding hands behind closed doors.

"Not yet," Jamie admitted, scrolling back to the top of the page. She couldn't remember now how she had found her way to *SCOTUSblog*, a site that live-blogged Supreme Court opinions and orders—Facebook link? Twitter post? Google search?—but two days down the rabbit hole and she was thoroughly hooked.

Emma rubbed her shoulder. "Didn't the blog people say it was probably going to be on Monday?"

"Yeah, but no one actually *knows*. Today's the anniversary of the DOMA case, so other people have been saying the justices might pick today. You know, for reasons of historical resonance."

"It'll only resonate if it's good news, though," Maddie said as she walked into the hotel room, Angie, Britt, and Ellie on her heels. And, wait, was Jodie allowed to be in a team member's room? Then again, Ellie was the team captain. What would Jo do, suspend her on today of all days for hanging out with her fianc—*wife?*

"I'm telling you guys, it's going to be good news," Jamie said as she hit refresh again.

The Supreme Court, true to form, had left their same-sex marriage ruling until the last week of the current SCOTUS term, along with a handful of other hotly contested cases like state redistricting, the Clean Air Act, and the death penalty. You know, just a few light questions about life, liberty, and the pursuit of happiness.

"Isn't it the anniversary of the Lawrence decision, too?" Emma asked.

"The what decision?" Angie asked, flopping down beside Rebecca while Britt stretched her long body across the foot of the queen bed.

"*Lawrence versus Texas*, 2003," Jamie said without looking up. She had done a senior project at Stanford on the history of LGBTQ+ rights in America and could still recall most of the details that had gone into her presentation. "It's only been twelve years since SCOTUS struck down the sodomy law in Texas to make gay sex legal everywhere."

Angie frowned. "Are you honestly saying gay sex was still illegal like ten years ago?"

"Yep—at least, in a dozen states or so. And most of those still haven't gotten rid of the laws that *Lawrence* invalidated."

Several audible expressions of disgust echoed across the room as Jamie hit refresh again. Then she gasped as a single word flashed across the screen: MARRIAGE. "Oh my god, you guys! Kennedy's got the opinion. Shhh!"

From Emma's other side, Maddie murmured, "Why do we need to be quiet?"

"So she can think," Emma replied. "I think."

Britt and Angie snickered, but Jamie ignored them and

read aloud, "Holding: The Fourteenth Amendment requires a state to license a marriage between two people of the same sex! *Holy crap!*" She lifted her eyes to Emma's as her girlfriend's arm tightened around her. "They did it! They freaking legalized gay marriage! Like, everywhere!"

The stunned silence that had fallen over the room broke when Angie leapt off of Rebecca's bed, whooping, and proceeded to dance around the room while everyone else cheered. Maddie soon joined her, and if they kissed? Well, they could be forgiven. After all, gay marriage had just been legalized in every single state in America. Even in the Bible Belt.

Jamie read aloud again over the cacophony: "It also says the Fourteenth Amendment requires states to recognize a marriage between two people of the same sex when their marriage was lawfully licensed and performed out-of-state. Oh my god, you guys. We won! We totally won!"

Britt leaned over to give her a high five, and Jamie captured her friend's fingers and held on for an extra-long moment, grinning. This win was even more important for Britt, given she was involved with a foreigner. Allie was careful to abide by the rules of her tourist visa, but if she and Britt were to get engaged or married, her path to citizenship would be easier to navigate.

Emma hugged Jamie against her side, breath warm against her ear. "I feel like this is a good sign, don't you?"

"Um, yeah! A great one!"

"I love you," Emma added, her voice almost a whisper.

"I love you, too." Jamie leaned in and pressed her lips against Emma's for a brief, heady moment. They had actually won. Not just the battle, but the entire war.

She sat back, smiling around at her happy friends. SCOTUS—thanks to Kennedy and the four awesome liberal judges—had once again acted to protect the dignity of queer Americans. In a matter of minutes, the legal realities of gay and lesbian couples across the country had shifted. From now on, no matter where they went in the United States, a married lesbian or gay couple could not be denied their basic rights. Not legally, anyway. As one *SCOTUSblog* reader helpfully commented, this decision effectively legalized same-sex marriage in all 50 states, and forced each state to recognize one another's licenses.

Just like that, the war over her right to marry the person she loved had ended, and the right side—the only side, as far as Jamie was concerned—had emerged victorious.

The raucous noise settled into a dull chatter as everyone grabbed their phones and proceeded to text friends and family members and post celebratory messages to Facebook and Instragram. As she and Emma huddled together, heads nearly touching over their phones, Jamie was happy to see the rainbow wave of posts on both of their personal Facebook feeds. The outpouring of support was unsurprising given how carefully they curated their feeds, but still, it was something to see.

Eventually, she clicked back over to the live blog to review additional details of the decision. The vote had been 5-4, as expected; the ruling took up three of the day's four boxes of files; each of the dissenters had written an opinion, including Chief Roberts—his first ever; the majority opinion relied on the dual rationales of fundamental rights and equal protection; and, last but not least, the ruling had established as fact that the Fourteenth Amendment's Equal Protection Clause and Due Process Clause prohibited the unjustified infringement of the right of gay and lesbian couples to marry. She couldn't stop smiling as she followed a link to supremecourt.gov and skimmed the majority opinion. *Obergefell v. Hodges* had

176

determined without a shadow of a doubt that marriage was a fundamental, constitutional American right, and that any discriminatory attempt to prohibit same-sex marriage was an unlawful violation of the Constitution.

Jamie was in shock. She may have told everyone that she anticipated good news, but honestly, she'd been *hoping* for this decision, not expecting it. No one had known which way it would go. The anti-gay marriage arguments had been pathetic at best, with arguments based on astonishing levels of prejudice without any legal footing of note. But those same bullshit arguments had worked for decades, in and out of courtrooms across the country. Jamie still couldn't get her head around the fact that Kennedy, a Catholic social conservative who had been nominated to the court by Ronald Reagan, had swung the same-sex marriage vote to the liberals. This was the same justice who had sided with the court's conservatives two years earlier when they gutted the Voting Rights Act; the same justice who had agreed in Citizens United that corporate donations to political campaigns were protected by the First Amendment.

And yet this man, this deeply problematic, openly conservative judge, had written eloquently about the hopes and dreams of same-sex couples:

It would misunderstand [the petitioners] to say they disrespect the idea of marriage. Their plea is that they do respect it, respect it so deeply that they seek to find its fulfillment for themselves. Their hope is not to be condemned to live in loneliness, excluded from one of civilization's oldest institutions. They ask for equal dignity in the eyes of the law. The Constitution grants them that right.

Her eyes caught on the final line of the ruling: "It is so ordered."

It is so ordered.

She released a breath, feeling the weight of years and years of hatred and persecution falling away as she exhaled. If she and Emma were to get married, it would be legal right from the start. They wouldn't have to fight for the right to be treated equally because all of the amazing couples who had stepped up in *Obergefell v. Hodges* had taken the fight for recognition of their marriages to the highest court in the land. And before them, there was Edie Windsor, who took the fight for her 40-year relationship with Thea Spyer all the way to the Supreme Court. And before them were the couples in Massachusetts who had won the landmark 2004 decision that had first signaled the turning of the tide. And so on and so forth, the wave continuing back farther and farther, all the way to the 1969 Stonewall uprisings when a bunch of New York queers rebelled against police brutality and started the modern gay liberation movement.

As much as Stonewall was a flashpoint in history, this day was too, and Jamie was thankful to have Emma and Britt and Angie and their teammates beside her at the moment when LGBTQ history in America changed.

Voices sounded in the hallway, and then Meg and Todd were pushing the unlocked door open and Jamie's older sister was standing there in the entryway, her arms upraised in triumph over her messy bun, eyes bleary from the weeks of travel but elated behind her chunky glasses.

"Gay marriage is legal, bitches!" she announced, and the room dissolved into cheers once again.

Jamie had a feeling Emma was right. Today was going to be a good day, after all.

#

The wave of exhilaration carried her all the way to warm-ups that evening before petering out in the face of her World Cup suspension. She and Gabe were allowed to be in the locker room and on the bench before the game, but they would have to be in the stands before the playing of the national anthems.

"This sucks," Jamie said glumly as she and Gabe sat on the red cushioned seats of the US bench at TD Place Stadium.

"I know," Gabe agreed. She watched their teammates practicing small-sided keep-away games, her shoulders and head dipping slightly as if she were trying to control the ball's movement through mental telepathy.

The rest of the team was dressed in cleats and the black and neon green warm-up uniforms that fans seemed to either love or hate, but Jamie and Gabe weren't allowed to dress like their teammates. Instead, they were clad in sneakers, jeans, and matching blue collared US Soccer shirts, an outfit that clearly marked them as separate. Jamie had like the shirts when Nike delivered them. Now, she was pretty sure she never wanted to wear it again.

"But at least we get to be here at all," Gabe added.

Jamie only shrugged. At that moment, she almost wished she were sitting alone in her hotel room. Every once in a while she caught a journo with their telephoto lens focused on the bench, and she was pretty sure they weren't taking pictures of the comfortable individual seats or the scratch-resistant glass arch that protected the players from potentially unruly fans. You really had to look out for those soccer moms and dads, as Angie and Lisa liked to joke. Never knew what a toddler in a USWNT jersey might throw. A used popsicle stick in the wrong hands could be—well, super sticky.

Why exactly did the teams need to be protected by the kind of chemically strengthened glass used to make smart phone screens? Jamie had yet to hear a reasonable answer. It wasn't like the women's game caused riots. More than likely, someone at FIFA had a cousin or brother whose company had won the contract to provide player benches at the World Cup, and with cash cow FIFA footing the bill, only the finest would do.

So many assumptions governing the administration of women's World Cups derived from lessons learned at men's World Cups, but personally, Jamie thought that comparing the two was like comparing apples and oranges. But the business of soccer was not something she wanted to think about right now. Although, maybe dwelling on FIFA's idiocy was exactly what she needed to distract herself from her current situation. Certainly there was a nearly endless supply of source material to draw on.

"Good thing Ellie didn't get suspended, too," Gabe said, her eyes on her ex-girlfriend chasing down an errant pass from the center of one of the warm-up groups.

"No kidding."

She had come close, though, and not on the field of play. Ellie's post-Colombia commentary hadn't remained restricted to the team's progress toward peaking. The team had learned later that she had shared her opinion that the referee seemed to target Gabe and Jamie, going after players the ref knew were already sitting on yellow cards. Criticizing a match official was just as risky after a match as during one, given FIFA's well-known touchiness when it came to suggestions of match-fixing. While Jamie had secretly appreciated being defended by her captain, she'd also worried that Ellie could be censured, possibly even suspended by the tournament's highly reactive governing body.

When Jamie told Ellie of her fears, the team captain had only shaken her head and said confidently, "Isn't going to happen. Even Beth Scott was allowed to play in the bronze medal match in London. I was significantly cagier than she was."

Beth Scott should have been suspended, as far as Jamie was concerned. The Canadian captain had gone on the record accusing the referee of the US-Canada game in the semis of the 2012 Olympics of giving the game to the American side, stating that "the ref had already decided the outcome before she blew the starting whistle." Meanwhile, Scott's teammate had gotten away with a red-cardable foul—nay, *assault*—on Emily Shorter. Catherine Beaumont was already carrying a yellow card for one of the seven fouls the referee hadn't missed when she purposely stomped on Shorter's head. If the official had truly been intent on giving the game to the US, red-carding Beaumont ten minutes into the second half—or, really, at any point in her deluge of fouls—would have been easy enough. Jamie was sure the Canadians would have whined about that too, though, intent as they had been on blaming everyone but themselves for their loss in that epic match.

The day after the US downed Colombia, federation reps informed Ellie she would need to make a formal apology, so she did. A day after that, FIFA officially gave her a warning rather than a suspension, but Ellie appeared to shrug it off. The coaches didn't seem bothered, and neither were the players. Ellie had only said what everyone was thinking—and by doing so, Jamie couldn't help noticing, she had taken the heat off Jamie and Gabe for fucking up so royally. That was just the kind of teammate she was.

"You know, Ellie wasn't wrong about that freaking ref," Gabe said now, her eyes on their teammates pacing themselves through warm-ups.

"I know," Jamie agreed. "After the disaster at the Algarve, what were they thinking letting her officiate a match in the knockout round?"

They bitched about the previous game, bandying about statistics like it was their job. Which, Jamie had to admit, it pretty much was. The US had been called for 22 fouls while Colombia had only been tagged for 12, which didn't make any sense seeing as the US had dominated possession. More than one person at team breakfast the morning after Colombia had wondered aloud who had paid off the ref. Cheating wasn't unheard of at the World Cup. The final group stage matches were played at the same time so that teams wouldn't change their tactics to achieve a particular result. FIFA had adopted this practice after the 1982 Men's World Cup, when West Germany and Austria had appeared to conspire to ensure they both advanced while Algeria was eliminated.

"Can you imagine Jo asking us to tie or lose on purpose?" Jenny had asked as she'd polished off a giant omelet. "Better yet, can you picture our reaction if she did?"

Jamie had been amazed by the number of stories they'd come up with that morning about scandals in international (men's) football. The most famous incident had taken place in 1989 during a Men's World Cup qualifier in Brazil, when the Chilean keeper Roberto Rojas had hidden a razor blade inside his glove. Near the end of the game, with Chile losing 1-0, Rojas pretended to be struck by fireworks that landed on the field. Head bloodied, he was carried off, and his teammates refused to return due to the "unsafe" conditions. When video revealed that Rojas had intentionally cut his own forehead with the razor blade, Chile was not only disqualified from the 1990 Men's World Cup, they were banned from the 1994 Men's World Cup, too. Rojas, meanwhile, was banned for life.

Match-fixing wasn't only restricted to the World Cup. Various plots had been discovered and prosecuted in men's professional leagues around the world, from Serie A and B in Italy to Australia's Premier League. In Germany, a Bundesliga referee had coordinated with players, coaches, and other officials to fix matches, while in Brazil, two referees known as "The Whistle Mafia" had been paid by outside investors to throw games. Ellie's mistrust of the Romanian official—and even Beth Scott's over-the-top accusations around the sketchy Olympics calls—weren't entirely unjustified, that much was clear.

When warm-ups ended, Jamie and Gabe stood up to join their team for the final pre-game locker room talk. Jamie tried not to think about how it could be the last team meeting of its kind for this World Cup, and she wouldn't even be dressed in her USWNT kit.

Freaking ref. Jamie hoped never to meet her again, but she figured FIFA probably wouldn't let that happen. Some drama was good for the game, she'd heard more than one federation official opine.

"Don't worry," Ellie said, ruffling her hair as they neared the locker room. "You'll get another chance to play."

God, Jamie hoped so. She'd tried telling herself it was okay if she didn't. Tried forcing herself to feel grateful just to be here in Canada as part of the team. But gratitude wasn't something you could force. Or, at least, she didn't seem able to do so. At Emma's mother's house in Minnesota six months earlier, she had assured everyone she would be here in Canada, even if it meant sitting in the stands. But once she'd made the roster, it had never occurred to her that she might end up doing that, anyway.

Her mind refused to focus during Jo's pep talk and again during the captains' speeches. Then she was participating in the unmelodic singing of the birthday song to Jenny, who was turning 29 that day, and the less inharmonious final cheer—"Oosa-oosa-oosa-ah!" A moment later, she was filing out of the locker room with the other non-starters. Except instead of returning to the comfy seats on the American sideline, she and Gabe left the team in the tunnel and retreated into the stadium, accompanying a team rep and a FIFA intern to the US Soccer box midway up the stadium, where player agents, federation staff, and other team insiders could watch the game in relative privacy.

A handful of other people were already seated, but Jamie didn't recognize them. She followed Gabe to the front row and slouched into an empty seat, resting her feet on the metal railing that almost but not quite compromised her view of the field. Her knees jumped throughout the playing of the national anthems as a sense of unreality washed over her. She was supposed to be down there on that field right this second, her throat thick as "The Star-Spangled Banner" played and she stood shoulder to shoulder with her teammates ready to give everything she had to keep their World Cup dreams alive. But no. She'd screwed up—again—and here she was in street clothes reduced to watching from afar.

The federation hadn't let her wear Emma's jersey, nor had they allowed her to pick her own seating. She'd wanted to sit with Meg and Todd, down in the lower deck in the seats Jamie had gotten for them. But they would be surrounded by non-US Soccer approved fans, and the federation—and FIFA—couldn't risk an incident of any kind, she'd been told.

An *incident*? What did they think, that she would get drunk and go off the rails? Then again, professional athletes weren't always reliable on that front.

"Why would you even ask that?" Gabe had muttered as they'd walked away from the final pre-game meeting with their FIFA and US Soccer reps.

"Sorry," Jamie muttered back. "It wasn't that I didn't want to sit with you."

"My feelings aren't hurt," Gabe had said, shoving her sideways with her shoulder. "At least, not much. I meant why would you think they would let you watch the game without an official babysitter?"

"Um, hello, have you met my sister?" Jamie had asked. "She's pretty much the definition of babysitter. Besides, Emma says you don't get—"

"—what you don't ask for," Gabe finished. "Yes, Max, I may have heard that once or twice. Really drinking the Blakeley Kool-Aid, huh?" As Jamie cocked an eyebrow at her, Gabe had winced. "Gross. Clearly I did not think that sentence through."

Now Gabe touched her jiggling knee. "Dude, chillax. Pulling a quad isn't going to help anyone."

"Ha, ha," Jamie said. But the lame joke somehow helped ease the tight knot in her midsection of—jealousy? Anger? Self-recrimination? Whatever it was, the tightness didn't ease much, but even a slight abatement allowed her to take a breath and hold it while the US team—*her team*—got together on the sideline for one final pre-game cheer before jogging onto the field.

The only good thing about this whole fiasco was that the coaches had finally been forced to tweak the line-up. Instead of a 4-4-2 with Ellie and Jenny up front, they lined up in a 4-5-1 formation, the same as China—not to mention Colombia, Germany, Brazil, and Australia. Angie had earned the start in Gabe's left midfield slot, flanking Maddie with VB in her usual spot on the right. Rebecca had been added to the line-up as the right attacking midfielder while Jenny played the same position on the left. This formation, Jamie genuinely felt, had the potential to be a far better use of their individual talents. Of course, there wasn't a place for her on the field currently, but she was a team player. What was best for the team was what mattered.

She heard her sister's voice in the back of her head: "Sure, Jan."

What was best for the team was what mattered, god

damn it.

The starting whistle blew, interrupting Jamie's internal battle, and she glanced down at the field. This was going to be the longest game she'd ever watched, she was pretty sure.

Go USA.

CHAPTER THIRTEEN

Actually, Jamie realized shortly after the game started, their bird's-eye view allowed her and Gabe to watch Jo's game plan unfolding from above: Press, press, and press some more. In the second minute of the match, Maddie sent a beautiful through ball between two Chinese defenders into the path of an onrushing Rebecca. Gabe half-rose in her seat as Rebecca struck the ball from inside the 18—only to shank it wide.

Nerves, Jamie thought as Gabe dropped back into her seat and Rebecca sent an apologetic thumbs-up to Maddie. That had long been Rebecca's challenge, Jamie knew: to silence the stubborn doubts at the back of her head long enough to finish in the offensive third.

"I swear," Gabe said, "you give a striker too much time to think and they screw it up nine times out of ten."

"Why is it then you seem to have a thing for strikers?" Jamie asked, smiling sideways at her teammate.

"I mean, it's not like they're bad people," Gabe clarified. "They may not be the sharpest tactically, but they're usually fast and strong and they always have a nose for goals."

"Or maybe a 'head' for goals is more accurate," Jamie offered.

"So maybe off the field they tend to speak in overly simplistic soccer metaphors like 'The game of life isn't over until the final whistle blows."

Jamie laughed. "Or 'We're taking it one step at a time,

one game at a time.'"

"Or 'We just need to give one hundred and ten percent.'"

The conversation paused when Taylor sent another through ball into the box, this time for Jenny to run onto. But the sideline official's flag went up. Less than a minute later, Ellie's shot from the top of the box went wide. Maddie launched a rocket over the crossbar a couple of minutes later, and Jamie and Gabe groaned at all the near misses. Still, it was only ten minutes in and already the US had created more chances than they'd managed in the first half of their other games.

Apparently subbing Jamie (and Gabe) had been the key to success.

Sighing inwardly, Jamie pushed the self-pitying thought away and said, "My favorite soccer cliché is 'Life is like football: You need goals.'"

"But it is," Gabe said. "You really do!"

That was the thing, they agreed as the game continued at the same breakneck speed: Strikers genuinely believed their soccer metaphors. Jamie had to admit that she loved their unshakable faith in the beautiful game.

"Same," Gabe said. "But even so, sometimes I can't help cringing at some of the interview clips."

"And yet the media eats that crap up."

"Right? Sometimes," Gabe confided, "I'm tempted to get real with reporters. Like, 'Our shit stinks just as much as the next person's.' In fact, it probably stinks even more given those protein shakes Lacey pushes on us like our federation-provided dealer."

Jamie hid her laughter behind her hand. Somehow such a crude statement emerging from the mouth of one of the team's more uptight players struck her as particularly hilarious. But if a resourceful journo caught her guffawing during a game from which she'd been suspended, the reaction would not be good.

Down on the field, China was finally seeming to adjust to the onslaught and had managed a few offensive breaks of their own. But the US defense, who hadn't allowed a single goal since Australia—345 minutes and counting—handled the attacks with seeming ease. Jamie watched Emma slide-tackle a Chinese striker and lifted her fist in solidarity. *Yes*! Her girlfriend was amazing.

And speaking of girlfriends…

"So, your thing for strikers," she said, bringing the conversation back around. "First Ellie and now Rebecca?"

Gabe shrugged noncommittally, a smile lurking at the corners of her mouth.

"That's exactly how Rebecca reacted when I asked her. You two are massively on the down low, huh?"

Jamie didn't mean anything by the comment, but Gabe straightened up in her seat and folded her arms across her chest.

"We don't feel the need to broadcast who we are," she said, her tone defensive, "in order to feel like a responsible member of the community."

Whoops. Jamie had put her foot in her mouth on this one. "I don't either," she assured Gabe. "I'm just trying to live my life. But hiding who I am with the way I look would take massive amounts of energy that I can't afford. Not if I want to be the best football player I can be."

Gabe's shoulders loosened as she uncrossed her arms. "I honestly don't know how you and Ellie do it. My family would freak if I came out publicly."

Jamie shrugged. "I've had people telling me to tone down the gay forever, but that's the thing—I'm not performing an identity. I'm just being me. If people don't like that, well, as my aunts like to say, fuck 'em if they can't take a joke."

Gabe smiled, finally, and Jamie counted it as a win.

China had been pressing for the last couple of minutes, but now the pro-USA crowd gasped in unison. One of Jenny's shots had just been cleared off the line by a defender. Dang it! Another close call.

"Speaking of jokes," Jamie added, "what do you call a defender who just ate a big dinner?" Gabe side-eyed her skeptically but didn't say anything. "Duh, a fullback!"

"Dude." Gabe shook her head.

"Who's the best player in history?" Jamie asked, and then answered her own question: "George Best! Get it?"

"Yes, I get it, Max. But who's he? Some British wanker?"

"Yeah, actually. He played for United and the Irish National Team a while ago."

Gabe's eyebrows arched. "Did you just call a United player the best player in history? I'm totally telling Emma."

"Feel free," Jamie said. Since Arsenal had finished ahead of United and claimed the FA Cup title the previous month, Emma had been more than happy not to talk about their respective Premier League teams.

Another collective gasp sounded. Angie's corner kick had found a crashing Taylor at the top of the box—just as they'd been practicing the last few days—but O'Brien's header had a little too much power and sailed over the crossbar.

"Dang," Gabe said, glancing over at Jamie. "They don't really seem to need us."

Jamie nodded. Obviously she wasn't the only one who'd noticed the shift in the team.

The rest of the half continued on in the same vein, with the US exploiting the seams and narrowly missing their scoring opportunities. China dug their heels in and tried to knock the American players off their game by occasionally knocking them off their feet, but there was a momentum about the game that couldn't be avoided, Jamie thought, with the US dominating possession and limiting China's offensive chances. It was only a matter of time before the American side scored.

Not in the first 45, though. Injury time closed out with China missing the US goal only for Jenny to get another chance at the opposite end less than a minute later. But the Chinese keeper corralled that shot, and the half ended.

"Jesus," Jamie said, expelling a breath.

"I know. This is a really good game. Sort of wish I was playing in it!"

Same, Jamie thought. So, so same.

She pictured the Romanian ref again, as she had been doing late at night and early in the morning when sleep eluded her, and imagined knocking her to the ground with a well-placed strike of the ball. The image of the hated ref going down flailing mollified her anger slightly. It wasn't like Jamie would do anything like that in real life. But fantasizing about it made her feel better, so she wasn't going to feel guilty about that. Not much, anyway.

At halftime, their official babysitters reminded them that they weren't allowed to join the team in the locker room. Which was a lame FIFA rule, Jamie and Gabe agreed, glaring at the unlucky FIFA intern. To distract themselves, they wandered the concourse a bit, accompanied by their tireless babysitters. Jamie picked up an order of garlic fries because why not, and then proceeded to worry about parsley flakes in her teeth as a few brave fans stopped them to say their yellow cards had been bogus—*they totally had*, Jamie thought but couldn't say with their FIFA shadow lurking nearby—and pose for selfies. As much as it pained her, Jamie smiled and nodded and made polite conversation with the fans. They were the reason she and Gabe and the rest of the team were here at all, and that bore remembering even on a crappy day like today.

But was it a crappy day? As they headed back toward US Soccer's team box, Jamie remembered the feeling that had come over her earlier when the Supreme Court ruling was announced. She would remember that moment of immense joy and overpowering relief for the rest of her life. Meanwhile, the frustration and gloominess she was experiencing now would fade, especially if the US won and she got a chance to play in the semis. A win by the US in Vancouver ten days from now would be magical for the players and inspiring for tens of thousands—maybe even hundreds of thousands or, possibly, *millions*—of people around the world. But the Supreme Court decision? That was life-altering history with a capital H.

If the plaintiffs in the cases that eventually made it all the way to the highest court in the land could take the months and years of battling on behalf of all queer Americans, Jamie was pretty sure she could handle the disappointment of missing a single soccer game, as important as this match might be.

Back in their seats with the halftime clock winding down, Gabe gestured at Jamie's fries. "Good choice?"

"Perfect. What about you?"

Gabe smiled around the Polish sausage slathered in relish she was currently devouring. "Totally."

The second half started the way the first had ended, with Rebecca earning three quick chances, none of which she managed to finish. In between jumping up and clutching their heads, Jamie and Gabe discussed their favorite stadiums of the tournament so far—Vancouver was definitely the best, they agreed, and not only because they were Pacific Northwesterners at heart—before moving on to their potential competition.

With the US in control of the match so far, it didn't

feel like a potential sports jinx to talk about the next round. If they did win tonight, the US players would spend time in the morning recovering from today's match before driving to Montreal in the afternoon to begin getting ready for Germany, who had defeated France in penalty kicks earlier in the day. Meanwhile, Australia would be playing Japan in Edmonton and England would be facing Canada in Vancouver to determine the other semifinal match-up.

"Only two more games after this one," Gabe commented, eyes on the field where their teammates were battling against China's renewed pressure.

Gabe was right, Jamie realized. She'd been so focused on missing the quarters that she hadn't thought much about the countdown. The final match in Vancouver was only nine days away. Nine days were all that stood between them and potential glory. Or heartbreak. They wouldn't know until they got there—assuming they managed to finish even one of their many chances against China.

"It's too bad we'll meet Germany in the semis," she said. "That should be the real final."

Germany had seemed nearly unstoppable throughout the tournament, whereas England and Canada were still definite underdogs. Japan, ranked fourth in the world currently, had struggled to win games throughout the tournament. On the day the US squeaked past Nigeria, Japan did the same against Ecuador. *Ecuador*, who had lost to Cameroon and Switzerland by a combined score of 16 to 1. Somehow their old rivals didn't seem quite the threat the US had expected. But like the American side, Japan had found a way to advance at every stage so far. Jamie had a feeling they would continue that trend in the week ahead.

"Yeah," Gabe said, "but beating Japan would round out the perfect redemption story, you know?"

Jamie definitely knew, even if she hadn't been on the squad four years earlier. It wasn't just the veterans obsessing over a rematch. The press kept focusing on the optics, too. It was hard not to, especially since the only real surprise in the knockout rounds so far had come when Australia eliminated Brazil. And even that wasn't entirely shocking. Brazil was known not only for its technical style but also its defensive lapses. Germany had beaten Sweden by three, France had defeated South Korea by the same margin, England had come back from being down a goal against Norway, and Canada had downed Switzerland. For the most part, the knockout rounds were proceeding as expected. Now, if only the US could freaking score!

Just as Jamie thought this, another promising build-up started from the US midfield. She held her breath as Taylor O'Brien received the ball from Emma and took two steps forward, head up, eyes roving the field before her. Jamie could anticipate the play's development almost as if she could read the players' minds. Beside her, Gabe tensed, too, her hands gripping the metal railing as she leaned forward. They watched in strained silence as Taylor took another step and then launched the ball into the Chinese box where the American players outnumbered their opponents. In the center of the box, one foot on the penalty spot, Ellie gathered herself and leapt into the air, all grace and muscle and perfect timing. Jamie and Gabe were already rising, their voices shouting in wordless tandem as Ellie's head connected with the arcing ball and drove it firmly past the keeper's outstretched hands and into the corner of the goal.

She had done it! After 51 minutes of knocking on the door, the US had finally broken through.

"And that's why I love strikers!" Gabe said, laughing as she turned to hug Jamie.

Jamie hugged her back, grinning. At least they wouldn't be alone in the stands, Gabe had said after Colombia. At that moment, as they celebrated Ellie's historic goal—every goal she scored was historic since she'd broken the scoring record—Jamie appreciated Gabe's presence beside her even more.

"Oh, look," Gabe said, pulling away. "They're doing it!"

Jamie gazed down at the field as their teammates finished hugging and jogged over to the bench, where all 21 players, starters and non-starters alike, lined up facing the stands—and, more importantly, the TV cameras—and arranged their arms parallel across their chests to represent an equal sign. They held this pose for five full seconds before Ellie called out something, and the players' stance shifted. This time, they held their hands up in the shape of a heart, smiling widely while the clock ticked away another five seconds.

"Man," Gabe said, her voice low and thick, "that's so cool."

"Yeah," Jamie agreed. "It really is."

More than anything, she wished she could be down on that field with her teammates, celebrating not only Ellie's goal but the most important ruling in LGBTQ American history. But in sport as in life, there was no going back. She contented herself with standing ramrod straight beside Gabe, their arms and hands mirror images of those of their teammates.

And then the moment had passed, and the officials were waving at them to retake the field while China milled around, heads down.

"Damn," Gabe said as they sat down again. "The girls are playing really well. I wasn't sure if they would keep it up in the second half."

"I wasn't either. But you know what?" she added, elbowing Gabe.

"No, what?"

"Gay marriage is legal in America. Even in Texas."

"Hells yes!" A grin spread across Gabe's face again as she gazed back at Jamie. "Even in Alabama."

"Even in Utah. The Mormons must be so pissed!"

"*So* pissed!" Gabe laughed and held up her hand. "Go USA, and go gays!"

Jamie slapped it. "Go USA gays!"

As they leaned back in their seats, Jamie realized this was the most time she had ever spent with Gabe. Her previous impressions—that Gabe was stodgy as hell and a prim rule follower, possibly even socially conservative—were being pleasantly turned on end. Gabe, she now realized, was simply more reserved than the average national team member. Jamie had already begun to guess as much since joining Gabe's Game Day meditation circle, but sharing their mutual banishment had given her a window onto the other woman she probably would never have sought out on her own.

As if reading her mind, Gabe nudged her and said, "You know, you're not so bad after all, Max. Even if you've never gotten a red card."

"You would say that," Jamie returned, smiling a little as she watched China rush a throw-in and deliver the ball directly to Maddie, who sent it back to the defense to restart yet again.

"What does that mean?"

"You play for the Reign, don't you?"

"Ha ha," Gabe said, rolling her eyes. But she was smiling, too.

The US never let down the rest of the half. The coaches used all three subs, swapping Ellie in the 60th minute for Emily Shorter, who came in at midfield and pushed Angie up to the front line. Jamie was happy to see her back in action, since it hadn't been clear if Emily would even make the squad. Rebecca and VB came off for a break as well, with Lindsay Martens (a surprise roster addition who hadn't seen a single minute of play so far) coming in and pushing Taylor up to the midfield, where she continued to challenge for every single ball that came near her, much to the Chinese players' dismay.

Once again, Jamie was psyched that Taylor, a literal bruiser, was on their side.

And then the remaining time was dwindling, and China was launching a series of desperate, last-minute attacks that the American defense shut down every time. As soon as injury time was announced, Jamie and Gabe rose.

"Um, I think you're supposed to stay here until the final whistle blows," the young FIFA intern said in her Canadian accent, blowing her bangs out of her eyes.

"Actually," Gabe said, "the rule is that we stay in the *stands* until the final whistle. It'll take us a few minutes to get down to the field, and this way we can avoid most of the crowds. It's actually safer if we go now."

Their US Soccer rep smiled slightly before saying, "Absolutely. Let's go!"

What could the FIFA rep do? She followed. At least, Jamie assumed that was what happened. She was too busy trying to watch monitors as they zigzagged their way down to field level, the US Soccer crests on their shirts and the FIFA passes dangling at their necks allowing them past any and all security. The final whistle had just blown when they emerged from the tunnel to join their team on the sidelines, and while it wasn't the best field-side celebration Jamie had ever experienced, it was pretty damn good.

The first person she hugged was Britt, grinning and whooping at her as she reached the bench. Next was Ellie, tired and sweaty but sporting a smile that was more content than Jamie had seen in a long time.

"Way to go, hero of the match!" Jamie said, pounding Ellie on the back.

"Easy, killer," Ellie replied, laughing. "See? I told you that you would get another chance."

Jamie hugged her again. "Thanks," she said more quietly.

"You're welcome," Ellie said, and smacked her on the back.

A moment later she found Angie, who she lifted into the air and spun around despite her smaller friend's protests. "Way to go, Ange! You were awesome against the Motherland!"

That was how Angie jokingly referred to her parents' native China. Jamie and the other U-23ers were the only people on the team she allowed to invoke the term of affection.

"Put me down, Max!" she said, but she was laughing, her dimple seemingly permanently carved into her cheek. "Dude, we did it!"

"I know! If I had to watch a game, I'm glad it was this one. You guys played lights out, I'm serious."

"Thanks," Angie said. "Missed you out there, though. Both of you."

Jamie didn't think that was really true, but she nodded. "Thanks, man."

They bumped fists, and then she was turning, looking for a familiar golden ponytail. There. Emma was standing near midfield with Maddie, talking to a pair of Chinese players who Jamie vaguely recognized from her own brief stint in the Women's Professional Soccer league, the precursor to the NWSL. Jamie waited until the conversation had ended and the Chinese players had turned away before launching herself at Emma.

"Hey!" she said, hugging her girlfriend briefly from behind. "Great game, you guys!"

"Thanks, Max," Maddie said, her smile glowing with

contentment just like Ellie's. "See you guys in a bit."

"See you," Emma said even as she turned in Jamie's arms. "Hey, babe."

"Hey," Jamie said, smiling brightly down at her. "You guys were awesome! 423 minutes!"

"What? Oh, you mean without being scored on?"

Jamie nodded. "You guys are seriously the Department of Defense!"

"Whatever," Emma said, dismissing the nickname Phoebe had come up with during a recent ice bath recovery session. She started to lean in even closer, and for a second Jamie thought Emma might give her an ordinary, run-of-the-mill peck on the lips. But at the last minute she shifted away. Whoops. Couldn't let themselves get too carried away by the joy of victory. Jamie was in the doghouse enough as it was.

"Anywaaay," Emma said, drawing out the final syllable as she slipped her arm through Jamie's and tugged her toward the sideline, "how was it?"

"It was fine. I liked watching you guys play," she said honestly.

"Right," Emma said, sounding affectionately suspicious, if such a thing were possible.

"No, really," Jamie said, laughing.

"But…?"

"But it also sucked."

Emma nodded, as if that was the answer she had expected.

The mood in the locker room was buoyant. Jo and the other coaches congratulated them on the victory and gave them time to discuss amongst themselves what had worked in the match and what hadn't, what lessons they could take into the semifinals. They would have a few days to prepare in Montreal, Jo reminded them—three, to be precise. On the last day of June, they would meet their old nemesis Germany, the current number one ranked team in the world, to determine who would play for the gold medal in Vancouver on July 5th.

"From here on out," Jo said, looking around the room with that steady, confident gaze of hers, "the competition only gets steeper. We created a lot of chances tonight, and that's what the coaches and I have been hoping to see from you. Now the next step is to finish those chances. Let's make that our goal for the next match, eh?"

Some of the players laughed at the teasing tone in her voice, or maybe at the pun, but Ellie didn't, Jamie noticed. Neither did Phoebe, or Emma, or Maddie. They only nodded, their expressions dead freaking serious. It had been sixteen long-ass years since the '99ers had won the World Cup. Clearly, the veterans saw nothing remotely amusing about their current run for gold.

Jo nodded, short and decisive. "All right, then. Time to lock this game down, athletes. Your families are waiting to celebrate with you back at the hotel. You've got two hours before curfew. Use them wisely. Oh, and one more thing." She paused, a smile slowly spreading across her face. "Happy equality day, my friends. Love is love, and the laws of our great nation have finally caught up!"

A cheer rose up through the concrete- and metal-lined room, echoing and rebounding until Jamie couldn't tell which sound waves were coming and which were going. As she shouted herself hoarse and jumped up and down with her teammates, she decided she didn't really care. Love was love, and she wasn't going home yet. The Supreme Court had made same-sex marriage legal throughout the land, and the US would live to play another day in Canada. Whether or not Jamie ever saw another minute of playing time, she could think of plenty to celebrate.

At the hotel, they were greeted by fans who provided a cheering gauntlet through the first-floor corridors, chanting "U-S-A!" and singing the national anthem. It reminded Jamie exactly whom they were playing for, and she smiled at the crowd, even though she hadn't done anything today to deserve their recognition. As they headed toward the team's meal room, Taylor O'Brien and Lindsay Martens, genuine newbies, slapped the hands of girls and boys dressed in red, white, and blue headbands and tank tops. But Jamie noticed that Emma, Jenny, and Maddie were less enthusiastic, eyes assessing the crowd shrewdly as they moved from one corridor to the next.

When they finally reached the meal room, they found their friends and family members waiting just like they'd done in Edmonton after the match against Colombia. There was also a buffet dinner waiting, since match time had forced them to eat mid-day, but for once the players bypassed the food to embrace and be embraced by the family members who had, as the cliché went, gotten them this far. And yet, like many clichés, this one was accurate. Without the parents in this room committing to their daughters' soccer journeys, the USWNT roster would be much, much different.

As she wove through the tables toward her own family, Jamie saw Angie and Ellie greeted by theirs, the hugs awkward and seemingly superficial. But she didn't have long to worry about her friends because her parents and Meg and Todd were before her, smiling and jostling each other to see who could reach her first. Predictably, Meg won, but then the rest of her family joined the hug and she sighed, her shoulders falling as the last of the tension in her chest eased away.

"Good job, honey," her mother said.

"What? I didn't do anything."

"I think we all know that isn't true," her father said.

And, yeah. He was probably right.

Emma's brother and his fiancée were at the next table, and they arranged the chairs so that the Maxwells and the Blakeleys were mostly sitting together. Emma and Jamie even switched places after they'd demolished their first helpings of food, in order to get caught up with each other's families. In fact, they were sitting in each other's seats when the hotel staff rolled in a giant cake decorated with a rainbow heart, a soccer ball, and the number 29.

"That's right, it's Jenny Latham's birthday, isn't it?" Bridget asked.

Jamie nodded, belting out the birthday song with the rest of the crowd.

When they'd finished, Jenny bowed to the crowd and took up the cake knife, as team tradition demanded. "I asked for this design," she announced, "because as most of you know, today is a historic occasion, and not only because it's the anniversary of my birth."

Jamie whistled French-fan style at her former WPS teammate, who smiled and nodded regally.

"Anyway," she continued, brandishing the knife in a somewhat alarming manner given that Jamie had noticed the empty beer bottle at her place setting, "while we are obviously celebrating our win tonight, we are also rejoicing—yes, I said *rejoicing*—because today, at last, love has won. Gay marriage is now legal in all fifty of the United States, and even more than our win tonight or my birthday—*I guess*—" she paused for the wave of laughter that rolled across the room, "we are celebrating a court decision that affects all of us in this room. Look around you. There are women and men sitting shoulder to shoulder with you who will now be able to marry the person they love. So without further ado, let's eat some cake and have a party, my friends!"

A cheer erupted, forks clinking against glasses in

accompaniment, and Jamie was pretty sure she heard the ubiquitous "U-S-A" chant from somewhere in the far corner. Jenny bowed once more and commenced cutting the cake.

A few minutes later, as Jamie stood in line with Emma waiting for a slice of cake, she watched Ellie carry a couple of plates back to her table. Jenny had given her part of the rainbow heart, and as Ellie lifted her fork, Jamie heard Mrs. Ellison say, "I don't understand why she would put a rainbow heart on her birthday cake. It's not like it really applies to her, is it?"

Ellie winced while most of the players in earshot immediately looked at Jenny to gauge her reaction. The birthday girl finished cutting the piece she was on and then paused, her eyes on Ellie's mother.

"Actually," she said, her voice carrying, "who says I won't end up marrying a woman? It's a free country, last time I checked."

Audible gasps sounded across the room while Jamie bit back a smile. Beside her, Emma leaned her head against Jamie's shoulder to hide her own mirth. Things were never dull when Jenny Latham was part of the team.

The surprises weren't over yet, though. Jamie was next in line when she heard Lisa's mother asking if now she and Andre would finally get married. They'd been waiting until same-sex marriage was legal, Jamie knew, out of solidarity. Apparently Lisa's mother knew that fact as well.

"I don't know," Lisa said, her eyes on her longtime boyfriend. "What do you think, Andre? Should we get married?"

"Is this you proposing?" he asked.

"Maybe," she replied impishly.

"Hmm," Andre said. He folded his napkin and set it on the table. Then he stood up. "Well, I don't think that's good enough of an answer." He reached into the pocket of national team, that is."

Everyone within earshot laughed, and Jamie smiled as she gazed around at her friends and family. This day had been almost perfect. Or no, actually, it had been perfect. Even Jessica North's vitriol—and the active hatred of people far worse than her—couldn't touch them. The only ones who could rain on their parade were the Germans, and Jamie didn't intend on letting that happen.

The semifinals were four days away. Tomorrow they would begin video review, position scouting, and strategic offense and defense preparation. For now, though? For now, Jamie was going to scoot her chair closer to Emma's and sip the glass of wine the team's nutritionist had approved. For now, she was going to celebrate a double win on this extra-historic day with the friends and family she loved most in the world.

"To winning!" she said, holding up her glass.

Voices responded immediately all around her: "To winning!"

Boo-yah.

CHAPTER FOURTEEN

Emma gazed out the window as the coach glided through Montreal, taking in the city's eclectic mix of Gothic, Art Deco, and modern architecture. She hadn't been here in years, not since she'd been a teenager traveling across Canada for CONCACAF's Under-19 qualifying tournament. That was the summer when she and Tori Parker... She winced slightly and glanced sideways at Jamie, who gave her a quizzical smile. Probably best not to remember the last time she'd visited Montreal. She smiled back at Jamie and returned to the view outside their window, sunny and idyllic and different somehow from her memories of the largest city in Quebec, Canada's only predominantly French-speaking province.

To be fair, the last time she'd been here, she'd still basically been in shock from losing her father a couple of months earlier. Emma had changed immeasurably in the years since, though thoughts of her father's death still occasionally reduced her to a stuttering mess. This time around, Jamie would be with her, their relationship solid despite the difficult spring. If her teen self could see her now, she'd be ecstatic. Of course, she'd also be pissed because, really? No World Cup title since '99?

I'm working on it, she thought to her hypothetical annoying younger self. Honestly, this World Cup was looking better and better, even with Germany looming ahead in the semis. They just needed to keep improving, game by game. So far, so good.

accompaniment, and Jamie was pretty sure she heard the ubiquitous "U-S-A" chant from somewhere in the far corner. Jenny bowed once more and commenced cutting the cake.

A few minutes later, as Jamie stood in line with Emma waiting for a slice of cake, she watched Ellie carry a couple of plates back to her table. Jenny had given her part of the rainbow heart, and as Ellie lifted her fork, Jamie heard Mrs. Ellison say, "I don't understand why she would put a rainbow heart on her birthday cake. It's not like it really applies to her, is it?"

Ellie winced while most of the players in earshot immediately looked at Jenny to gauge her reaction. The birthday girl finished cutting the piece she was on and then paused, her eyes on Ellie's mother.

"Actually," she said, her voice carrying, "who says I won't end up marrying a woman? It's a free country, last time I checked."

Audible gasps sounded across the room while Jamie bit back a smile. Beside her, Emma leaned her head against Jamie's shoulder to hide her own mirth. Things were never dull when Jenny Latham was part of the team.

The surprises weren't over yet, though. Jamie was next in line when she heard Lisa's mother asking if now she and Andre would finally get married. They'd been waiting until same-sex marriage was legal, Jamie knew, out of solidarity. Apparently Lisa's mother knew that fact as well.

"I don't know," Lisa said, her eyes on her longtime boyfriend. "What do you think, Andre? Should we get married?"

"Is this you proposing?" he asked.

"Maybe," she replied impishly.

"Hmm," Andre said. He folded his napkin and set it on the table. Then he stood up. "Well, I don't think that's good enough of an answer." He reached into the pocket of his leather jacket, pulled out a small velvet box, and knelt down on one knee. And just like that, the room of two hundred people fell silent. "I've been carrying this around for more than a year now, and I don't want to wait another second to ask you. So this is it, Lee. Will you allow me to spend the rest of my days showing you just how much I love you?" His gravelly voice was breaking by the end of the speech, and Jamie could see the tears in his eyes more than reflected in Lisa's as he smiled up at her, the literal embodiment of heart eyes.

"Oh my god, yes!" she practically shouted. She launched herself at him, and he stood up, wrapping his arms around her as the oohs and ahhs swept across the crowded conference room.

Jamie turned her own not exactly dry eyes to Emma, only to find her girlfriend watching her. As they shared a secretive smile, Jamie thought that someday, somewhere down the road, they would be starring in their own version of this same ritual. Today's court decision confirmed that they had just as much right to do so as Lisa and Andre, and while Jamie hadn't expected legal recognition to mean as much as it did, she was willing to take it.

"Did you see Jessica North's Instagram post?" Meg asked, leaning across the adjoining table to catch Jamie's eye.

"No." She winced preemptively, bracing herself for what would no doubt be homophobic douchebaggery shared for all the world to see.

Sure enough: "She wrote some pseudo-Christian BS about the world needing to pray like never before," Meg confirmed.

"Pretty sure the research proves you can't pray away the gay," Tyler said, scraping up cake crumbs with his fork.

"The only one who needs to pray is Jessica North," Emma said. "That she ever gets another call-up to the

The coach slowed as they approached a swank downtown hotel not far from Olympic Stadium, where the semifinal would take place. At least they were nowhere near the stadium where they'd played their qualifiers nearly a dozen years earlier.

And yet, a lack of proximity didn't prevent Angie from piping up, "Ah, the hotel that shall forever live in US Women's National Team infamy. Right, Blake?"

"Wait." Jamie's eyes narrowed. "*This* is the hotel where you guys stayed during under-19 qualifying?"

"Of course not," Emma said, glaring at Angie who was snickering openly now. "Shorty's just messing with you."

The insult didn't appear to phase Angie's amusement. She only smirked harder and elbowed Maddie, who said without looking up from her phone, her tone long-suffering, "Yes, Ange, I saw her face."

That was the best way to handle one of Angie's pranks, Emma knew: simply ignore her. Jamie, somehow, didn't seem to have learned that lesson during the many years of her friendship with Angie.

Outside the hotel, a sizable contingent of fans cheered as they disembarked, pillows clutched to their sides. That was one of the small improvements Lacey had implemented: Everyone now traveled with their pillows from home. Emma nodded at the gathered fans and resisted the urge to look over her shoulder as she followed her teammates into the hotel. Just inside the double doors, the friends and family who had beaten the team bus to Montreal waited—including one family member Emma hadn't expected to see just yet.

"Mom!" she said, and rushed to where her mother was standing with Ty and Bridget.

"Emma, sweetheart," her mom said, tugging her into a warm hug, Emma's pillow smushed between them.

"What are you doing here?" she asked, pulling away to slap hands with her brother. "I thought you couldn't get here until Tuesday."

Her mother shrugged. "I decided they could do without me. It's only work, honey, while this is the World Cup."

"I'm really glad you're here," Emma said, blinking back sudden tears. "I just have to get settled, but then could we maybe go for a walk?"

"That sounds perfect," her mom said, smiling. Ty and Bridget flashed her a thumbs-up, and Emma started to turn away only to find Jamie brushing past her to hug her mom, too. Jamie was so much more of a hugger than she'd been when they were younger that it still sometimes startled Emma.

"You made it!" Jamie exclaimed.

"I did," Emma's mom agreed, her eyes warm as she gazed from Jamie to Emma. "I wouldn't miss out on this time with my girls. Nice work, you two, in getting the team this far."

My girls. While Jamie characteristically minimized her role in the US team's advancement, Emma blinked back more tears. Geez. It wasn't even the end of the tournament yet, and here she was ready to break down at the smallest provocation. Or, not the smallest, exactly. But still. Clearly she needed to pull it together.

Her mother made that goal exponentially harder a little while later while they were strolling through the Parc Maisonneuve, a large city park not far from the team hotel. Emma was walking arm in arm with her mom, talking about the dog her mother and Roger were planning to adopt—a little Maltipoo named, predictably Emma felt, Mollie Mae—when her mom gestured toward a bench.

"Can we sit?"

"Of course," Emma said.

They sat together for a few peaceful minutes, watching pedestrians pass. In her cut-off jean shorts, baseball cap, and sunglasses, Emma was dressed not to be noticed, but that didn't stop the occasional passerby from clutching their companion unsubtly when they recognized her. Emma, for the most part, ignored the attention as she and her mom shared fond memories of Lucy, her dad's sweet dog who had died of cancer Emma's first year of college. She had always felt guilty for not being there, but at least Ty and their mother had been with her at the end.

"Speaking of your dad," her mom said, reaching over to take her hand, "remember how he thought you could be the next Mia Hamm?"

Emma laughed, though there might have been a slightly watery quality to the sound. "If that isn't an example of parental blindness, I'm not sure what is."

"He genuinely believed you could be," her mom insisted. "I did, too. Still do, truth be told."

Emma shook her head, but she couldn't deny the way her shoulders straightened at hearing of her mother's—and father's—confidence in her soccer abilities.

After a pause, her mom asked, "Do you still feel like your life will be incomplete if you don't win the whole thing? Because from where I'm sitting, winning seems almost inevitable at this point."

"Mom!" Emma half-turned toward her. "You can't say things like that!"

Her mother regarded her blankly for a moment before her brow cleared. "You mean because of the sports jinx phenomenon. This is you being superstitious, right?"

Emma sighed a long-suffering sigh. She would bet Mia Hamm's family knew better than to call such beliefs mere superstition. "If we lose," she groused only half-jokingly, "I guess we'll know why."

"Oh, sweetheart, I'm from Minnesota. You know I

don't believe in all that you-know-what kind of hooey."

Emma tried and failed to prevent the laugh that burst out of her, and she had to admit that it felt good, just for a minute, to think about something other than soccer.

"By the way," her mom added, reaching into her sizable purse and pulling out a tightly folded gray sweatshirt, "I wanted to give you this. I found it when I was cleaning out the Shoreline house a few years ago, and I've been waiting for the right time."

Squinting slightly, Emma took the proffered sweatshirt. As she undid the rubber band compressing the material, her curiosity morphed into confusion. A brand new UNC Women's Soccer sweatshirt with a branding design that was at least a decade old made little sense. Unless…

"Your dad bought it right before he died," her mother explained, her voice as soft as the hand that brushed back the stubborn curls that had managed to escape Emma's ponytail. "He just, well, he never got a chance to wear it."

Emma's grip on the crew neck sweatshirt tightened before loosening again. She smoothed it across her lap, surprised to note that it didn't seem much bigger than her own many UNC Soccer sweatshirts. Had her dad been smaller than how she'd always remembered him?

For a moment, the busy Montreal park faded away and she was back on a Chapel Hill practice field on an early Sunday morning, the August day already hot and humid, the cicadas keeping time to her labored breathing after a sprint rep. But instead of listening to her coach talk about how the work they were putting in now would pay dividends in November, she had been picturing her father doing wind sprints with her the previous summer on her high school field, trying his best to keep up until finally he'd flopped down in the grass and lay on his back, laughing. Had his heart been in trouble even then? She'd thought he was just traveling too much and not exercising enough, but maybe she'd simply missed the signs.

"I know how cold you get in hotels," her mother said, her voice more hesitant now. "And also, I thought it might be a way you could feel your dad here with you. Because he wouldn't miss this World Cup for anything. Even I, a science-believing secular humanist, know that much."

The tears refused to be blinked away this time. Eyes still hidden behind her sunglasses, Emma leaned her head against her mother's shoulder. "You really think so?"

"I do," her mom said, stroking her hair. "I really do."

Maybe that was why she'd been missing her dad more during this World Cup than any other—because his spirit or his energy or his *soul*, even, was somewhere nearby, watching over her. It was a nice thought, even if she couldn't quite convince herself it was true. She'd long suspected that it would be easier to believe in a god, in heaven, in an afterlife, like Emily and Rebecca and the other members of the God Squad. To simply have faith. But like her parents, she had been blessed with an unwavering belief that most of life's mysteries could be explained by science, even if human beings didn't always get their hypotheses correct. The beauty was there in every drop of water, in every molecule of air, in every cell that made up a human body or an insect's carapace or a bird's wing—not because a book written long ago said so, but just because it was.

She was still pondering the mysteries of the universe when a group of park-goers dressed in varying derivations of the American flag stopped a few feet away, elbowing each other eagerly. Emma swiped surreptitiously at her lingering tears and lifted her head from her mother's shoulder to smile at the Americans who had come to Canada presumably to watch her and her teammates play soccer.

"Are you Emma?" a girl with braces and skinny legs asked, her voice shy.

"I am," she said, and squeezed her mom's arm before rising to meet her fans.

The three kids in the group, wearing Jenny's and Lisa's numbers, crowded around Emma to tell her how AMAZING the defense had been so far and how they KNEW FOR SURE that she and her teammates would win THE WHOLE THING.

"Well, thanks," Emma said, smiling down at them. "You play, don't you? I can tell."

The girls blushed and grinned and told her all about their AYSO teams back in Michigan, where they were still in elementary school. Emma listened and offered a bit of her usual advice: "Keep working hard even when no one is watching, and you'll do great. But most of all, have fun because soccer is the best game in the world."

"And you and Lisa are the best defenders in the world," the oldest girl declared, braces glinting in the sun. "Even that jerk Tony Aiello says so."

Tony Aiello was a former US men's national team player who now worked as a FOX Sports commentator—a fact that wasn't universally appreciated by the American soccer community.

A woman who looked like an older, less awkward version of the girl, complete with a matching Afro and faint freckles, stepped forward quickly. "Alexis, baby, that's enough."

Emma caught the mother's eye and smiled. "Let's be honest. She's not wrong, is she?"

As the group of adults laughed, the smallest girl grabbed her father's hand and leaned into his side, wincing at the sudden noise. Emma started to smile down at her, but then a wave of longing swept over her. She could remember being that shy kid, clinging to her dad's side whenever she had to navigate a new social situation. Even as an adult, even after all these years, she still sometimes noticed the empty space beside her where her father should have stood.

She managed to smile for the requisite selfies—there was a reason she never left a team hotel without brushing her hair and teeth—and then the family wished them luck and walked away, the girls' voices squeaking in excitement at seeing "Blake from Seattle."

Emma felt her mother's eyes on her as they began to stroll in the opposite direction, back toward the team hotel.

"What?" she asked, quirking a brow.

"I think you might actually be more famous than Mia Hamm," her mother announced.

Emma only smiled and walked on through the green, green park. The tears were threatening again, and she wasn't sure she could trust her voice. Her mom squeezed her arm but didn't press her. In the summer sunlight filtering through the trees, her eyes looked a little bright, too.

When Emma could manage it, she leaned into her mother's side and said, "I love you, Mom."

"I love you too, Emma boo."

Something unseen brushed against Emma's other side. No doubt it was only the breeze, but that didn't stop her from whispering, "Love you too, Dad."

#

Emma sipped her coffee, leaning against her and Jamie's usual table in the hotel restaurant. "You know," she said as Jamie joined her with a steaming mug of green tea, "I have a good feeling about today."

It was already Game Day, and in a matter of hours, the die would be cast. Either Germany would be going home tonight or the US would. Whoever won the match, it was bound to be awkward because, once again, they'd been assigned to the same hotel. Thanks, FIFA. Or, as Emma had mentally christened the world football federation, Freaking Incompetent Football Association.

Jamie stared at her. "Dude, don't say things like that! You'll jinx it."

"Will I? Like, seriously, I just believe that we will—"

"Not another word, Blakeley. I'm serious."

Ooh, her last name. Jamie really was serious. Emma sipped her coffee and gazed over the top of her mug. "Superstitious much?"

"Says the 'psychic' one," Jamie said.

"Hey, lose the air quotes. You know I am."

"Sure, Blake. Whatever you say."

Even though she was only teasing Jamie, Emma really did have a good feeling about the coming match. Germany might technically be the better side, but that didn't necessarily mean the European powerhouse would win. Sure, they had scored more goals than anyone else, but the American defense had allowed the fewest number of goals, so really, they should match up well—no matter what the naysayers in the sports press said.

Not that Emma had spent much time in Canada reading the sports press. She hadn't been on social media much either, mostly because she'd freaked herself out by posting that photo of her and Jamie on top of the Empire State Building. According to the company she paid to manage her public accounts, the response had been overwhelmingly positive. Maybe after the World Cup ended, she would check for herself. Or maybe she'd let the management company keep on doing their thing. Honestly, it had been nice to only communicate online with people she knew and loved. If her stalker was still out there—and he probably was—at least she wasn't giving him power over her life. Instead, she was staying focused on what mattered most: this team and their World Cup journey.

She could tell as the day went on and everyone went about their Game Day routines, from ice baths and hot tub soaks to massages and meditation circles—her teammates were brimming with the same confidence she could feel lifting her shoulders and giving her seemingly boundless energy. Which was good. Because if you didn't believe you could do something, then you probably couldn't.

"The corollary of that philosophy, athletes," Jo said in their pre-game discussion in the locker room late that afternoon, "is that if you do believe you can do something, you more than likely can."

"Boo-yah!" Phoebe said, but without a fist bump because the trainer was currently taping her wrists.

"Boo-yah," Jo agreed, and the locker room broke out in laughter. "Seriously, though, the coaches and I have decided to scrap our previous line-ups and go with the one you've been pestering us about for ages." She turned to the nearby whiteboard and arranged the ten white player pieces in—Emma grinned at Maddie—an actual 4-3-3.

As the players around her broke into excited chatter, Emma noticed Jo and Mel exchange a small smile. Was that why they'd held off on the formation until now? To give the players the extra motivation they would need to beat a resurgent Germany?

"All right, all right," Jo said, holding up a hand. "Bear with me for a few more minutes. Then we'll get out there and kick the ball around. The turf is cooling down, so let's let it do that, yeah?"

Emma nodded and settled back into place on the bench in front of her assigned cubby. They had been lucky to play mostly in the evening, which gave the turf a chance to release the heat it accumulated over the course of a day. During one Round of 16 match in Vancouver, the turf's temperature had come in at above 120 degrees. Midday games in Edmonton had taken place in even hotter conditions, and Emma had heard that several players had posted images on social media of their burned feet. She would be happy to delay in the coolness of the locker room for as long as the coaches deemed wise.

"As you know, " Jo went on, moving the player magnets around the board as she spoke, "the 4-3-3 was designed for offensive production, but when we don't have possession it'll need to look more like a 4-4-1-1, with Jenny and Ellie remaining central and VB and Gabe dropping back to help out Jamie and Maddie as needed. The back four is playing well as is, so your shape doesn't need to be tweaked. But as we discussed at our last video review session, I want everyone out there to look for Germany's ability to explode out of their formation, particularly on the flanks. Got it?"

Players around the room nodded even as they worked through their pre-warm-up routines. Germany's 4-2-3-1 formation had made them highly dangerous on offense, but previous offensive output meant very little. What mattered was what Germany did today. The Department of Defense, Emma was pretty sure, would have something to say about that.

"Really, anyone on Germany could score at any time," Jo reminded them. "That means first and second touches are going to be key, as will your ability to transition quickly from defense to offense and send numbers up the field."

She turned away from the whiteboard to regard the players gathered before her. "We've been here before, athletes. It's no accident that this team has made it to the semifinals of the World Cup seven times in a row. But Germany is no stranger to this stage of the game, either. What it comes down to is simple: Who wants it more? Who wants the spotlight, the pressure, the eyes of the world upon them? There are plenty of people who don't think you can do it. In fact, I heard Tony on air earlier claiming he hadn't seen any reason to think you could pull off this victory, and I doubt there's anything I could say to sway him."

Groans and nearly audible eye-rolls rang out across the locker room. Tony Aiello was only too happy to use his Fox-sponsored bully pulpit to weigh in on every aspect of the women's program—and on any other team or soccer organization mentioned in his presence.

"But that's okay," Jo continued, "because the time for talking is over. Now it's time to play. What do you think? Is he right? Are you going to let Germany dictate pace, pressure, possession?"

"No," came the resounding reply.

"Are you going to let Germany send you home tonight?"

"No!" The cry echoed through the locker room.

"I'm sorry, I don't think I heard you. I said, ARE YOU READY TO GO HOME?"

This time their response made the walls shake as all 23 members of the US Women's National Team screamed, "NO!"

Jo surveyed them, a smile almost curling her lips. She nodded once. "That's what I thought. So let's go fucking do this."

The cry in response was almost deafening, and Emma exchanged a grin with Maddie. They were ready. *So. Fucking. Ready.*

CHAPTER FIFTEEN

Fucking Canadians, Emma thought, glancing over her shoulder at Jamie who only widened her eyes in response. The Montreal stadium's staff had started the American anthem mid-stream around "—early light..." Was it purposeful? Were they pissed about the long list of transgressions—wait, make that the long list of WINS—the US had notched against their home team, who had been knocked out of the tournament by England three days earlier?

Whatever. If it was a purposeful gaffe by the host nation to get inside their heads, it wouldn't work. Seriously, was Canada new here? If anything, the slight would only make the Americans play with a bigger chip on their shoulders.

In the sideline huddle, Ellie spoke low and urgently. "Win or go home—that's where we're at, guys. Leave everything on the field. Let's win this fucker! Oosa on three: one, two, three!"

"Oosa-oosa-oosa-ah!" the team chanted in perfect unison.

Emma strode onto the pitch, noting the blur that was Jamie streaking past her to the center of the field. They were going to win this, she thought confidently. But then she looked at Germany on the other side of the field and remembered that they were ranked ahead of the US; were currently leading the tournament in scoring; and had beaten the US 3-0 the last time they'd met in the World

Cup semis. Admittedly that had been in 2003, and other than Ellie, none of the current US players had been on the squad then, but still.

Emma lifted her gaze and focused on the stands, another sell-out crowd at more than 50,000 tickets sold. Just like China in the previous match, Germany had a decent number of fans rooting for them. But their pockets of supporters couldn't begin to compete with the sea of fans dressed in blue and white. Germany was wearing their red uniforms, and the American fans had come prepared, clearly. These people, with their faces painted and wardrobes dotted with eagles and flags, with their smiling children and their proud signs and waving flags, these fans were the reason the American team even existed. They were the reason Emma could stand on this pitch in her US national team jersey, her name and number emblazoned across her back marking her as a member of an elite club. These fans were the reason the US team was given a slightly better margin of victory in the odds—because their energy, their love and light, would carry the team through.

She thought of the three little girls she'd met in the park a few days earlier, and her shoulders straightened. They were going to win this or die tryi—well, not *that*, she hoped. But they would damn well give everything they had to beat Germany.

Leave it all on the field. Give it your all. WIN.

Her eyes met Jamie's as she neared the top of the penalty area where the rest of the defense was gathering for their pre-game cheer, and she nodded once. Jamie nodded back. *We got this.*

The Germans had lost the coin toss, which, of course, Emma found promising. Ellie had selected the end of the field that Phoebe had requested, closest to the German cheering section. The jeers of their opponents, Phoebe always said, fueled her even more than the cheers of their supporters. Plus this way she would have their fans at her back for the second half, when the stakes of the game usually became more clear. Nothing like a clock winding down to kick you into gear.

Emma and her fellow defenders gathered together and stuck out their arms, hands stacked one on top of another in the same order as usual. Phoebe nodded around the small circle and said, "One, two, three, hold the line!" Then they were pushing off each other, tight and coiled, game faces ready.

Just another game, Emma told herself, jumping in place and trying not to notice how much she had to pee as the head referee, a woman from Russia, waited for the signal from the sideline that the television broadcast was set. And then, before Emma expected it, the starting whistle blew and the game was off.

Germany had come ready to play, it was immediately clear. Borrowing a page from the US team's playbook, they threw high pressure at the American side right from the whistle. Two minutes in, that pressure got some help by a bad call near the American defensive end. Emma knew this ref, though. She was competent and collected, exactly what was needed in a World Cup semifinal, and would likely be fair. Quickly, Emma let go of her irritation over the missed call and focused on defending in their end.

Turned out there was a lot to defend in the first few minutes as Germany drove the US back, closer and closer to its own penalty area. On the outside, Ryan got beaten by one of the German strikers, and Emma had to step up from her loose double team to knock the ball away. It caromed off the striker's shin guards and earned the US a goal kick, but that had been too close to a German corner for Emma's liking. Only a minute and a half later, another German striker tried to turn the corner into the box, forcing Taylor to knock the ball away.

Crap, Emma thought, looking to Phoebe for direction. Germany had just earned their first corner kick only two and a half minutes into the game. That was not good. Not good at all.

Not good became even worse a moment later when Lotte Schneider, Germany's center midfielder and a familiar face from Emma's WPS days, delivered a perfect lofted ball to a wide open Mila Friedrich. Germany's star striker rose up, flicked her head, and delivered a solid strike toward the net. Phoebe scrambled to cover the space in time, but she barely had one hand up when the ball arced just over the crossbar. *Whew.* Germany had very nearly scored, and the game hadn't even been underway for five minutes. That would have been a rough blow to recover from.

As Phoebe passed Emma the ball and she and Lisa started the attack out of the backfield, Emma heard her college coach's head in the back of her mind, as she often did: "Don't panic. Weather the storm. Possess the ball and build your own attack."

And yet, it was hard not to panic 15 seconds later when Taylor launched an ill-advised long ball that Germany neatly corralled and used to launch a quick counter. Ryan unaccountably dove in as a German midfielder dribbled at her—the US defender's second error in nearly as many minutes—and suddenly Emma was racing backwards again, trying to delay the all-out attack. Before she could reach her, Ryan's player sent the ball into the center, where Lisa stepped in to clear it away.

Maddie received the ball in the midfield, turned, and passed to Jenny, who one-timed the ball outside to an overlapping Gabe on the left flank. Gabe slowed the ball down to allow their teammates to catch up, and then sent a lofted cross toward Ellie that Germany—*damn it*—once again intercepted. And, great, Germany was on the counter again. Jamie shut down the attack, though, dropping the ball back to Lisa who was immediately run over by Friedrich. The referee whistled the obvious foul, and Emma paused for what felt like the first time all game to take a breath.

"Let's settle down," she called as she helped Lisa up. "Slow it down, guys. Let's play at our pace, not theirs."

The US players near enough to hear her nodded. They had 85 minutes to go, Emma reminded herself as Phoebe prepared to restart play, and there was no way Germany could keep up this punishing onslaught, especially not when they'd played 120-plus minutes only a few days earlier on a hot as hell turf field. Maybe that was why they had come out pressing so hard—because they, too, knew that they would only have so much gas.

The frantic pace continued, though, somehow, with both sides earning chances in their offensive ends. Taylor's targeted header on one of Jamie's picture-perfect corner kicks forced Annike Lange, the longtime German goalkeeper, to make a kick-save in traffic. A minute later at the other end, Phoebe had to palm a shot over the crossbar just to be safe. And they were still only SEVEN minutes in.

Phoebe slapped her hands together, clearly frustrated. That was a shot she would normally hold onto. Given the collective case of nerves they all seemed to be suffering from, Emma would take safe over a potential costly error that could cost them a berth in the final. Fortunately, the Germans bumbled the corner kick, and the US was off and running again.

The crazy pace continued unabated, each side trading offensive opportunities and defensive stops. In the fifteenth minute, Gabe slotted a perfect through pass between two German defenders to Jenny charging into the German box, and Emma's fist clenched preemptively as Jenny took her shot. But—*damn it again*—Lange cut down the angle and made another kick-save, sweeping the ball away at the last minute.

"Shit," Emma muttered to herself, careful not to react in a way the cameras would pick up and replay. But seriously, the US couldn't afford to miss a golden opportunity like that one. The offense needed to get themselves in gear, and soon.

The half continued, both teams probing and pressing, falling back and defending. Emma's heart rate barely had a chance to recover from anticipation over a scoring opportunity for the US before Germany was sprinting at them with numbers. She honestly couldn't remember the last time she'd played in such an even, high-paced match. Occasionally one team would foul the other, but the fouls mostly occurred because both sides were battling all out for each and every possession, not because they were being dirty. The referee, as Emma had expected, held her whistle and let the players work it out. At least, until an almost innocuous play ten yards outside the US box when Maddie turned her back to her mark and got whistled for knocking the German player down. To Emma, it seemed as if her mark went down a bit too easily in scoring territory, but that was what the Germans were known for, wasn't it? For knocking heads sometimes literally with their opponents and then crying foul as soon as anyone on the other team dared lay a finger on them.

Later, Emma would regret that thought, as if she had somehow caused what happened next.

Phoebe called a three-person wall just inside the box with another player one step off while everyone else picked a German player to mark closer to goal. Emma shouted, "Hold the twelve!" and her teammates immediately stepped up so that they were even with the penalty mark, forcing the Germans to come with them to avoid being called offsides. Now, as long as no one on the US side got sucked behind the line…

When the whistle blew, Schneider struck the ball toward the back post. Emma watched the ball sail over her and her mark, a surge of pride rising as Jamie leapt into the air and headed the ball—only to be headed herself by Mila Friedrich, whose forehead connected with the back of Jamie's head with a sickening *thunk*.

"No," Emma gasped as Jamie's face contorted in pain. She watched helplessly as Jamie dropped to the ground and lay face down, unmoving. The referee blew her whistle, but Emma barely noticed as she hurried to Jamie's side. Phoebe was already kneeling beside her, one hand rubbing her back gently. As Emma approached she moved aside, giving her unrestricted access.

"Jamie," Emma said, her voice urgent as she knelt beside her. Jamie was still face down, but her legs were moving, and both hands cradled her head as she pressed her face into the turf.

"Ow," Jamie moaned, her hands rubbing the back of her head. "What the fuck? Did Phoebe punch me or something?"

"Or something," Phoebe said, her tone light. "I was nowhere near you, Rook."

"It was Friedrich," Emma said, relieved Jamie was conscious and talking. "She headed you." She glanced around to see Mila still on the ground too, blood dripping from her scalp. Head injuries could be notorious bleeders.

"Christ! What are German skulls made of?" Jamie's voice was muffled but distinct, and Emma chose to see that as another good sign.

"Are you okay?" she asked. "Do you have a concussion?"

Maddie and Ellie were crowding around Jamie now too, Gabe and Ryan and the rest of the team milling about nearby.

"I don't know," Jamie said, and rolled over onto her back, holding her arm across her eyes as if the lights overhead hurt too much.

The team doctor and his assistant reached them a moment later, and the rest of the players backed away. Not Emma, though. She simply held Dr. Brandt's gaze and remained where she was at Jamie's side, one hand covering her girlfriend's protectively.

He nodded at her and then bent over Jamie. "Hey, Maxwell. Took a little hit to the noggin, did we?"

"You could say that, Doc," Jamie said, squinting up at him.

"Do you know what city you're in?"

"Montreal," she said, and shot Emma a look. "Kind of hard to forget."

Emma ignored the dig, if that was what it was.

"And what game is this?"

"World Cup semis," Jamie said. "Also hard to forget."

"You'd be surprised," the team doctor commented.

He asked her a few more questions that Emma recognized from the Standardized Assessment of Concussion (SAC) test that all players in the pool had on file with the federation, and then, after checking her neck and the point of contact at the back of her head, asked if she wanted to try sitting up. She complied, and though Emma watched her carefully, Jamie didn't visibly react to the change in position. Another good sign. Even better was that she didn't report any concussion symptoms—no loss of consciousness, no blurred vision, no ringing in the ears, no nausea. She wasn't bleeding, either, so Dr. Brandt had her stand up and administered a vision check and a strength test, both of which she appeared to pass.

And yet... And yet, Jamie had suffered a mild concussion while training with the Thorns before the

World Cup. Shouldn't the doctor pull her out? Shouldn't he take her into the quiet locker room and administer a full concussion assessment there? Head injuries could be serious, Emma knew. More than one former national team star had quit the game due to lingering side effects from too many concussions. But Jamie wanted to continue, and the coaches obviously wanted that as well, and soon Dr. Brandt was sending a thumbs-up to the coaches on the sideline, who returned the gesture.

"Are you sure you should keep playing?" Emma asked Jamie as Dr. Brandt conferred briefly with the referee while the German doctors fastened gauze around Friedrich's head wound. She, too, appeared to have passed her team doctor's examination.

Jamie frowned at her. "Yes, Emma. Of course." And then she walked to the sideline with Dr. Brandt and waited to be waved back on.

The long delay seemed to shift the game's momentum. For the next five minutes, the Americans pressed, peppering the German penalty box with services and shots. Finally, with less than ten minutes to go before halftime, Emma saw her chance. On a quick counter off a missed American shot, Schneider sent a through ball to Friedrich at midfield. Emma closed the space quickly and slide-tackled the German striker. She caught her just above the ankle, smiling grimly at the satisfying *thwonk* of the connection. Friedrich went down, rolling dramatically like Europeans were wont to do. She needn't have bothered, Emma thought, rising and stalking away as the ref blew her whistle shrilly. That had been what the commentators would call a "professional" foul. To the average onlooker, it probably looked like Emma had simply been concerned with slowing down the counterattack, not with obtaining revenge for the late hit on her girlfriend.

Professional foul or no, the referee whipped out a

yellow card that Emma accepted expressionlessly. When Friedrich popped up after a full minute of grasping her lower leg as if it had been broken in two, the gauze at her forehead still intact, Emma only quirked an eyebrow at her. Unlike with Beaumont at the Olympics, she hadn't tried to take the German striker out of the match. After all, Friedrich probably hadn't meant to injure Jamie.

As Germany restarted, Emma avoided looking at the US bench. She had a feeling she didn't want to see the looks Jo and her assistants were undoubtedly exchanging.

For the rest of the half, both teams continued to exchange attacks—and fouls. Gabe got taken down on three separate occasions in the space of five minutes, but she managed to get up and keep playing each time. It was the World Cup semis. You didn't go off the field unless you were on a stretcher.

Which was exactly what worried Emma.

At the whistle for halftime, Jamie ran off the field and into the tunnel as if to demonstrate how perfectly okay she was. Or, possibly to avoid Emma. She started after her girlfriend, but stopped when she heard her name called. It was Melanie, waving her closer.

"Walk with me, Blake," she said, her voice more of a command than a request.

Dutifully, Emma fell into step beside the defensive coach as players jogged past, headed toward the tunnel.

"So. I see you followed my advice."

"Um," Emma said.

"I have to say, this wasn't the situation I had in mind."

She winced. "I know. Sorry?"

"You're carrying a yellow card, Emma. From an intentional foul."

She swallowed. Hearing it out loud like that... "I know, Mel. I really am sorry."

"Jo wants to sub you."

"She… What?" Emma stared at the assistant, barely feeling the smack to her shoulder Maddie gave her as she jogged past.

Melanie held up a mollifying hand. "I convinced her to hold off for now, but no more bringing your personal crap onto the field. That's your one free shot. Got it?"

"Got it," Emma said meekly. "Thanks, Mel."

Mel shook her head. "I'm glad my wife and I never played on the same team."

"Well, I mean, you kind of do, right?" Emma asked, wriggling her eyebrows.

Mel bit her lip, but her smile shone through anyway. At least, a little.

In the locker room, players met with the training staff while the coaches chatted with individuals and amongst themselves. Finally, Jo took up her usual position near the whiteboard and cleared her throat.

"Okay, athletes. Overall, your coaches and I are happy. We're solving the pressure, and we're dominating in possession, shots on goal, pretty much every category across the board. You all have committed to defending on every line, from the back to the front. But…" She paused, glancing around the room. "What do you think I'm about to say?"

"We have to finish our chances," Ellie said.

"Exactly. Because as we all know, playing well does not always correlate with victory. But I honestly think we're having our best game of the tournament, so keep it up." Her gaze sharpened momentarily as Jamie emerged from a side room with the team doctor. "All right, get ready, athletes. We only have forty-five more minutes guaranteed at this World Cup. Let's get it done for Vancouver, yeah?"

"Yeah," a chorus of voices rang out.

The energy in the room was upbeat, positive. As ankles were re-taped and bloodstained jerseys traded for clean backups, team members chatted about the German attack and how to capitalize on turnovers. Germany was weakening, they were sure of it. If the US could keep up the pressure, the German side would crack. It was only a matter of time.

Emma nodded in agreement even as she drifted closer to Jamie, Melanie, Jo, and Dr. Brandt.

"Are you sure, Rick?" Jo was saying as Emma sidled over.

He nodded. "She passed the SAC with flying colors both times."

"I'm good, Coach," Jamie said. "I would tell you if I wasn't."

Jo's eyes narrowed as she regarded Jamie's flushed cheeks and sweat-soaked hair, and Emma could almost hear the older woman thinking, "Would you? Would you, really?"

Because if it was Emma, she was pretty sure she'd say anything, do anything not to get benched during any World Cup match, let alone the semis. Especially if she'd just sat out the quarters.

But Dr. Brandt wouldn't lie. If he said Jamie had passed her concussion protocols, then she had passed her concussion protocols, both outside on the field and here in the comparatively quiet training room. Jo seemed to reach the same conclusion because she nodded once. "Glad to hear it." And then she turned away, clapping her hands to get the team's attention.

As Jo went over a few last details—they were starting the second half the way they'd ended the first—Emma leaned into Jamie's side, not realizing how much she'd needed the contact until she felt Jamie's lean, muscled form press back against her.

"You okay?" she asked, her voice low. "Really?"

"I'm good," Jamie said, and slipped her arm around Emma's waist for the briefest of moments. "I promise."

Emma nodded, reminding herself that injuries were a risk they all shared equally. But seeing Jamie go down like that and knowing it was possible she could have a concussion—or worse—had kicked Emma out of the dream that was the World Cup. Her fear for Jamie's safety had reminded her that they would only play this game for a few more years, and then they would retire, each of them, and go about finding a way to spend the rest of their many years (if they were lucky) on this amazing planet. The game of soccer, however beautiful, was temporary. Their bodies, on the other hand, were as close to permanent as they would experience in this lifetime.

Forty-five minutes to go, she told herself as the team drew together for a cheer. That was all she needed to focus on. She could freak out about head injuries and human mortality later.

Lord knew she would, too.

#

The second half began the way the first had ended, with both teams trading feints and bursts but with the possession and energy favoring the US side. Every play seemed to bring Germany closer to breaking. The further she got from Jamie's injury, the more Emma could feel the anticipation of victory buzzing beneath her skin again. Jo was right—they really were playing their best game of the tournament.

And then, with just over ten minutes gone in the second half, what seemed like catastrophe struck. Off a German throw-in at midfield, Schneider sent an absolute Hail Mary pass to the front line, a lob that dropped into Taylor O'Brien's path as she raced back into the US penalty box. A moment of indecision was all it took for Friedrich to surge past Taylor, her foot snaking out to claim the ball for a run at the goal. Emma was only a few feet away, covering her own mark, when she saw it: Taylor, in her desperation, reached out and grabbed Friedrich's jersey, tugging her backward just as the German striker lined up her shot. Her limbs flailing exaggeratedly, Friedrich went down, as she was always going to do inside the penalty box.

Fuck.

The referee blew her whistle, hand pointing decisively at the penalty mark. A penalty kick. She had just awarded Germany a penalty kick, and Emma couldn't even pretend that it wasn't warranted. Friedrich might have gone down a bit too easily, but Taylor had undoubtedly made contact in a way that allowed the striker to sell the foul, if that was even what she was doing. Honestly, Taylor was lucky that when the referee reached for a card she chose yellow, not red.

Maddie and Ellie both had words for the ref, but it wasn't like they were going to change her mind. Taylor, meanwhile, was pacing the top of the box, tears visible in her eyes.

"It's okay," Emma said, and slipped an arm around the younger player's shoulders. "Don't beat yourself up. We need you to stay focused, okay? There's a lot of game left. Besides, we have Phoebe, remember?"

While Lisa echoed Emma's encouragement and Schneider stepped up to the penalty spot, Phoebe casually walked away from the goal, pausing to take a long drink from her water bottle and swinging her arms around as if to loosen up. Really, Emma knew, she was just trying to get inside Schneider's head. More power to her, in Emma's opinion. If all was fair in love and war, then this was definitely war.

The referee made sure the field players were arranged outside the box, and then she turned to Phoebe and blew her whistle, pointing at the goal. Phoebe pointed at an imaginary penalty box infraction, but the referee ignored the gesture and kept pointing at the goal. Finally, Phoebe shrugged and took up her position on the goal line. Schneider, who had looked increasingly nervous the more time Phoebe wasted, shook her head to herself and stood waiting for the referee's whistle.

Emma exchanged looks with Jamie and Maddie. This shot was everything. Personally, Emma was glad she wasn't Schneider.

It felt like it had been 84 years by the time the referee blew her whistle. Schneider must have felt the same way because instead of taking a calming breath, she immediately stepped to the ball and struck it toward the left goal post. Phoebe guessed wrong and dove right, but it didn't matter because the ball skimmed wide of the post.

Schneider had freaking missed!

"Yes!" Emma cried, brandishing a fist as the partisan crowd erupted.

"Oh, thank you god," Taylor O'Brien gasped, falling to her knees.

Really, Emma thought, she should be thanking Phoebe. Wordlessly, she and Lisa went to pick up their younger teammate.

"Head in the game, Taylor," Lisa said, slapping her on the back.

"Let's make that miss count," Emma added.

Taylor nodded and wiped away more tears. But Emma was fairly certain they were tears of relief this time.

Jamie grinned at Emma as she jogged backwards up the field. "We totally got this!"

"Don't jinx it," Emma said, but she was smiling too.

How could she not?

Phoebe didn't smile, though. She just nodded vehemently as if to say the miss was exactly what she'd expected. Given Schneider's shaky body language before the shot, it very well might have been.

The game continued. Oddly, instead of letting down, the Germans' confidence seemed to surge after the missed PK. But Emma couldn't help feeling that the German side only had this one last desperate push to offer. If the US could weather it, Germany would likely exhaust themselves. She said as much to Lisa during a brief stoppage when one of Germany's defenders took Jenny out near midfield.

"Totally," Lisa agreed. "We only need one goal. Or if we do go to penalties, my money is on Phoebe."

Emma's money was pretty much always on Phoebe. Not only was the US keeper excellent at mind games—an often overlooked component on PKs—but she was also widely considered the best goalkeeper in the world.

We got this, Emma thought as she moved up the field for the US free kick.

As it turned out, they did. Less than ten minutes after Germany's missed penalty, Jenny earned a PK of her own when a German defender took her down hard on a slashing run into the box. Ellie calmly stepped up to take the penalty. Emma hung back with Lisa while the rest of the team jockeyed for position around the box in case of a rebound. On the US bench, the players and coaches stood in a line, arms around each other's waists—just as Germany had done ten minutes earlier.

The referee created the delay this time, taking extra time to lecture the players pushing and shoving each other around the penalty box, but Emma noticed that Ellie didn't look nervous like Schneider had. She kept her body relaxed, her gaze focused on the ball. When at last the referee blew her whistle, Ellie paused for a long moment before moving forward and striking the ball like a rocket into the right corner. The keeper dove left, and the ball surged into the back of the net unimpeded.

"Fuck yeah!" Ellie shouted, and sprinted toward the sideline where she slid forward on her knees, pumping her fists.

Emma and Lisa grinned at each other and rushed forward, joining their teammates in a pile in the corner. Ellie had done it. She hadn't cracked under the pressure but, instead, had dealt Germany a blow that would be difficult to recover from. And oh, by the way, she had just tied Marisol's World Cup scoring record.

"Way to go, Elle," Emma said, hugging her friend tightly as soon as the crowd had cleared.

"Thanks, Em," Ellie replied, her eyes shining. "Let's fucking do this!"

Holy crap, Emma thought a moment later, hugging Jamie to her side briefly as they jogged back to their end of the field together. They were really going to win the World Cup.

#

Emma stood outside Jamie and Gabe's room, her hand raised but unmoving. It was nearly an hour past curfew, and they were probably already asleep. But Emma hadn't been able to sleep, so here she was, breaking team rules only days before the World Cup final. Was she crazy or merely stupid? Hard to tell, really.

Intellectually, she knew that Jamie was probably fine. Jamie had played the entire match and had even assisted on Angie's insurance goal in the 83rd minute after Jo subbed Angie in for Jenny. Back at the hotel, Jamie had seemed perfectly fine throughout their post-game celebratory meal with friends and family, and had assured Emma more than once that her head barely hurt. And yet, here Emma was, shivering in her sleep leggings and her dad's UNC Soccer sweatshirt, afraid to knock on the door because what if Jamie had been lying and now she was unconscious, maybe even—

Before the thought could coalesce, Emma rapped softly on the door. She waited, but there was no sound from inside, so with a glance up and down the corridor, she knocked again a little louder. This time she heard a thud and a muttered curse followed by familiar voices speaking words she couldn't quite make out. At last, footsteps approached the door, and after a moment it swung open to reveal a sleepy Jamie, her boxers and T-shirt wrinkled, her hair mussed.

"Emma?" she said, blinking in the light from the hallway.

"Can I come in?" Emma asked, and stepped inside without waiting for an answer.

Jamie turned on the light in the bathroom before turning back to her, face half-lit and half in shadows. "What's going on? Did something happen?"

"No." She started to reach for Jamie, but let her hand drop. "I was just worried about you. How's your head?"

From the depths of the room she heard Gabe sigh, long and loud, and mutter something about the World Cup and priorities.

"I told you, I'm completely fine," Jamie said, her eyes narrowing.

Emma twisted her hands together. "I know you said that, but I was thinking maybe I could stay. You know, just to keep an eye on you? I don't think the coaches would mind."

"Did they actually say that?"

"Well, no." She had considered asking, but her dad used to say it was better to ask forgiveness than permission. Though, come to think of it, that wasn't such a reassuring approach in a surgeon.

Jamie grabbed Emma's restless hands and held them in place. "Emma. Come on. What's really going on?"

"I told you, I was worried about you, okay?"

In the dim light, she could make out Jamie's pursed lips. "Yeah, but I've told you a bunch of times that you don't have to worry. Dr. Brandt told you, too. I'm totally fine."

"That's what that actress from *The Parent Trap* told everyone, and look what happened to her!" The words were out before she could think about them.

"*The Parent Trap*?" Jamie repeated, frowning.

Emma sighed. "Yes. She was snowboarding, and she fell and hit her head, and even though they tried to convince her to go to the hospital, she insisted she was fine. Except she wasn't fine, and two hours later she was dead." The words came out in a rush, which was surprising given that she hadn't realized how much of that story she'd committed to memory. It had happened shortly after she'd graduated from college, and she remembered being struck particularly by the image of the actress's teenage sons at her funeral. One moment they were on a ski trip with their mom, and the next she was literally dying, and there had been nothing she—*they* could do about it.

"Hey," Jamie said, pulling her into a hug. "I'm not going anywhere. Not yet. I promise, Em."

"You can't promise that," Emma whispered, hiding her face in Jamie's warm neck. Her skin smelled like a combination of the detergent the team's equipment manager used, the hotel's bar soap, and something that was pure Jamie. Emma clung tighter, her eyes closed against the tears that never seemed far away lately.

"No, you're right," Jamie agreed, her lips in Emma's hair. "But I can promise you I'm not in imminent danger of dying from a head injury tonight. Can you accept that?"

No. Emma sighed, her shoulders dropping. "Yes. I think so. I mean, I'll try."

"Seriously, you guys, just go to bed," Gabe muttered. "It's too late for this."

Emma pulled away and said, "Sorry, Gabe. You're right. I should go."

"Oh for Christ's sake, that's not what I meant. Just no funny business, all right? Jesus."

Wait. Gabe was saying she should stay, despite the very clear rules that most definitely said otherwise? She stared up at Jamie, whose eyebrows rose in matching surprise.

"You're obviously not going to be able to sleep in your own room," Gabe explained, sounding more practical than irritated this time, "and we really can't afford a weak link in the Department of Defense on Sunday. So get your asses in bed, both of you, and go to sleep."

Jamie smiled at Emma and squeezed her hand. "Yes, ma'am," she said.

A few minutes later, the bathroom light was off and Emma was burrowing into Jamie's already warm bed, pressing her cold feet against Jamie's bare legs and laughing quietly when she tried to squirm away.

"You okay?" Jamie whispered after they had settled down beside each other.

"No," Emma whispered back, and pressed her face into Jamie's shoulder. "But I will be."

"Love you," Jamie said, kissing her forehead.

"Love you."

"Love you guys too," Gabe said, and they all laughed. But quietly so as not to draw attention to their curfew-busting room.

Emma closed her eyes and listened to Jamie's heartbeat, strong and steady and constant. Jamie was fine, she told herself. Maybe if she repeated the mantra enough, it would calm her racing mind. What was it Jamie liked to say? Oh, right: Fake it 'til you make it.

It was worth a try, anyway.

CHAPTER SIXTEEN

Jamie stared out the hotel conference room window at the crowd chanting "U-S-A! U-S-A! U-S-A!" The fans had been amassing outside the team hotel since that morning, playing music, beating drums, and singing popular soccer anthems. It almost seemed as if they were more excited for the final against Japan than the team, Angie had joked. In a way, Jamie thought that might be true. The fans didn't have to worry about disappointing anyone, nor did they have to think about sponsorships or the business end of the game. No matter the outcome, these people could go home and resume their normal lives. But if the players didn't come away with gold...

They weren't going to lose, Jamie told herself, squaring her shoulders. They were going to beat Japan and attain the highest pinnacle of their sport. Today. This afternoon. In just a few hours, in fact.

"You okay?" Emma asked, leaning in to bump her shoulder.

"Totally," Jamie said. "I'll be right back."

In the restroom down the hall, she locked herself in a stall and leaned over the gleaming white toilet bowl, its medicinal perfume only making it harder to fight against the heaves. Sweat broke out on her forehead, and she silently cursed as the exterior door opened. Then she heard Britt's voice.

"It's okay if you get sick. Lacey has a shake for that, too."

Jamie snorted in laughter and almost lost control of the contents of her stomach. Normally a salmon burger and salad was the perfect meal before a game, but then she'd never played in a World Cup final, had she? Oh, god. THE WORLD CUP FINAL.

"Can I come in?" Britt asked.

Jamie thought about asking to be alone, but then she reached back and flicked open the lock. "Sorry," she said, wondering if she looked as green as she felt. Judging from her friend's furrowed brow, that would be yes.

"Don't be. Did you throw up?"

"Not yet."

"Want to try some tai chi? The hall is super wide, and I'm getting better. Bet I could kick your ass."

Which was so typical of someone on this team, Jamie thought, tossing her head in slight irritation. Also typical was her own need to show Britt up, even though motion was probably the last thing she needed at this juncture.

Surprisingly, it worked. After a few minutes of focusing on her breath and trying to move through her favorite relaxation routine as smoothly and deliberately as possible, Britt only barely staying upright beside her, the nausea subsided along with the nervous sweat and, she hoped, the green tinge to her skin.

"Okay, I'm good," she told Britt as she finished an intricate pattern.

"You sure?"

"Totally. Thanks, man," she added as they headed back to the conference room.

"You're welcome, bud," Britt said, slapping her shoulder.

Emma caught her eye from across the room and lifted an eyebrow. *You okay?*

Jamie nodded slightly. *I'm good.*

Emma nodded back and smiled at her, her eyes conveying the message that everything would be fine. And yeah, Jamie knew that in theory it would be. No matter what happened today, she would be with Emma and Britt and Angie and the rest of their teammates, who had coalesced over the past month and a half into the greatest group of friends she could ever imagine having. That wouldn't change, whether or not they won.

But that was exactly why they would win, she thought a little while later as they walked the gauntlet of cheering fans from the hotel to the team bus, its "ONE NATION ONE TEAM" banner blending into the colors of the gathered crowd. They would defeat Japan because they cared about each other individually and collectively, and because they wanted this win more than anything else they'd ever wanted—individually or collectively. Emma and Ellie had both said that this team felt more cohesive than any other World Cup squad they'd been part of. That camaraderie would help them rise above today, Jamie was sure of it.

She nodded at various fans as she approached the bus, checking automatically for suspicious activity. But the faces that gazed back at her were uniform in their enthusiasm, and it was difficult not to get swept into their emotions. She steeled herself, breathing deeply to keep from being overwhelmed. It was just another a game, just another match in a long string of matches before sell-out crowds in summertime Canada.

Her nightmares from the night before sorely undermined that notion. In one, Jamie had shown up to BC Place without her shin guards. In another, she'd been missing her cleats *and* her uniform. And in the last one she could remember, she had been on the field without any shorts on; whenever she tried to run, her feet seemed stuck to the turf, too heavy to move. For a soccer player, this was like the classic college nightmare where you find out on the day of the final that you were enrolled in a class you'd never attended. Jamie still had those dreams sometimes, too.

At least she didn't have to actually worry about not having her cleats or her uniform, she thought as she filed onto the bus behind Emma and followed her to their usual seats. Tad, the equipment manager, and his staff took care of transporting everything they could possibly need—and more—to the game ahead of their arrival. That way the players could focus on getting ready to play.

They had flown into Vancouver on Wednesday fresh from beating Germany in the semis. The World Cup mascot, Shuéme, a great white owl, had greeted them on the tarmac, and the players had posed for photos with her before heading to their hotel in downtown Vancouver. They'd arrived just in time to watch Japan defeat England in the other semifinal. Or, rather, to watch England self-destruct. Honestly, that match had been painful to watch. But Emma and the other veterans on the team had fist-bumped prolifically at the outcome. At last, the stage was set for redemption.

After a day of rest and recovery, they'd spent Friday and Saturday training and talking to the media ahead of the big event. Today, Sunday, was only their fourth full day in Vancouver. Talk about a whirlwind. A surreal whirlwind—Jamie kept having to tell herself that yes, she was really here, and not as a spectator. She, Jamie Maxwell, was starting in a World Cup final. This was literally the culmination of everything she'd been working for since attending her first and only World Cup final sixteen years earlier.

Now they just had to win.

The bus on the way to the game wasn't as noisy as usual, probably because Lacey had given them strict instructions to practice Mary Kate's visualization exercises. Even though the hotel was less than a mile from BC Place, the roads were jammed with traffic, and certain streets were closed altogether so that fans could parade down them to the stadium. Jamie glimpsed the crowds as the bus traversed downtown Vancouver, cars honking at them and pedestrians pointing and waving animatedly as the US Soccer bus crawled past.

Lindsay Martens and Tamara Keys, a backup defender and one of the younger players on the squad, waved back. There was little chance either of them would see playing time today, and for a moment, Jamie was almost envious of them. Then she shook her head to clear the traitorous thought. Of course she wanted to play. That didn't mean she wasn't legitimately terrified to make a mistake like the one the English centerback had made against Japan, scoring an own goal in stoppage time and singlehandedly destroying England's chance to advance.

But no, she told herself, rubbing her eyes fiercely, there was no room for negative thoughts right now. Only positive self-talk. She should be visualizing herself making fabulous plays, not career-ending errors.

Beside her, Emma was quiet, eyes closed and headphones clamped over her ears. Jamie couldn't begin to know what was going through Emma's mind. She'd spent nearly the entirety of her twenties on this team, traveling the world in pursuit of a World Cup title. In 2007, they'd bombed out in the semis, and more than one pundit had suggested the USA's glory days might be behind them. Four years later, they'd lost in the final, and the world had proclaimed that Japan had been destined to win. Emma had told her once that people used to ask her which loss was worse, but there was no way to choose. They were each terrible in their own right. This World Cup might be her last chance to attain her ultimate soccer goal. Not that

Jamie thought Emma would be too old to play in the next World Cup, but there was no guarantee that any of them would be on the team four years down the road. Injury, illness, coaching changes, and federation politics all meant that nothing was guaranteed. Nothing except this moment right now.

From across the aisle, Angie caught Jamie's eye and smiled. Her fantastic, point-blank goal against Germany in the waning minutes of the semis had launched her into the public eye—and, what was more, had earned her the start today. She was eating up the scrutiny, flaunting her tomboy style on FOX Sports and ESPN and amusing various hosts with her usual jokes and general ebullience. Surprisingly, her family hadn't seemed overly displeased with the attention she'd drawn, so that was good. Angie deserved this moment. She'd had to fight not only everyone in their age group to get to this time and place, but her own family's expectations as well.

Next to Angie, Maddie was gazing out the window, headphones over her ears. Like Emma, Maddie had long spoken of this final as a chance at redemption. She'd made her penalty kick against Japan four years earlier, too, but it hadn't made a difference. Jamie wondered if she was going through MK's visualization exercises now or if she was simply trying to lose herself in her psych-up mix. Some players preferred to use the ride to the stadium to think about anything other than soccer.

Ellie definitely was not one of those people. Neither was Jenny. Right now they were seated beside each other with their eyes closed, and Jamie didn't doubt that their visualizations involved scoring massive amounts of goals. Although perhaps Jenny was picturing other things. She had been struggling to finish, yes, but she had managed to contribute in other ways—earning corner kicks, penalties, free kicks. She'd also played more intense pressure defense than Jamie could ever remember seeing her do. Coming into the World Cup fresh off an injury meant she had started the tournament off-kilter, and she still hadn't seemed to find her usual brilliant form. Maybe today that would change.

In the seat behind Ellie, Britt winked at Jamie before returning to her conversation with Rebecca, her seatmate, and Lisa and Ryan. None of them seemed nervous as they chattered away on the way to the stadium. Lucky bastards.

Jamie's gaze drifted across the aisle to Phoebe, the best goalkeeper in the world for the last decade, sitting silently beside her longtime backup, Avery. Like Ellie, she had yet to win a World Cup. Also like her co-captain, she wasn't getting any younger. Her shoulders were "like a 90-year-old's," she liked to joke. Was this her and Ellie's last chance to make good on the legacy of the '99ers? Would the team be letting them down if they failed to fulfill the promise of redeeming their 2011 loss?

Jamie closed her eyes and took a deep breath. It was perfectly normal to be nervous. Who wouldn't be on the day of the biggest game of their life? The trick was to prevent her nerves from controlling her thoughts. And the best way to do that was to interrupt her negative thinking and replace it with positive. She ran through a couple of her mantras, and then she focused her mind and thought, *I believe that we will win. I believe that I will score.*

As the bus finally approached the stadium, she visualized both positive outcomes in careful detail. On any given day, she knew, any team could defeat another. The difference was in preparation, fitness, and most of all, belief. Confidence was the most important mental factor in sport, MK had told them time and again. In Jamie's experience, the national team's sports psychologist was absolutely right.

When the coach pulled up under the stadium

overhang, Ellie rose at the front of the bus and called out, "Come on, you guys. Let's fucking do this!"

"Let's fucking *go!*" the team responded almost as one.

And yeah, Jamie thought, feeling a terrified joy bubble up inside her chest. They were ready.

#

For the pre-game walk-through, a slight haze hung high up inside the stadium, the result of wildfires blazing in the mountains outside Vancouver. Fortunately, the brownish haze hanging over the city that morning had mostly burned off by now. Their FIFA rep assured them that the local particulate measurements weren't dangerous (yet), and that the stadium's climate control features would keep the interior more comfortable than a typical outdoor stadium. If anything, the slight haze lingering high over the city meant that the turf temperature wasn't as high as it might have been under more direct sunlight. The humidity had been dropping all day, so a temperature in the upper 70s didn't feel all that hot, either.

With game time still a couple of hours away, the stands were nearly empty. But as the US went through their warm-ups, the fans slowly trickled in. A huge Jumbotron hung above the field showing clips and images of each side's progression through the tournament, but Jamie noticed that most of the early arrivals were more interested in clustering around the edges of the field taking photos and videos of the two teams as they prepared for the match.

Every once in a while a sign caught her eye: "U-S-Eh"—a shout-out to Canadian pronunciation—was one of her favorites. A young girl clutched a handmade poster that read, "Hey FIFA: It's not about being beautiful. It's about how you play the beautiful game." Nearby, a bearded dude held up a sign that read, "I wish I could play like a girl!" But the best sign of all (in Jamie's opinion) was the one held by a cute gay girl that read, "Marry me, LATHAM, in ANY of the 50 states!"

Mostly, though, Jamie tried to ignore the crowd and focus on her warm-up. It was just another match, she told herself again, but this time her mind rebelled. No, it absolutely wasn't just another match. It was the World Cup final, and she had better bring it. The hope—the expectations—of an entire nation were upon them, as represented by the growing crowd of American-flag bedecked supporters. And yes, the USA would still love them if they lost; 2011 had proven that much. But if they could win, after failing to bring the trophy home for more than a decade and a half? Americans loved winners. It was in their cultural DNA.

But it wasn't just winning that the team's fans loved, Jamie knew. They appreciated effort and fearlessness, boldness and creativity. They admired the passion and dedication that the US women brought to the game. Jamie remembered how she'd felt as a kid, watching the '99ers lift the World Cup trophy at the Rose Bowl, how the joy at watching that group of women play soccer had buoyed her through the next few years. Had even, possibly, helped her heal from the assault in Lyon. She'd fallen in love with soccer before the 1999 World Cup. But watching the American team win? That had given her a high standard of play—the highest—to aspire to, a goal to set her sights on. How amazing if she could help provide that inspiration for even one of the many girls and women who would be watching this game today.

The thought of all the kids out there watching and waiting for something special from this match lifted Jamie's spirits even as the team's warm-up routine calmed her. As she focused on stretching her already loose limbs, she reminded herself of the quarterfinals, when she and Gabe had had to watch from the stands. Playing in this match was an absolute privilege. Like Britt, she could have been reduced to watching from the bench, if Jo and the coaches so chose. Or she might have gotten injured—AGAIN—and had to sit out the entire tournament. Instead, here she was getting ready to play in the single most important game of her life. And what was more? Emma would be with her on the field, fighting behind and beside her to win every 50-50 ball, to maintain possession, to press Japan when the ball turned over. To win a World Cup title, just like they'd dreamed about all those years ago in Pasadena when they didn't even know each other existed.

Definitely a privilege, she told herself as Mel blew the whistle and the team reconfigured in the usual pre-game keepaway groups. As they passed one another on the way to their separate groups, Emma caught her eye and smiled. Jamie smiled back. Her girlfriend, she was pretty sure, really was psychic.

#

Almost too soon they were filing off the field for a last bathroom break and a final check-in with the coaches. As they stood in their pre-game circle, arms around each other's waists and shoulders, Jo gazed at each of them and said, "All right, athletes. The moment we've all been working toward has arrived. You know what you need to do. The one thing I will tell you is to enjoy yourselves. Enjoy the match. Enjoy each other. Because moments like this come along once or twice in a lifetime. Grab it while you can. And play some fucking beautiful football, yeah?" The team laughed in response, giddy and keyed up, energy bouncing off the tiled walls around them. Jo glanced at Ellie and Phoebe. "Captains?"

Ellie said, her voice and eyes clear, "If we want to reach the top of the podium, guys, we have to believe. In ourselves, in each other, in our ability to bring this home. We just have to believe."

Phoebe added, "And fight. Fight for the ball, fight for each other, and then fight some more. I'll be behind you every step of the way."

Jamie gazed at the circle of women and a few men, at the players and coaches she'd basically lived with for the past five weeks, and drew in a deep breath, feeling tears prick her eyes. The emotion of the moment was almost too much, until Jenny said, "God damn it, you guys, I fucking love you all. Let's go win this motherfucker!"

So that, of course, became the team chant: "Let's go win this motherfucker!"

Jamie was pretty sure that wouldn't make US Soccer's web series.

And then the FIFA rep was knocking on the locker room door to tell them it was time, and the non-starters were leaving the room along with the coaching and training staff. Time seemed to spiral away out of control, and Jamie had barely caught her breath when the signal was given for the starters to leave the locker room. As they filed out into the hall, passing the line of coaches and support staff, Jamie's eyes caught Jo's. The head coach nodded at her as she clasped Jamie's hand, squeezing it warmly. Jamie nodded back, her spine straightening, her head clearing. Jo had called her not just a survivor but a warrior, one among many. And that, too, was why they were going to win: because they were a team of badass warriors, and they wouldn't accept anything less.

Boo-fucking-yah.

Jamie kept her shoulders back and her head lifted proudly as they filed out of the stadium, as they lined up for the anthems, as she took her final sideline sprints while the team captains met for the coin toss. No wonder Emma had such a good feeling about this game. The energy in the stadium was practically crackling. The turf was hotter than she would have liked and the air was a bit hazy from wildfires, but mostly all Jamie felt was STRONG. She was ready, damn it.

Which was a good thing, because it was time to get the show on the road.

"We won the coin toss," Ellie said as she jogged back into the huddle.

Another good sign, Jamie thought. Just like Germany.

"Did you get my end?" Phoebe demanded.

"Of course," Ellie said, grinning.

Phoebe fist-pumped, and the entire team whooped. The sun and shadows at one end of the stadium were ridiculously difficult. But the light would be in the Japanese keeper's eyes for the first 45, not Phoebe's.

"Nicely done, Elle," Jo said, holding Ellie's gaze for a second.

Ellie nodded at her, and then as the coaches retreated to the glass-covered bench, the players moved closer for the final pre-game huddle. Jamie found herself sandwiched between Emma and Britt, and leaned her head against Emma's strong back, waiting for Ellie to bestow her final words of wisdom.

"This is it, guys," Ellie said, raising her voice to be heard above the sound of the singing and chanting crowd. "This is our chance to take the trophy back. So let's get out there and fucking do this! Oosa on three. One, two, three, oosa-oosa-oosa-ah!"

Britt clobbered Jamie on the back as she headed toward the field. "Do it, James!"

Jamie nodded back at her, trying to keep her game face but unable to stop the grin that spread across her face as she caught her oldest soccer buddy's eye. And then she was sprinting out onto the field, past Emma and the rest of the defenders, past Angie who was smiling her own effervescent grin, past a grim-faced Maddie and an even more serious Jenny. She stopped in the center of the field and closed her eyes, turning in a half-circle. With her eyes closed, she could feel the waves of sound cascading from the stadium down to the field and back up again. It actually felt like a storm of sorts, buffeting her as she stood motionless, waiting for the most important game of her life to begin. Somewhere up there were her parents, her sister, and Todd; aunts and uncles and cousins from California and Colorado; old friends from Berkeley and newer ones from Stanford; and Shoshanna, the woman who had made it possible even more than her parents for her to be standing here on this pitch, getting ready to do battle with her sisters in arms.

Let's fucking do this, she thought as the referee's whistle sounded, and opened her eyes.

Since the US had chosen the end of the field they wanted, Japan kicked off. They ran the play the US scouts had identified as most likely, a long ball toward their right striker. But Ryan stepped up to intercept and sent a looping header into the air. Jamie beat her mark to the ball, turned, and sent an angled pass to Maddie, who carried the ball into Japan's defensive half before hitting Angie on the right flank. Angie dribbled forward and picked out Jenny with a superb through ball, and Jamie held her breath for a moment as Jenny stretched out—and deflected the ball to a Japanese defender, who cleared the ball nearly to the center circle.

Still, it was a good start. Angie had always been one of the most technically gifted players on their youth teams, and Jamie was psyched she was finally getting a chance to shine.

The ball fell to Taylor, who dribbled outside and hit Angie again up the line. Angie juked one defender, but a double team sent the ball trickling back to the Japanese centerback who cleared the ball once again directly into

Taylor's path. Taylor panicked and chucked the ball up the field, and Jamie paused as Kimura, the Japanese keeper, took possession. This was feeling a little bit like pinball, to be honest. But that too was a good sign—Jo had challenged them to start fast, and less than a minute into the game, they had already achieved that goal.

Kimura dribbled into her box and waved her team upfield, taking the opportunity to slow the pace that had so far favored the Americans. Only after Ellie pressured her did she pick up the ball and punt it into the US half. The ball once again careened around before Angie finally corralled an errant header and switched fields, sending it out to Gabe on the left flank. They worked the ball through the midfield, and eventually Jamie hit Taylor on the right sideline before sprinting into the box for a give and go. Taylor gave her the ball and she drove toward the endline, intending to pass it into the center. But before she could, two Japanese defenders collapsed to her, and her cross was deflected out—for a corner kick.

The crowd cheered, drums beating and voices chanting, and Jamie couldn't help grinning as she sent Taylor a thumbs-up. She could feel herself being swept into the energy pouring from the stands, but this time she didn't try to fight it. This time, she thought she just might use it to fuel her play.

Gabe took the corners on the right side of the field, so Jamie dropped into her spot on the six with several of her teammates, leaving the twelve open. She saw Gabe make eye contact with Ellie, who was standing ten yards outside the box, and knew that the corner they'd been practicing the past few days was on. Gabe lifted her hand, and out of the corner of her eye, Jamie saw Ellie streaking into the box just as Gabe sent the ball to the twelve on the ground. Before Japan could react, Ellie streaked from a patch of shade into the sunny penalty box and lunged, striking the ball perfectly in stride halfway between the penalty spot and the six-yard-box. Disbelieving, Jamie watched the ball shoot a thousand miles an hour into the net past Kimura's outstretched hand.

She had scored! Ellie had freaking scored—and, while she was at it, broken Marisol's World Cup scoring record. Not bad for the first two minutes of the match.

The cheers were practically deafening as Ellie, yelling all the way, sprinted toward the corner where the American Outlaws supporter group was sitting and leapt into the air, pumping her fist. When she landed, Gabe wrapped her up in a hug. Jamie and her teammates got there a moment later, and soon they were embracing in a dynamic, moving group hug.

"Fuck yeah!" Jenny shouted.

"I love you, man!" Angie yelled.

"Holy shit!" Jamie said, laughing.

"Ellie!" Emma called, and leapt into the fray.

The defenders had made it. The team hug was complete.

As Ellie extricated herself, she pulled Jamie toward her, hands on her shoulders, foreheads almost touching. "That happened because of you," she said, grinning. "You earned the corner. Way to go, Max."

Jamie stared up at the national team captain, barely breathing. Was this real life? Or just fantasy? Seriously, had Rachel Ellison, the all-time leading scorer in the world—men or women—just given her, Jamie Maxwell, partial credit for a goal in the World Cup final while 50,000 fans screamed and cheered around them?

Ellie just laughed at the look on her face and clapped her on the shoulder. "Let's go. There's still a lot of time left."

Jamie could only shake her head. Ellie had scored less

than three minutes into the World Cup final, and yet she was already thinking about the next play and the one after that. Probably that was how she'd become the leading scorer in history—by never resting on past accomplishments, even if those accomplishments were literally seconds old.

Emma slipped an arm around her neck as they followed their teammates back to their half. "Way to earn the corner, James."

"Thanks, Em."

They shared a smile, and it was the best moment between them Jamie could ever remember, even though they were surrounded by 50,000 strangers. She was happier in that moment, walking beside Emma back to the US side, than she'd ever been in her entire life, maybe even happier than she ever would be again. Ellie was right. There was a ton of time left. Most of the game, in fact. But this moment, this perfect, shining 60 seconds of life, was seriously the best ever.

Japan was already waiting at the center circle when the American players settled back into position. The crowd was still screaming, but Ellie was all business again, her game face even more intense after scoring. Jamie could imagine the FOX broadcasters covering the play: "And that's why she's the best finisher in the world. Her ability to focus is unparalleled."

And then the referee was blowing her whistle, and the game was back on.

The Japanese players hadn't given themselves time to settle back in, and Jamie thought it showed. They tried an odd little lofted ball down the center that Lisa easily headed down to Maddie. Maddie turned to her right, dribbled up field, and sent it outside to Angie, who surged forward, headed toward the endline. She quickly drew two defenders, but with a stutter step, managed to split them.

Except that the next minute she was going down and the referee had whistled the foul. Another set piece only a few feet outside the box.

Good thing they'd practiced set pieces.

"Jamie!"

She glanced over at the sidelines, and Jo was pointing at her. Then the coach flashed three fingers, and Jamie nodded.

The referee was spraying her magic line spray as Jamie jogged up. Heart pounding in her ears, Jamie waited until the ref was done to set the ball on the turf, rotating it backward half a spin the way she always did. Then she positioned her left foot beside the ball, took two and a half steps back on a slight angle, and waited.

It was only a free kick, and this was just another soccer game, she told herself. She'd played this sport her entire life, sacrificed for it, worked her butt off for it, traveled around the world and back to play it. This game had made her stronger than she'd ever thought she could be, had wrung emotions from her she would have preferred never to experience—loss and disappointment and failure—and given her the best moments of her life. Soccer had given her Britt and Angie and Lisa and Rebecca, Ellie and Maddie and even Phoebe Banks. Most of all, soccer had given her herself—and Emma. Because of this game, she had met the love of her life, lost her, and found her all over again.

While the referee lectured both teams in the center of the box, Jamie glanced back to where Emma and Lisa stood a quarter of the way down the field, waiting for the ball to pop out. As if she felt Jamie's gaze, Emma looked over. Their eyes caught and held, and then Emma gave her a small nod. *You got this.* Jamie nodded back. *I do.* And she did, because she had trained for this play in the Northern California rain, in the Southern California sun, in the

Florida humidity, in the London snow. She had practiced crosses with school teams, club teams, pro teams, and the national team. She had prepared for this game as much as any human being could, and now, yeah, she totally had this.

By the time the referee finally blew her whistle to resume play, Jamie's heartbeat had steadied, her breathing calmed. She took a long look at where everyone was lined up in the penalty box, lifted her arm, and struck the ball low toward the near post. Taylor faked one way and then moved to meet the ball, flicking it with her back heel toward the six the way they had practiced for what had felt like hours the previous day. Jamie, moving to get a better line of sight, gasped as the flick deflected off Taylor's defender and popped into the middle of the six yard box. Jenny narrowly missed it, but once again Ellie was in the right spot at the right time. She caught the ball on a half-volley and redirected it toward the corner. She had done it. She had actually scored again!

The ball had barely gone in when Ellie started sprinting toward the same exact corner as before, her finger raised on one hand, her face contorted in joy.

"Fuck, yeah!" Jamie shouted, and ran to meet her.

Ellie picked her up and spun her around. "Fuck, yeah!" she echoed. And then she all but thrust Jamie aside and kept running, less of a sprint this time and more of a purposeful run toward the US bench on the other side of the field. Jamie followed her, and so did Angie and Jenny and the rest of the starters. Adrenaline carried them across the field, and within seconds they were gathered on the sideline in a full team celebration. Even Phoebe was there, embracing Ellie and pounding her on the back. In the chaos, Emma hugged Jamie against her, laughing and shouting with the rest of the team. Jamie wasn't sure what anyone was saying, though. The sound of the madly cheering crowd was overpowering.

About that best moment ever? This one just might cancel it out.

While the Americans celebrated, Japan's starters gathered at the edge of the center circle for a team huddle. Jamie had no idea what they said, either, but whatever they did to refocus seemed to work. Within moments of kicking off, Japan's star midfielder Ichika Yamamoto had her first shot on goal. Phoebe corralled it easily, but the shot was a reminder that Japan wasn't going away. They were a world class team, and a two-goal lead could be lost as quickly as it had been gained.

Jamie settled in, tracking Yamamoto and positioning herself where she could best support Maddie's offensive runs while assisting the back line defensively. Over the next few minutes, Japan and the US traded possession. Every time the American players drove into their offensive end, the crowd roared as if a goal were imminent. Honestly, Jamie couldn't blame them. She sort of felt that way herself. Buoyed by the adrenaline borne of scoring twice in less than five minutes, she and her teammates kept up their high press, forcing turnover after turnover. But Japan had regained their composure and shut down each US foray. They were known for their patience in building out of the back, and in the twelfth minute, Japan created their best chance yet. But Phoebe again handled the dangerous cross easily, and then it was the US team's turn to build an attack.

Thirty seconds later, Ellie dumped a Japanese defender near their box, ending a promising chance. Japan took the free kick quickly and changed fields, working up their left flank. But at midfield, Jamie read the upcoming pass and stepped in front of Yamamoto to steal the ball back. Taylor immediately broke up the flank, and Jamie hit her on the run. Taylor took three touches and then crossed the ball toward the opposite side of the 18, aiming for a sprinting

Jenny. The cross wasn't quite high enough, though, and Jenny's defender had the inside angle on the ball. But the shadows from the Jumbotron on that section of the field were horrendous, and Jamie could see the defender struggling to find the ball in the sunlight. She tried to clear it away, but her header popped straight up in the air—and came down directly in Maddie's path. Maddie didn't wait for it to bounce, simply took the full volley on her laces and buried it past Kimura's outstretched hand.

Holy shit, Jamie thought, her grin impossibly wide as she stood, stunned, at the center of the field. What was this, even? They had scored AGAIN. The World Cup final wasn't even a quarter of an hour old, and somehow the US had already scored three times.

The crowd erupted as Maddie turned, her hands upraised triumphantly, and jogged toward the sideline, looking more stunned than anything. She slapped hands with Jenny and Ellie as she ran, and then Angie appeared in front of her and Maddie finally broke into a smile. She opened her arms and Angie jumped into them, practically knocking her over. They were laughing when Jamie reached them, and then the rest of the team crowded around to congratulate Maddie and bask in the unreality of being up 3-0 less than 14 minutes into the World Cup final.

The crowd was still cheering a minute and a half later when Japan tried another odd little flick in the mid third that Maddie knocked away, sending it into Ellie's path. Ellie touched the ball past her defender, took one look up the field, and launched the ball from the center line toward the Japanese goal. Because, you know, why the hell not? Kimura, who was playing well off her line sweeper-keeper style, back-pedaled furiously. But the lofted ball passed in and out of the Jumbotron's shadow, and Kimura seemed to lose it in the sunlight. At the last minute she appeared to recover, but then she slipped and stumbled on the turf, falling just as the ball reached her. Jamie couldn't believe it when Ellie's shot bounced off Kimura's fingertips, smacked against the inside of the goal post, and went in for goal number four.

Judging from her incredulous smile, Ellie couldn't believe it either as she ran back toward the American goal, shaking her head and pointing her fingers at the sky. The crowd's reaction was even louder than before, if possible, as Phoebe ran to meet her, crushing Ellie in her strong arms and shouting something Jamie couldn't hear. But she could guess. Ellie's ridiculous performance was almost guaranteeing that the co-captains, the two oldest players on the roster, would be standing on top of the podium in a little over an hour.

But again, there was a lot of time left, Jamie thought as they lined up for the fifth Japanese kickoff of the half. No need to get ahead of themselves. Or was there? Seriously, how could Japan come back from this?

"Keep pressing!" Jo yelled from the sideline. "Don't let down!"

They didn't. Less than a minute later, Ellie narrowly missed another goal with a header that went just wide. She might have a hat trick already, but she clearly had no intention of letting off the gas. Japan continued to try to slow down the pace of the game, to possess and build, but the American pressure made it difficult for them to execute the game plan that had made Japan one of the best teams in the world. Off a turnover, Jenny dribbled into the box, cut around two defenders, and rocketed a shot on goal, but Kimura made a big save. Jenny visibly expelled a frustrated breath before turning away, and Jamie couldn't help thinking that was pretty much how Jenny's entire World Cup had gone.

Japan wasn't letting off the gas, either. Their refusal to go away became obvious when a series of pinpoint passes culminated in a cross into the US box intended for Yamamoto. Taylor had waved Jamie off, so she was at the top of the box when the ball came in. She watched in alarm as Taylor dove for the cross—and missed. Before Jamie could track back, Yamamoto turned and coolly fired the ball past Phoebe.

FUCK. That was why defenders were told to stay on their feet—you couldn't defend from the ground. The one thing they had to do was not let Japan back into the game. Instead, they'd given up their first goal since the opening match against Australia. More than five hundred minutes of accumulated shutout time down the drain, just like that.

Jamie was too pissed to console an obviously distraught Taylor, but Emma and Lisa picked her up and dusted her off while Jamie brought the ball up to Ellie.

"We're fine," Ellie told her. "We just need to keep pushing forward."

Jamie nodded. "Let's go."

They didn't go. Japan had finally found their form, and two minutes later, they created another strong chance inside the US box. Fortunately, Phoebe shut this one down. The US got their own chance a few minutes later, and the end-to-end nature of the game continued. It felt more like a 0-0 match than a blowout, Jamie thought when Gabe was called for a ticky tack foul shortly after Ellie had been dumped on a no-call, and turned to practically shout at the ref. The fans booed and whistled too, and then broke into a "U-S-A" chant. Despite the score, everyone was still into the match.

The intensity remained right up until halftime. When the whistle blew, the Japanese players jogged off the field as if they weren't actually down by three. Jamie followed her teammates toward the tunnel, scanning the crowd as she went. A sign caught her eye as she left the stadium—"The USA Strikes Back." Sounded about right. But she pushed down the giddiness trying to hijack her brain. There was still an entire half to be played, and if the US could score four goals in a half, Japan probably could, too. At least, in theory.

Britt caught up to her in the tunnel and slung an arm around her neck. "Holy goals, Batman! Can you believe this?"

Angie burrowed between them. "Oh my god, right?"

Jamie allowed herself a grin and a vehement, "Hells yeah!" They were up 4-1 at halftime of the World Cup. Surely they could celebrate a little, couldn't they?

In the locker room, a couple of other players were laughing and joking, too, until Phoebe slammed her gloved hand into a locker with a resounding metallic thunk.

Beside her, Ellie leveled a glare at the room. "This game is not over," she said into the sudden silence. "There are forty-five more minutes to play, and Japan's not going anywhere. Let's focus, okay?"

"Okay, athletes," Jo said, picking up from Ellie. "As your captains have noted, we have forty-five more minutes to play, and Japan is a quality side—as I think some of you recall more than others."

At this, Jamie saw Maddie, Ellie, Phoebe, Emma, and a few other veterans grimace. No doubt they were remembering the previous World Cup final when Japan had come back again and again only to win on penalties.

"So let's talk," Jo continued. "First on the list of what's working is the way we started. Four goals in the first half of a World Cup final ain't half bad, my friends. The same goes for your hat trick, Ellie." She nodded as Maddie whistled shrilly with her fingers and Ellie just shook her head. "Everyone out there took their performance against Germany and improved on it, just as we challenged you to do. At least, at the outset. That brings me to what isn't working. Midway through the half, we lost momentum and stopped pressing. In the second half, we need to regain our shape and work on transitioning with numbers."

Jo turned to the whiteboard and used the player magnets to talk tactics for the next few minutes, stressing the changes Japan had made to their line-up thirty minutes in and the more offensive shape the substitutions had given them. Then she turned back to the players and paused, looking around the room.

"This tournament is inherently a challenge in and of itself. We've traveled thousands of miles to play seven games in a little over a month—on *turf*—while our critics found fault with every little thing, as if they expect us to be perfect. Well, perfection is not real life. But you? You are real, and you have risen above the challenges we've faced every step of the way. Today is the culmination of everything we've been working for. Your final challenge in this World Cup is to stay focused in the second half and bring us home." She glanced around the room. "What do you say, athletes? Think you can do that?"

"Yes!" the players chorused. *Hell yes.*

Jo nodded. "Good. Then get back out there as soon as you're ready. We have forty-five more minutes left in this World Cup. Let's make every one of them count."

Jamie used the restroom and headed back out the tunnel, visualizing herself defending beautifully, passing precisely, and even scoring. Emma had walked out before her and was chatting with Mel on the sideline when Jamie got there.

"Hey, Blake. Wanna pass?" Jamie asked, half-smiling at her.

Emma smiled back. "Absolutely. Just give me a sec."

Jamie grabbed a ball and juggled until Emma joined her. Then they passed the ball wordlessly, back and forth one-touch, the rhythm and familiarity settling Jamie's second half butterflies.

"Remember the first time we ever did this?" Emma asked.

Jamie looked up at her, one foot on the ball. The first time they'd trained together had been in Seattle the week after Emma's dad died. Her extended family had come for the funeral, as had Jamie, and one morning Emma had asked if they could run away. They couldn't, of course, so instead they'd gone for a run and kicked a ball around.

"Did you think then that we'd end up here?" Jamie asked, holding Emma's gaze.

"No," Emma said, and then added before Jamie could respond, "I *knew* we would." And she winked.

Sassy Emma was so hot, Jamie thought, laughing.

CHAPTER SEVENTEEN

Jamie jumped in place, waiting for the fourth official to send in the signal. Finally, the head referee blew her whistle, and the second half was on.

The US kicked off. Almost immediately they found themselves with a chance on goal as Taylor sent a long ball to Ellie and she nearly scored again from a crazy angle. Obviously they were taking Jo's message to heart.

Off the goal kick, Jenny and Gabe combined to create another chance, this time for Maddie. But the Japanese defenders smothered the cross and tried to build up. The American side kept pressing high, though, and soon they'd earned another chance. Kimura made the save, but Japan was scrambling. They'd come out on their heels, or maybe it was just that the US was starting the second half the way they'd begun the first. There wasn't anything Japan could do but try to survive and wait for the momentum to shift.

Four minutes in, Jamie saw her first real chance of the game. She and Angie did a give and go on the right flank, with Jamie overlapping on the inside, when Ellie cheated over. Jamie saw her coming and sent a through ball to the corner. Ellie caught up to it just before it went out. She could have crossed the ball in, but instead she turned toward goal and took on the nearest defender. Because when you had already scored a hat trick, why not try for more. She stutter stepped and executed a perfect scissor fake past the frozen defender, only to be met by a double team. Changing directions, she dribbled toward the corner of the eighteen and squared up for a shot. At the last second, she touched the ball with the outside of her foot back toward where Jamie was waiting at the top of the box.

It was a perfectly weighted pass, smooth and slow enough that Jamie had plenty of time to set up. The sounds in the stadium faded away, and her vision narrowed to the oncoming ball. She wound up and struck the center of the ball with the laces of her left boot, feeling the solidness of the strike resonate satisfyingly throughout her body. She watched, hardly breathing, as the ball lifted over the nearest defender, headed unerringly for the upper corner of the goal. At the last minute, Kimura leapt and managed to get one hand up in time to knock the ball up and over the crossbar.

"Ahh!" Jamie groaned to herself, holding her hands to her head. But she was smiling because that shot had felt awesome, and she was pretty sure she had more where it came from.

Ellie slapped her on the shoulder. "Keep 'em coming, kid."

If she did manage to score in the World Cup, would everyone please stop calling her *kid*? Yeah, probably not.

Momentum could be fickle, though, and a game could hinge on a single play—if you let it. A minute and a half later, Taylor O'Brien dumped one of the Japanese strikers in the US defensive third, giving Japan their first dangerous set piece of the half. The defense held the line at the eighteen, where the shadow from the Jumbotron meant Phoebe was looking directly into the sunlight. Jamie glued herself to Yamamoto. The hell if she was giving up her mark again. Taylor didn't argue, just found another Japanese player to mark.

Later, Jamie wondered what would have happened if she had let Taylor take Yamamoto. The younger woman would have been in an entirely different position in the box, and maybe then she wouldn't have leapt to head the inswinging ball out and instead flicked it into her own goal. But either way, what was done was done, and though Phoebe and Emma both scrambled to block the mishit, the ball trickled into the side netting anyway. Taylor, who the press had deemed the breakout star of the Cup, had just scored an own goal.

Yamamoto all but wrestled the ball away from Phoebe, and the Japanese team ran back to the center circle to force a quick restart. They were only down two with forty minutes to go. Jamie doubted she was the only one thinking the once unthinkable: Japan might just be able to pull themselves back.

The thing about momentum is that once you've had it, you can always find it again, even if you think you've lost it for good.

As soon as the US kicked off, Ellie was a blur of motion, driving forward into the center of the Japanese defense and pulling her teammates with her. Jamie followed willingly, and soon an overlapping Ryan was in the box earning a US corner kick. They hadn't sat back after the goal. Rather they were continuing to move forward, to press whatever advantage they could find.

Maddie wanted the corner, so Jamie let her have it and set up instead on the six. She was glad she did because Maddie's left-footed inswinger very nearly scored. Kimura just got a hand on it and deflected it wide, directly into Angie's path on the corner of the six. Angie one-touched the ball across the goal mouth to where Jamie, absurdly, found herself completely unmarked. She didn't even have time to think. She simply stuck out her near foot and redirected the ball into the back of the net. FOR A GOAL. HER GOAL.

The ball had barely crossed the goal line when Jamie leapt into the air with an inarticulate yell and an Ellie-style fist pump. She had scored in the World Cup final. SHE HAD SCORED IN THE WORLD CUP FINAL.

Angie rushed at her, grinning. "Dude!" she screamed. "You fucking scored!"

Normally Jamie would have been offended by the surprise in her friend's voice, but now she only clutched the smaller woman's shoulders and shouted, "Dude, you fucking assisted!"

Then they laughed and hugged and got swept up into Ellie's arms as the captain shouted unintelligibly. Soon they were surrounded by the rest of their teammates, including Maddie who dropped a kiss on both of their heads.

"I fucking love you guys," she said, her voice tight with emotion.

Jamie fucking loved everyone at that moment, especially Emma who was staring at her with tears in her eyes, her smile even wider and happier now, if that was even possible.

"Now we just have to get you a goal," Jamie told her as they jogged back to their end, the stadium literally shaking around them in raucous celebration.

"That's okay," Emma said. But she was grinning too.

The game continued with more of the same frantic end-to-end play with multiple chances at both ends. The Americans kept up their pressure, though, and Ellie in particular seemed like she was everywhere on the field. Phoebe stood confidently against the Japanese attack despite the sun in her eyes, and Emma and Lisa were as stalwart as they had been all tournament.

In the sixtieth minute, Jo subbed Taylor out, replacing her with Emily Shorter's fresh legs. Honestly, Jamie felt better having the veteran defender behind her because while they didn't need to score again, they definitely had to make sure Japan didn't find the net. And their best way of doing that was to press and probe, cross and shoot, the same strategy that had brought them this far.

Jenny nearly scored on a cross from Angie in the sixty-third minute, but missed wide. Ellie and Yamamoto exchanged a series of fouls in the sixty-fifth and seventieth minutes, as if neither superstar wanted to be outdone by the other. But the fouls were the result of hard play, not dirty conduct, and each player helped the other up after the call in a show of obvious respect.

Jamie kept checking the clock, elated each time to find that they were four or five minutes closer to the end of the match, when they would lift the troph—*Focus, damn it. Finish the match.*

Japan continued to possess and press, but down by three this late in the game, most of their shots smacked of desperation. Time was winding down, and everyone could feel it. Even the crowd seemed to be holding its breath between chants of "U-S-A" and the newly reworded, "I believe that we have won."

Japan never gave up, Jamie had to give them that. They forced the American side to play all the way to the end, even winning a corner in extra time as the players and coaches on the US bench stood shoulder to shoulder, arms wrapped around each other's waists, waiting for time to run out. But Phoebe and the defense shut down any and every challenge from the Japanese offense, and it was as if, Jamie thought, the American side could do no wrong. As if some sort of magic had found its way inside them and now it refused to let them lose.

Refuse to lose. Exactly.

When injury time ran out at last and the referee finally—FINALLY—blew her whistle, those three shrill, beautiful tweets barely audible over the cries of the crowd, Jamie leapt into the air and looked around for Emma. Her girlfriend was mid-hug with Lisa, but she was looking at Jamie over her fellow defender's shoulder.

"We fucking won the World Cup, man!" Angie shouted, her arm forming a near choke hold around Jamie's neck.

"I know! We fucking rock!" Jamie replied, smiling so hard her face muscles ached.

And then the bench was emptying and the players and coaches were meeting in an almost scrum at the center of the field, hugging and laughing in pairs and small groups while the crowd roared and photographers and videographers captured every move. Britt practically tackled Angie and Jamie, and then Lisa and Rebecca were there too, and the longtime friends were hugging each other and yelling almost unintelligibly about the incredible perfect awesomeness of this day.

Nearby, Jo stopped in front of Ellie and held her at arm's length for a moment, and then they hugged and Jamie heard the coach say, "I am so fucking proud of you, Ellison!"

Ellie closed her eyes and held tight to the coach, and Jamie thought she knew exactly how she felt.

Then Jo moved on to her, and they smiled at each other before sharing an exuberant hug. "Way to go, warrior," Jo said in her ear. "I knew you could do it."

"Thanks, Coach," Jamie said, her giddiness only enhanced by the tears pricking her eyes.

When they found their way to each other, Emma grabbed Jamie in a tight hug and lifted her off the ground, spinning her around until she squealed in laughing protest. Then Emma set her down and smiled into her eyes.

"I love you," she said, not even trying to hide her emotions.

"I love you, too," Jamie said, and swept her into another hug.

Someone draped an American flag around their shoulders, and Jamie could see flashes going off against her closed eyelids, could hear the chanting of the crowd and the sounds of the American Outlaws drums. But as she held Emma close against her, all she could think was, *FINALLY*. They had finally made it to this place and time, and it was even more wonderful than she ever could have dreamt.

The moment was interrupted when she felt an elbow in her side and opened her eyes to see Angie and Britt both pointing toward the corner of the field. Jamie turned Emma slightly, and they both watched, smiling hugely, as Ellie stood on her tiptoes to reach Jodie, who was dangling over the side of the stands. Jodie's arms came around Ellie's head, and as the whole stadium watched on the live feed from the Jumbotron, Ellie kissed her wife proudly, passionately, happily. Because not only had they won the World Cup, but gay marriage was legal in the entirety of America.

A moment later, Phoebe leapt into the stands to kiss her husband, but in a move that seemed entirely fitting, the cameras panned away from them to focus back on Ellie and Jodie.

"Dudes, let's go," Angie said from behind Jamie.

She glanced back to see Angie holding up an American flag and gesturing to her and Britt. What else could she do? She grabbed one corner and joined her oldest friends on the team in a victory lap, smiling and waving as the fans cheered them on. She could hardly believe this was real, and yet, at the same moment, it was so real her heart hurt.

World Cup champions, oh my.

Their circuit brought them back to the family section in the corner behind the US bench, and as they stood in front of the packed stands, Jamie scanned the rows for her parents and Meg and Todd. Wait—there they were, her mom and dad and sister and brother-in-law, smiling and waving down at her, eyes alight with love and pride. Beside them were the Professors Thompson with Becca and Rhea, out on their first baby-free date, also waving enthusiastically. Jamie waved back and blew them all kisses, and then Emma was beside her and they were waving at her mom and Tyler and Bridget, and Emma was smiling but...

"You okay?" Jamie asked.

"Fine," Emma said.

Jamie could tell she wasn't, but Ellie picked that moment to lift her into the air from behind, and Jamie couldn't exactly tell an American treasure to put her down, could she? By the time Ellie had moved on and Jamie refocused on her girlfriend, Emma's eyes had cleared.

"Come on," Emma said, nodding toward the rest of the team. "Official ceremony first, family selfies on the field later."

Family selfies on the field? Jamie hadn't even known that was a thing.

#

Later, after the two teams had shaken hands and the portable stage had been wheeled out onto the field, after the fans had booed the procession of FIFA officials and Jamie had barely held back an unprofessional smirk, after Phoebe had received her Golden Glove award, Ellie had been given both the Golden Boot *and* Golden Ball awards, and Japan had claimed their runners-up medals, Jamie followed her teammates up the stairs and onto the stage. This was the hardest part of winning any tournament, she knew from previous experience: slogging through the official awards ceremony when all you wanted to do was celebrate your ass off. But this time, Rob Muñoz, US Soccer's president, was standing there waiting to drape the gold medal around her neck. This time, the most coveted trophy in the game was sitting on a table off-center stage just waiting for the American players.

Time dragged just as it had throughout the second half, until, at last, Ellie and Phoebe grinned at each other and lifted the trophy high into the air while gold ticker tape drifted around them and the crowd, which had slogged through the ceremony themselves, roared in approval and chanted, once again, "U-S-A! U-S-A! U-S-A!" The day was complete, and as she danced around the stage with Angie and Britt, flashes going off all around them, Jamie forgot about the incompetence of FIFA. She forgot about the raspberries that still stung her legs. She forgot about the exhaustion of traveling thousands of miles in a little over a month. She forgot her bruises and sore muscles and sunburn, and simply cheered herself hoarse.

When it came, she took her turn with the golden trophy, smiling sheepishly as she pressed her lips to the cool, smooth metal. There were individual kisses and group kisses, and even pairs—Maddie and Angie, Emma and Jamie, and Gabe and Rebecca, as well as BFFs like Ellie and Phoebe, Emma and Maddie, and Jamie, Angie, and Britt. Finally, the team clomped down from the stage to pose en masse before a banner that read, "World Cup Champions!" Those images, Jamie knew, would decorate posters licensed by US Soccer and sold in limited editions across the country to diehard USWNT fans.

This part of the celebration felt staged—literally—not to mention cliché-ish, but Jamie went through the motions anyway, feeling slightly surreal as she took her place in the relatively short line of athletes who had lifted this particular trophy in victory. The US had just become the only women's team in history to win the World Cup three times. Germany was next with two, and Japan and Norway each had a single title to their name. Jamie smiled harder as she remembered that this win combined with their defeat of Germany in the semis meant they were also back on top of the international rankings. The US was number one in the world again—first in FIFA's rankings *and* official champions of the world.

Nice.

Ceremony complete, it was finally time to start the real party. As non-VIP fans filtered out of the stadium, players' families came down to the field. As did a few others—the American Vice President and his family, for one. And—Jamie tried not to gasp as she turned around and came face to face with her childhood hero: *Mia Hamm.*

"Hey, Jamie," Mia said, smiling at her and holding up her palm. "Great game today."

"Um, thanks," Jamie blurted as she gave Mia Hamm—*Mia freaking Hamm*—a high five.

"Your goal was the nail in the coffin," Mia continued, seemingly unperturbed by Jamie's fish mouth impression. "When you came right back after that second goal and scored on that combination with Wang—"

"It's Wang," Jamie interrupted, correcting—*oh shit*—Mia Hamm's incorrect pronunciation. "Rhymes with wrong, because she usually is, ha ha." She said the last bit almost desperately, her grin a tad manic.

"Oh, sorry. *Wang.* Anyway," Mia went on, her smile relaxed, "that was the moment I knew without a doubt you guys would win."

"Really? I mean, thanks, Mia. Can I call you Mia? Is that okay?" Vaguely, Jamie was aware of Angie and Britt snickering in the background, but she ignored them. After all, Mia Hamm had sought her out, not them. Suck on that, losers.

"Actually, it's Miss Hamm," Mia said, and then burst into laughter and clapped Jamie on the shoulder. "Kidding. Ellie told me to keep an eye out for you. Obviously, she was right." And she winked and moved on to congratulate Angie and Britt.

Jamie made faces at them over the soccer legend's

shoulder because, yes, she was that mature. She couldn't help that meeting a *genuine soccer goddess* turned her into a fourteen-year-old stuttering mess. Surely that was only natural.

A little while later, when the stands were almost empty and even the field was beginning to clear, Jamie found Emma standing near the US bench, fingering her gold medal.

"Ready to go crack some champagne?" Jamie asked. But when Emma looked up at her, the slightly bruised look from earlier was back. "What's wrong? Did something happen?"

Emma shook her head, glancing down at the confetti-strewn turf. "No, of course not. I'm just being ridiculous." As she blinked rapidly, Jamie could see tears glistening on her eyelashes. Plenty of other players had been crying in the last half hour, but Jamie could tell Emma's tears weren't the happy kind.

"I doubt that," she said, one hand on Emma's shoulder.

Emma didn't reply, though, simply kept staring down as her fingers worried the World Cup medal.

"Are you hurt?" Jamie asked. "Did you get hit in the head? Seriously, how many fingers am I holding up?"

But her exaggerated concern didn't get the eye-roll she expected. Instead, Emma looked up at her, gray-green eyes awash in tears, and said, "I wish my dad were here."

So that was it. Jamie sighed and tugged Emma into her arms, kissing her brow gently. "Of course you do. I'm so sorry he isn't, Em."

Emma pressed her face against Jamie's shoulder and said, her voice muffled, "My entire life has been leading up to this moment. And now that I'm here and he isn't, I don't know what to do next. What do I do next, Jamie?"

"You celebrate," Jamie said, pulling away to peer at

her. "Just like you would do if he really was here."

Emma gazed up at her, eyes so full of pain Jamie almost forgot they'd just won the World Cup. "Really? Just like that?"

She nodded. "Just like that. Only, make sure you keep him in your heart while you do. He's always in there, isn't he?"

Emma nodded, her eyes clearing a little. "Yeah. I guess so."

"Good."

"Good," Emma echoed. She lifted her hand and touched Jamie's cheek. "You're amazing, you know that?"

She winked jauntily. "That's what Mia Hamm said, too."

Emma rolled her eyes. "Gee, how did I get so lucky?"

"Pretty sure I'm the lucky one."

"Are you guys talking about getting lucky tonight?" Angie asked as she passed by on her way to the tunnel. "Because hells yes!"

"Fuck off," Jamie said, laughing, and then, as Angie waggled her eyebrows, added, "I know, that's what she said."

In the locker room, bottles of champagne were passed around along with the instructions that they were only allowed to spray them in one corner where some enterprising staff member had erected a plastic barrier, which elicited snorts of derision from the team.

"What the hell?" Angie said, rolling her eyes. And then she promptly shook a bottle of bubbly and popped its cork in the designated champagne-spraying zone. "We're world champions, baby!"

Soon they were all drinking and dancing to the brand new post-game cool-down playlist that Jenny had mixed the night before when she couldn't sleep. Even Jamie took a few gulps of champagne, ignoring Angie's hoot of approval. You only won the World Cup once. Or maybe twice, if you were lucky.

Squad goals, for real.

Caroline, the PR rep, wanted photos for the USWNT twitter account before they stripped out of their uniforms, so they obliged, raising their champagne bottles and shouting for the picture. Emma knelt near the front, tears apparently forgotten as she flexed her impressive biceps for the camera, while Britt had one arm around Jamie and the other around Angie. For a moment, it was as if Jamie was outside of herself, seeing the group as Caroline might, sweaty and bubbly and freaking HAPPY.

Winning felt fucking good. No, scratch that. It felt incredible. And it wasn't just because as an American, winning was in her DNA. It was that she had stood shoulder to shoulder with this amazing group of women and shown that when it counted, they could rise above. They could do anything, she thought as she cheered for the federation's official photo.

The freaking incompetents at FIFA had better look out. That much was certain.

CHAPTER EIGHTEEN

Jamie opened the door and peeked inside. *Wow*. The Sheraton Wall Centre didn't mess around.

"Let me see," Emma said, ducking around Jamie to enter the suite only to stop short just inside the entryway. "Damn, this is gorgeous. Too bad we have to be downstairs in like three hours."

"No kidding." Jamie let the door fall shut behind them.

At their post-game dinner, Emma's mom had handed them key cards and said with a smile, "Congratulations, girls. I thought you might want some privacy later."

Privacy was a bit of an understatement, Jamie thought now. Emma's mom had rented out a suite near the top of the team hotel, complete with a sunken living room, a kitchenette, and floor to ceiling windows on one side of the room. A door across the living space led into a bedroom that appeared to have more huge windows and a king-sized bed. With thick ivory wall-to-wall carpeting and high ceilings, the space felt larger even than Jamie's new apartment—if she was remembering her apartment correctly. She hadn't been there in a while.

As Emma took a seat on the living room couch, Jamie went to the window and looked down at the avenue far below where earlier that day they had walked among a sea of fans to their waiting bus. That walk felt like days ago, given how much had happened in the hours since. Now, at three in the morning, the area was finally empty. She wondered how long the fans had celebrated outside the hotel. They had (still? again?) been out in force when the team returned from BC Place. Which, even dinner seemed like a million years ago now.

"Come away from there," Emma said, shuddering slightly.

Jamie didn't tease her for her fear of heights. She simply joined her on the couch, settling in beside her and immediately tugging Emma closer. It was nice to be able to touch her at last. No more team time now—at least, for a few hours. In the morning, the media whirlwind would begin. Angie would probably still be drunk, and she wouldn't be the only one, either.

It had been quite the celebration. First had been the ride from the stadium back to the hotel, with Queen's "We are the Champions" blasting on the bus speakers and everyone standing in the center aisle singing along with the most famous victory anthem of the past four decades, still champagne soaked and wrapped in American flags. Their meal room had been set up and waiting, their family members already more than halfway through yet another buffet-style celebratory meal. Only this time, the team hadn't been restricted to only one drink. The beer, wine, and champagne had flowed until Jamie couldn't distinguish between the champagne bubbles and the pure happiness bursting through her bloodstream.

Surprisingly, the speeches had been kept to a minimum, but Ellie had finally given in to the insistent sound of spoons clinking against glasses and risen, holding up her beer bottle in a mock salute.

"We are the champions, my friends, and we'll keep on fighting 'til the end," she had said in a serious, pedantic tone. As boos and whistles mixed with laughter, she'd smiled. "No, seriously, you guys, I'm standing here and it's still all just sinking in. Every single member of this team started this journey with a dream when we were little kids. Each of us managed somehow to hold on to that dream, to our belief in ourselves and, eventually, in each other, to get to this moment. And here we are, tonight, literal champions of the world."

She shook her head and smiled even wider, if possible, as the cheers and whoops echoed through the huge room. "It's dizzying, you guys, I'm serious. Or maybe that's just the smoke. I feel like there's a metaphor in there somewhere, something about how we were on fire today while actual wildfires blazed not that far away. Anyway, that's probably the booze talking. Speaking of booze…" She lifted her bottle of beer again. "To the most amazing group of badass women I've ever known—and that's saying something. Thank you for making my dreams come true. I love you all."

Jo had spoken too, and Phoebe at much prodding, but Ellie's was the only speech that brought actual tears to Jamie's eyes. Probably that had been the booze talking, too.

In truth, she hadn't had that much to drink. Alcohol and she had never gotten along well, and she'd had no interest in turning the best night of her life into a blurry, nauseating mess. The party had lasted for hours upon hours, so a few drinks spread out across multiple venues had kept her smack dab in the pleasantly tipsy zone.

After dinner, they'd finally had a chance to shower and get ready for the official US Soccer party at the Commodore Ballroom, an event space that was only a few blocks from the hotel. Under strict orders not to carry open containers or otherwise embarrass the federation, players made their way to the bar in small groups only to find their friends and family members already there, dancing to tunes served up by the DJ the federation had hired for the #FanHQ outreach program.

As soon as the entire team had assembled, they'd taken to the stage and Ellie had voiced their thanks to everyone who had helped get them there. A few other people had spoken, including Jo and a couple of federation officials, and then they'd danced. And danced. And danced some more. Each time Jamie had started to feel tired, she would remember the sensation of scoring; or of running around the stadium with Angie and Britt, carrying the flag between them; or of shaking hands with the Vice President and Mia Hamm, who KNEW HER NAME. And then a fresh wave of adrenaline would wash over her and she would shake her booty and laugh even more.

At one point, Angie had complained, "Jesus, you guys, this is like my high school's all-night graduation bash. You know US Soccer only wants us here so we don't go out and do something stupid."

Jamie hadn't actually seen anything wrong with that plan, either at the secondary school level or here in Vancouver. The Commodore was close enough to the hotel that there wasn't much chance for inebriated team members to get in trouble. Not that a lack of opportunity had ever stopped Jenny Latham.

Britt, glued at the hip to Allie, her permanently smiling girlfriend, had shrugged. "Yeah, but this party has large quantities of alcohol, so the comparison can't be entirely accurate. Then again, it is Jersey we're talking about…"

Ignoring the jab at her home state, Angie had suddenly switched gears—also the booze talking, Jamie suspected. "I mean, I guess it doesn't matter if Big Brother is watching. We won the freaking World Cup, and now we get to celebrate with all of these beautiful, amazing people?" She shook her head. "Enough said, man. Totally enough said."

Jamie had known what she meant. The sheer number of friends and family present at the game and at the party afterward had been incredible. In addition to Jamie and Emma's immediate family, they'd both had aunts, uncles, and cousins in Vancouver for both the game and the after party. Dani and Derek had made the trip up from Seattle, and stayed at the Commodore to celebrate the win almost as long as the team did. Becca and Rhea had put in a few hours as well, simultaneously relieved to be away from the twins and also mildly weepy despite the extended post-game snuggle fest they'd enjoyed with their babies during dinner. Jamie was actually surprised the two moms had made it out twice in one day, but Rhea was the youngest of three, and her parents were experienced grand-babysitters.

"Besides," Becca had said as she leaned against a pub table with her wife, "this party is once in a lifetime shit. Unless you win it next time, of course."

"I hope watching you cry into your beer while your babies sleep peacefully three blocks away is once in a lifetime, too," Meg had said teasingly.

"Whatever," Becca had replied. "It's the love hormone, okay? Just wait until you and Todd pop out a baby or two."

Rhea had started laughing at that. "Um, I don't think Todd will be doing the popping, sweets."

Becca had only pulled her wife in close, their smiles competing with those of the players around them.

The love hormone—that would be the perfect name for a club, Jamie had thought later, spinning around and around with her friends and family, love and victory heavy on the air. This was what her and Emma's wedding reception would be like, wouldn't it? Except without the One Nation One Team banner hanging behind the stage.

And without the federation brass, one would hope.

The memory lingered now as Jamie sat beside Emma on the couch, her ears still ringing from the dance music, her fingers toying idly with Emma's hair. "So you were serious in London when you said you wanted to get married, right?"

Emma didn't move for a long moment. "What?"

"Someday," Jamie added quickly, realizing how her middle-of-the-night curiosity had phrased itself. "I mean, the whole marriage and kids thing is still where you see yourself headed, right?"

"It is," Emma said, her voice calm and steady. "What about you?"

"Yeah. Definitely."

"Good."

"Good," she echoed, tracing the back of Emma's hand. "Can I ask you something?" As Emma's gaze shot to her, she added, "No, not—I meant about your dad."

"Oh." Emma nodded, her head falling back against the couch. "Go ahead."

"I just wondered if you felt like he was with you tonight."

Emma shrugged. "You know I don't actually believe in things like that."

"You're the one who talks about being psychic."

"Well, yeah," Emma said, "but I feel like that could be explained by science. We only use ten percent of our brains, as far as we know, so being psychic could easily be part of the other ninety percent. But my dad somehow being here after all these years? That, I can't see, no matter how much I might wish it were true."

"Okay," Jamie said, "I get that. So you didn't feel like he was physically present, but did you still think about him tonight?"

"Yeah," Emma admitted, her eyes on their linked hands. "Of course. There was this one moment when we were up on stage cheering and being all rowdy, and I looked over and saw my mom sipping her glass of champagne and smiling, and it was like all of a sudden I could totally picture my dad there with her. It felt almost like a memory that my brain didn't know wasn't real. Does that make sense?"

Jamie nodded. She had shared an article once with Emma about how when a person relives a memory, their brain experiences the event as if it's actually happening all over again in the present. That was why false memories could be so difficult to counter. The human brain, it turned out, could be truly terrible at distinguishing between reality and fantasy.

"You always make sense," Jamie said, leaning into Emma. "Well, usually, anyway. I mean, you are a United fan, and there's obviously no rational reason for that."

"Ha ha," Emma said, smiling sleepily. She tilted her head, allowing her temple to rest against Jamie's. "He would have been happy about all of this."

About their World Cup win? Or about their relationship? Jamie wasn't sure. Just as she started to ask, a huge yawn overtook her, and then her eyes desperately needed a break from the light; only a moment's rest, you see...

An indeterminate amount of time later, she jerked awake at the sound of someone snoring. Was it her or Emma?

Beside her, Emma laughed softly. Then she leaned in and kissed Jamie's cheek before tugging on her hand. "Come on, my little World Cup champion. Time for bed."

They should have sex after winning the World Cup, shouldn't they? Jamie was sure they should. Like, screw team time literally, heh heh. But she had barely enough energy to brush her teeth and set aside her gold medal—which she, like everyone else on the team, had been wearing all night—before falling into the soft as a cloud bed. She was still dressed in her Carhart's and a tank top Jodie had given her emblazoned with the word "TOMBOY," despite her luggage stowed by some unknown helper in the corner by the window, and honestly? She was fine with that.

Emma snuggled up next to her and turned out the bedside lamp. In the dark, she said, her voice low, "Thanks, Jamie."

"For what?" she asked, yawning.

"For being here with me."

"My pleasure," Jamie said, wishing once again that she had enough energy to make up for the weeks of federation-enforced abstinence. She reached under Emma's shirt, fingers brushing against her warm skin, and then her hand drifted to her girlfriend's hip where she knew Emma had inked a spiral sun compass into her skin as a tribute to her father—and to Jamie, too. Her thumb rubbed gently at the unseen tattoo, and she felt rather than heard Emma sigh. A moment later, Emma's fingers were warm against Jamie's bicep, tracing her Sanskrit tattoo in the dark.

"Someone has to look after you," Jamie said a little belatedly, smiling as she heard the amused huff of air escape Emma's lips.

"More like I'll be looking after you," her girlfriend said. "I'm serious, Jamie, we're in the eye of the hurricane right now. The media whirlwind was crazy after we lost in 2011. Now that we've won?" She shook her head, hair brushing against Jamie's bare shoulder. "I can't even imagine."

Jamie couldn't, either. It was hard to process that she would be one of the players being pursued by the press the way Angie had been all week after her goal against

Germany. Then again, Ellie had scored a *hat trick* against Japan. It was possible no one would even notice Maddie and Jamie's goals.

Except, nah. That didn't really seem like a thing.

In the quiet hotel room, with the lights of Vancouver sparkling outside seemingly close enough to touch, it was difficult to picture the craziness Emma swore—and Jamie believed—was coming. But she knew this moment would pass quickly, and they would be joining the rest of the team in a matter of hours to get their hair and make-up done before going on FOX Sports to receive their new three-star national team kits. After their appearance at the Fox Sports pavilion on the Vancouver waterfront, it was back to LA for a fan rally and celebration at Staples Center. Jamie had even heard rumors of a ticker tape parade in New York City—the first ever for a women's sports team—and an extended victory tour, so already their post-Canada schedule was shaping up to be a marathon, not a sprint.

Kind of like the World Cup itself.

And here Jamie had been worried about returning to the NWSL and trying to manage her long distance relationship with Emma while playing for rival professional teams. If US Soccer had its way, she and Emma wouldn't be apart much at all. Not that she minded that prospect.

Jamie snuggled closer to Emma, her eyes closed. In the morning—okay, in like two hours—the whirlwind would resume. But for now, they would lie here in each other's arms, and maybe they would even sleep, assuming Jamie could get the images of goal celebrations, of fans roaring, of the people she loved alternately cheering and tearing up to take a rest. Either way, she and Emma had made it. They were World Cup champions, and they were in love and thinking about one day, maybe down the road, getting married.

For now, Jamie thought, her arms encircling Emma's

warm, strong body, that was more than enough.

ABOUT THE AUTHOR

Kate Christie, author of thirteen novels including *Beautiful Game, Leaving LA, Gay Pride & Prejudice*, and the Girls of Summer series, lives near Seattle with her wife, three young daughters, and the family dogs. A graduate of Smith College and Western Washington University, Kate has played soccer most of her life and counts attending the 2015 World Cup finals game in Vancouver as one of her top five *Favorite. Days. Ever.*

To read excerpts from Kate's other titles from Second Growth Books and Bella Books, please visit her author website at www.katejchristie.com. Or check out her blog, *Homodramatica* at katechristie.wordpress.com, where she occasionally finds time to wax unpoetically about lesbian life, fiction, and motherhood.

To receive updates on her work, including future installments in the Girls of Summer series, sign up for her mailing list at katechristie.wordpress.com/mailing-list.

PATREON SUPPORTERS

Last year, one of the faithful readers of the Girls of Summer series suggested I start a Patreon account so that those with the means and desire could help support my work in ways other than purchasing titles. So I did, and the experience has been eye-opening. Not only do I worry less about the business side of writing, but I've also formed online friendships with patrons of my work. So much of writing is a solitary slog away from family, friends, and co-workers, but with Patreon I can interact with readers who I know care deeply about my work. That is a really powerful gift, even more than the financial support.

One of the benefits listed on my Patreon page—in addition to behind the scenes glimpses and free e-books, audiobooks, and paperbacks—is the publication of my patron list in the back of my books. So here goes with the inaugural list. Thank you to each and every one of you for letting me know that my books have found their way to generous readers who just might care about my characters as much as I do.

Amanda J., AZ, Barb B., Bernie C., Charley K., Chris Z., Cristina K., Ed M., Erica G., GZ, Hugh R., Jan B., Jessie W., MW, Pat G., Robyn H., Spencer K., Stephanie A., and Suzi S.

Made in the USA
Lexington, KY
09 August 2019